PRAISE FOR EIGHTH DIMENSION - FREQUENCY

Eighth Dimension: Frequency is one of the most intriguing stories I have ever read. I thoroughly enjoyed this book and highly recommend it to anyone interested in faith-based sci-fi, metaphysical mysteries, and the exploration of life's ultimate truths.

~Luwi Nyakansaila Readers' Favorite Reviewer

❧

If you're a fan of novels that revolve around human relationships and personal growth, this book is sure to leave a lasting impression.

~Alija Turkovic Readers' Favorite Reviewer

❧

Roberts weaves a plot exploring the themes of love, family, friendship, technology, extraterrestrial life, communication, and faith, among others. The biblical references and scientific details will enlighten young adults on concepts of Christianity and physics.

~ **Keith Mbuya Readers' Favorite Reviewer**

❧

Between ensuring her mother's late-night sleepwalking episodes don't end in tragedy and deciding whether she likes her colleague Judd enough to date him, Chumana Ironvein's days are hectic. Everything changes the day she receives a mysterious package with cryptic instructions on how to handle its contents. Nothing prepares her for the thrilling adventure that follows in Lorilyn Roberts's *Eighth Dimension: Frequency.*

~Essien Asian, Readers' Favorite Reviewer

I was on the edge of my seat throughout the story, thanks to its unpredictable plot and characters with diverse beliefs shaped by their experiences and backgrounds. This is a wonderful book that explores the profound mysteries of existence, divine purpose, and the potential hidden within each individual.

~Doreen Chomp, Readers' Favorite Reviewer

A YOUNG ADULT FANTASY

EIGHTH DIMENSION

BOOK I

FREQUENCY

LORILYN ROBERTS

OTHER TITLES BY LORILYN ROBERTS

SEVENTH DIMENSION SERIES

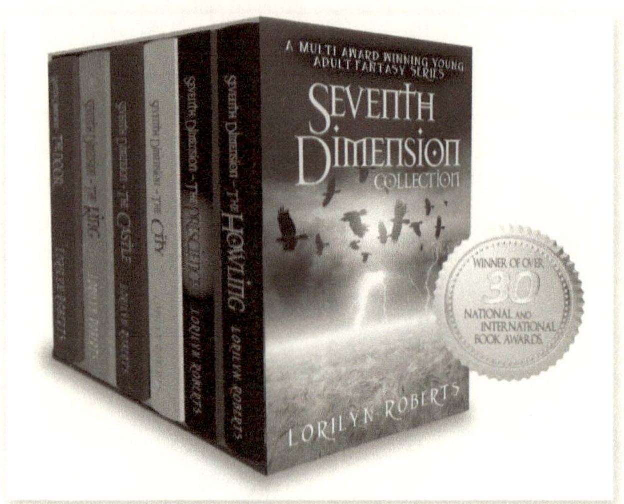

LorilynRoberts.com

Seventh Dimension - The Door, Book 1

As an Audiobook

Seventh Dimension - The King, Book 2

As an Audiobook

Seventh Dimension - The Castle, Book 3

As an Audiobook

Seventh Dimension - The City, Book 4

As an Audiobook

Seventh Dimension - The Prescience, Book 5

As an Audiobook

Seventh Dimension - The Howling, Book 6

As an Audiobook

Seventh Dimension Devotional Series: Am I Okay, God?

As an Audiobook

ADDITIONAL BOOKS

The Donkey and the King

Book Love

Tails and Purrs for the Heart and Soul

Children of Dreams

God's Good Works: Stories to Treasure and Tales to Ponder

The Night Cometh: 20 Fantastical Short Stories about Heaven, Hell, Life, Death and Eternity

Created in the Image of God: Missionary to the Chácobo Ignites a Revolution Without Guns

Food for Thought: Quick and Easy Recipes for Homeschooling Families

Taste and See, A Sampling of First Chapters by John 316 Marketing Network Authors, Vol 2

How to Launch a Best-Selling Christian Book

21 Stories of Gratitude: The Power of Living Life With a Grateful Heart (A Life of Gratitude)

Bloom in Your Winter Season

Remembering Christmas (Divine Moments)

Taste and See, A Sampling of First Chapter by John316 Marketing Network Authors, Vol 1

Celebrating Christmas With ... Memories, Poetry, and Good Food

Eighth Dimension - Frequency

Published by Rear Guard Publishing, Inc.

Gainesville, FL

Ver 1.3

Cover photograph - standard licensing agreement

Cover design by Lisa Vento

Library of Congress Control Number: 2025915807

ISBN: 978-1-964528-01-4 (ebook, Amazon)

ISBN 978-1-964528-05-2 (ebook, Ingram Spark)

ISBN: 979-8-223476-32-0 (ebook, Smashwords)

ISBN: 978-1-964528-02-1 (soft cover, Amazon)

ISBN: 978-1-964528-04-5 (soft cover, Ingram Spark)

ISBN: 978-1-964528-03-8 (hard cover, Ingram Spark)

Bound and printed in the United States of America

I mused over my insane dreams. How many planets in the solar system had I visited? How many children had I rescued? I was always searching. Perhaps all those children I rescued in my dreams were me—rescuing myself.

~Lorilyn Roberts

Dedicated to Scott Gallatin,
a man after God's own heart.

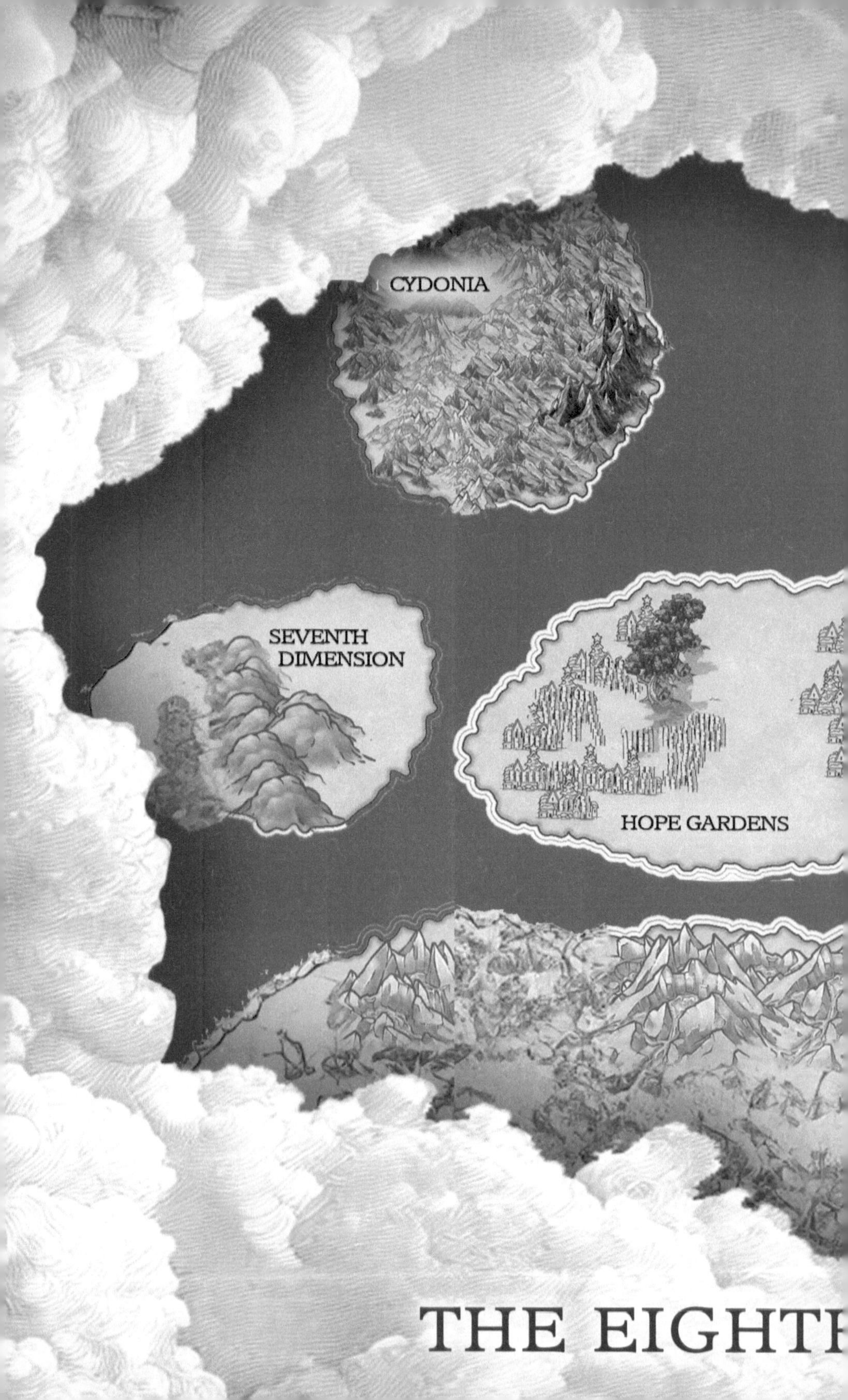
CYDONIA
SEVENTH
DIMENSION
HOPE GARDENS
THE EIGHTH

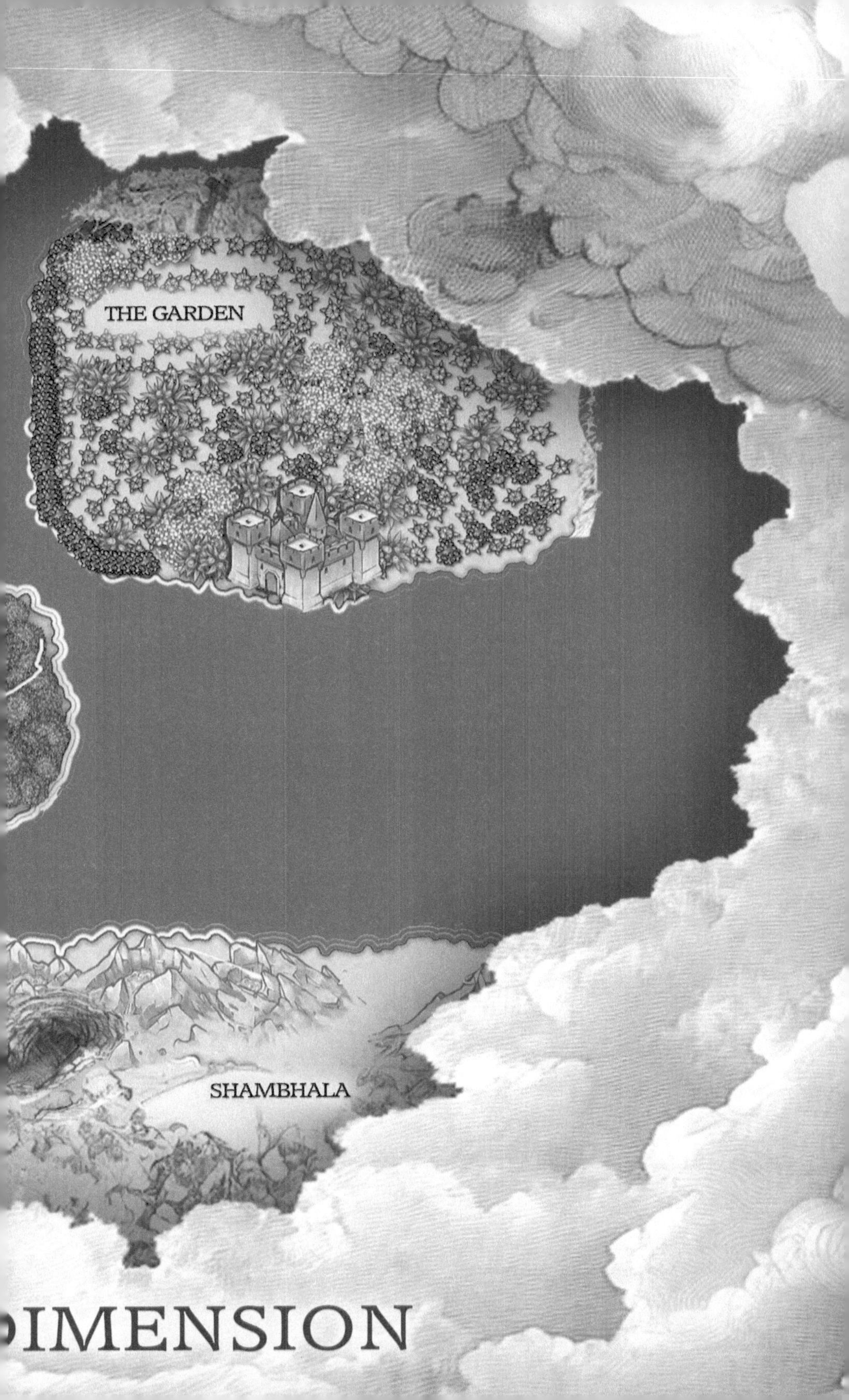

THE GARDEN

SHAMBHALA

DIMENSION

CHAPTER ONE

The alarm rang. I hopped out of bed and ran toward the bathroom. A gentle breeze streaming from the hallway caught my attention. I froze when I heard a whisper deep within my soul.

C-h-u-m-a-n-a.

Curious, I stepped into the hallway and saw the front door ajar.

"Mother?" I took a few steps and looked out, but I didn't see her. I shut the door and ran into her bedroom, but she wasn't there. Then I checked the kitchen. Where was she?

Fear seized me. I returned to the front door, reopened it, and gazed at the parking lot. Cars driving by blocked my view. I refused to imagine the worst.

Suddenly, emerging from the early morning shadows, I saw her in the distance. Mother was bent forward, trudging along at a slow pace. Should I run over to get her and bring her back? She didn't appear to be injured. Where had she gone before sunrise?

My hands sweated with perspiration as I clutched the doorframe. Cold air swept up my legs, and I shivered as I waited. I forced myself to think seriously, which scared me even more.

How many times had the door been unlocked in the morning when

I went to school? I tried to convince myself we were forgetting to lock it. Seeing the door wide open was too much. Someone could walk in. Suppose one day she left and never returned?

I waited, keeping my eyes focused so I wouldn't lose her if she wandered off again. When she arrived, she was oblivious to my presence, walking by me without saying a word.

"Mother, where have you been?"

She turned and faced me with a surprised expression. "What, Dear?"

"Mother, it's winter, and you're outside in your nightgown. Where did you go?"

She blinked. "I'm so tired. Can we talk about this later?"

Flustered, I bit my lip. Had this ever happened to anyone else, or was I the only one with a mother who walked in her sleep?

If I reported her strange behavior to a doctor or health professional, they would probably hospitalize her. Then what would happen? I had no other family. Not yet 18, I'd have to live in a foster home.

I tried again. "Just tell me where you went; that's all I want to know. Where did you go?"

A slight understanding momentarily crossed her face. "I'm sorry, Honey. I didn't mean to frighten you. I'm just a sleepwalker. Been one all my life."

"Sleepwalker, where?" I pressed. "Where do you go?"

She sat at the kitchen table with a vacant look across her face. "I don't know. I wake up as I'm approaching the apartment. I don't know where I go."

I believed her, so what was the point? Sooner or later, I would find out.

I quickly fixed her some oatmeal. After placing a breakfast tray before her, I clasped her fingers around the fork. "Mother, you need to eat."

She nodded. She lifted the fork to her mouth with uncertainty. I sighed. Soon, I would have to feed her.

I studied her wrinkled face, which was aged beyond its years. "I'm leaving for school. Don't go anywhere. I don't want to have to find you when I come home, okay?"

She nodded. Her fading eyes met mine. She knew who I was, but when would that change?

"Get some sleep."

I made sure she took a few bites, and then she went back to the bedroom. She would sleep most of the day and watch the news later. At least she didn't have to work.

My father supported us. To distract myself from his absence, I imagined I looked like him. Mother said he was good-looking, and he had to be smart because I didn't get my brains from her. Did he have red hair? A photographic memory?

I heated some oatmeal and milk in the microwave and ate at the kitchen counter. I would be late for school if I tarried. I quickly checked on Mother before leaving and found her already asleep. The red bruises on her arm startled me. Did they have anything to do with her disappearance?

My heart pounded. Was someone hurting her? Tears rose, and I whispered, "Mother, I love you." I gently stroked her head. "Don't go anywhere while I'm gone."

Peace enveloped her face, assuring me she would be safe until I returned. And then the panic would set in again. Should I lock the door so she couldn't leave? What if there were a fire?

I felt anger consuming me because I had no control over the problem and could do nothing about it. I blamed my absent father and wept. Where is your love, your presence, your care? This is your fault. Paying the bills and providing a roof over our heads isn't enough.

But the walls, lined with dozens of books Mother once read, remained silent. The healing crystals she collected long ago did nothing more than collect dust. I wanted to get rid of everything from the past. Perhaps long ago, they meant something, but now they were only stark reminders of a mother who once was vibrant, alive, and healthy.

The only sound I could hear was my mother's breathing. Suddenly, I remembered the voice calling me to the open door. Too many times, whispers called my name. From where did they come? The fleeting voice would always fade away, leaving me with more questions than answers.

I returned to the kitchen and looked at the microwave clock. I had precisely fourteen minutes and fifteen seconds to arrive at school without being late.

I grabbed my backpack and exited the front door, double-checking the lock. I would not be late. I was never late.

I reassured myself that Mother was safe. Nobody ever came around the apartment during the day.

As I shut the door, early morning sunshine greeted me. The darkness lifted, and the crisp winter air energized me. I shuddered as a breeze brushed my face. I should have worn a scarf. Thank goodness I wouldn't be late.

I hated Atlanta winters. When winds ripped decaying leaves from limbs, I hoped for snow to make the city white—but, sadly, snow rarely fell. Instead, the trees were naked for months, making the winters depressing. I couldn't wait for spring. I wouldn't think about Mother at school. At least, I would try not to.

CHAPTER TWO

I subconsciously counted my steps as I walked. Sometimes, I would close my eyes and pretend I was blind. I knew exactly where I was because I could feel the world's vibrations. Like soft music, their frequencies penetrated my soul, and I walked to the beat.

By contrast, death has no energy, vibrations, or frequency. Once, I rescued a dog that had been struck by a car. Even though everyone else dismissed me, I knew the helpless creature was still alive. The dog lived because I cared. My mockers could not perceive the dog crying. They were dead in the spirit.

Today, however, I carried a heavy burden. Did I dare tell Judd about my mother? He was the only one I felt comfortable confiding in. The problem was that he perceived me as his prized possession. I didn't feel that way about him. Perhaps I was being selfish and using him, not so much for my benefit but for my mother's.

I couldn't remember a time I was so concerned about her. Dementia was progressive, and as far as I knew, no cure existed. No one could reverse the damage already done. I lamented. My mother's mental issues started with depression. Now, she was senile. As bad as depression was, senility was far worse.

I had no one I could trust. No one.

If only Shale hadn't had the accident. Sorrow filled my heart. The accident changed everything. When we lived together, we had community. Laughter was our medicine when our moms drove us crazy.

Whenever I dwelt on the accident, I became depressed. Try as I might, I didn't have it in me to forgive her. Would my depression lead to senility like my mom's?

Cars breezed by. I was glad some people knew where they were going, even if their destinations were mundane. At least they were important enough to plot on a map. What was mine, beyond school?

How could I know my future if I didn't know my past? My mother said disclosure would be forthcoming when I was old enough to "handle the truth." At 17, that hadn't happened. However, when I turned 18, I would know.

My mother never talked about my father. Except once, a long time ago. She said he was good-looking, a genius, and always absent.

I'd only had one person I would call my friend, but Shale Snyder wasn't my friend anymore. Even though it was an accident, it hurt too badly. What do you do with hurts that won't go away?

My thoughts returned to school as I entered the glass doors. The bell rang—perfect timing. I wouldn't settle for anything less than perfection. I walked into my AP Chemistry class and sat next to Judd. He glanced at me, and I mouthed, "I need to talk to you after class."

He nodded.

I turned my attention to our narcissistic instructor, whose brilliance was only superseded by his self-love. No one liked him very much, including me.

With a photographic memory, I didn't have to study the material if I listened closely. I didn't get that gift from my mother. She couldn't remember anything, especially lately. I glanced at the other brilliant students. Otherwise, they wouldn't have qualified for AP Chemistry. Who knew what burdens they carried? I didn't want to know, but somehow, I did. If I wasn't careful, I could let everyone else's sorrows become mine.

AP Chemistry concluded, and the bell rang. Judd, Hollywood handsome, with his dark brown curly hair, brown eyes, and dark complexion, approached me. I could sense other girls' jealousy that I was Judd's favorite, but I ignored them. Judd could have anyone he wanted. Unfortunately, I sensed our motivations to be together were mutually exclusive.

We waited for the other students to exit as we approached the door.

"What's up?" Judd asked.

"Oh, it's my mom. I'm worried."

"She's getting worse?"

I nodded. "What should I do? You know I have no one else."

"We could get married."

"Seriously. I'm not joking."

"I am being serious."

Now I remembered why I didn't want to talk to him. He was thoughtful and stupid at the same time. He wanted more than to be friends. I didn't want a boyfriend, especially a serious one.

Sensing my irritation with his inappropriate response, Judd replied, "If you can make it another six months, you'll be 18 and in control of your destiny. You won't have to deal with the craziness anymore. You'll be old enough to make choices without fear of what anyone says you must do."

I was only getting partially through. I didn't care about my freedom. I cared about my mother. "I don't want her to be committed to an institution. What would they do to her?"

The hallway was loud, and it was hard to hear. "Can you meet me for lunch?"

Judd nodded. "Sure. See you then," and he headed to his next class.

I watched him disappear in the hallway amongst a sea of faces. I couldn't wait until I graduated.

CHAPTER THREE

I arrived first, and Judd joined me. "Hey, do you want to go to McDonald's?" he asked.

I glanced at the clock. "We won't have that much time—let's do it."

We hurried to the front office and signed out. Judd had his own car, and recently, the school had relaxed the rules, allowing juniors to leave school grounds over lunch, provided their grades were good.

I didn't have my license yet. I told everyone it was because I didn't have anyone to teach me, but the real reason was that I didn't care. I preferred to walk.

"Let's just go through the drive-thru," Judd said.

I nodded. Judd graciously paid for mine, and I felt relieved just unloading my burden as we talked. We sat in the McDonald's parking lot, eating fries and nuggets. Maybe he didn't have any solutions, but it helped to talk about it.

I sipped on the unsweetened tea. "If only I knew where Mother went. And the bruises on her wrists disturb me."

"Have you seen them before?" Judd asked.

I shook my head. "Maybe I'm imagining it. The room was dark, and I felt panicky about everything. I should have looked more closely, but I needed to get to school. Besides, she was sleeping. I didn't want to wake her up."

Judd reached over and touched my knee reassuringly. "If it happens again, let me know. Call me."

I nodded. "I will. Thanks."

He added, "Do you want a ride home from school later today?"

I shook my head. "No, I prefer to walk. Get the exercise."

He smiled, peering at me with his captivating eyes. "You don't need it."

I laughed. "I do it for my mental health."

"Ah, I see."

The twinkle in his eyes was alluring, but I still didn't want to be his girlfriend.

"What about tonight? Are you busy?"

I shrugged. "I just want to spend time with my mom."

Judd nodded. "Okay. If you change your mind, call me."

"Thanks." We chatted about meaningless stuff for a few more minutes before heading back. How would I survive one more year of high school? It was so dull, so unfulfilling, and so time-consuming.

"Before I forget to tell you," Judd said, "I got a new job."

"You did? I thought you liked it where you were."

"It was okay. Nothing to keep me there when I got offered something better."

"Where is it?"

We pulled into the school parking lot. "It's called The Ark."

I giggled. "Like Noah's Ark?"

"Ah, it's probably a takeoff from the name, but it's a prepper store. They sell food, batteries, generators—anything you might need if the power went out."

I rolled my eyes. "It's not like we live in Florida. When was the last time we had a power outage here?"

Judd cocked his head. "Well, they wouldn't have opened the store here if they didn't think they could make money. Maybe somebody knows something we don't know."

I shrugged. "Do you get a discount?"

"Yep, and I'm sure I'll buy some stuff."

I had enough to worry about without thinking about the apocalypse.

Judd parked the car and handed me a pamphlet. "These are some of their food packages. You can take a look later. The food lasts twenty years. And it's always good to stock up on essentials."

I glanced at the pamphlet before stuffing it in my purse. "Okay. Let's go before we're late."

I SURPRISED MYSELF. Later, I did look at the list that The Ark recommended for emergency provisions. Since English was boring, rehashing stuff I knew, I pulled it out to keep from falling asleep. Mother's escapades in the middle of the night had caught up with me. While it might be good to have extra food for an emergency, if things really got bad, did I even want to be here?

CHAPTER FOUR

The school bell rang, and everyone scattered. Buses waited out front for the freshmen and sophomore students who didn't have their driver's licenses. Juniors and seniors scurried to the parking lot to show off their cars.

I walked. I could have ridden the bus or gone with Judd, but I liked to walk. It cleared my mind of cobwebs, and I loved being alone, if one could call it that, with buses, cars, and trucks zooming past me on the busy street.

As I strolled along the worn path, my thoughts consumed me. What if Mother disappeared and didn't come back? Would the police blame me for her disappearance?

Should Judd and I get married so he could help me? How old did you have to be to get married? That was not my first choice, but it was a choice.

I was willing to do just about anything to avoid foster care. This was home. My friends did teenage things. I was a caretaker. If only I had someone to help me. Was Judd Luster that person?

I smiled when I thought about his last name. At least my last name sounded better than his—Ironvein, Chumana Ironvein.

I saw the weekly boxes stashed outside the front door when I arrived. They contained toiletries, Hello Fresh meals, milk, eggs, and whatever else we needed, provided by someone—I presumed my father.

I shouldn't complain. I had food to eat, a roof over my head, a mother I loved, and a boyfriend. Despite those things, something wasn't right. I always sensed I had grown up too soon. I barely remembered my childhood. Perhaps I didn't want to.

The only good times were when Shale and I lived together. We used to share our secrets and play soccer with Judd, Rachel, and other kids. When our moms drove us crazy, we could commiserate, laughing at how crazy they were. But the accident changed everything. Judd forgave Shale, but I didn't know how.

Sometimes, it seemed like life was just a chess game with two kings fighting to defeat the other, and I was a meaningless pawn on the big board. However, what if I weren't a meaningless pawn? What if I were a bishop or a rook?

I unlocked the door and announced my arrival. "Mother, I'm home."

I found her in the living room, drinking coffee and watching the news. What conspiracy theory were they broadcasting today?

Her eyes met mine, and she smiled. Although she didn't talk much anymore, she knew who I was. I took a deep breath, thankful there weren't any surprises.

I walked over and kissed her on the forehead. "Is there anything happening in the world I should know about?"

Not that I expected an answer, but this time she did reply. "UFOs."

I stopped. Why would that interest Mother? "So, what about UFOs?"

"I watch the news to learn about UFOs."

I scoffed. "As if they are real?"

She nodded. "They are real."

"Whatever." I paused. What if they were real? No, that was conspiracy stuff.

"I need to bring in the boxes, and then I'll fix supper."

She nodded.

I heard my phone chirp, so I looked to see who texted me. "Let me know if you need me. I'm free tonight."

On Friday nights, Judd and I often hung out together. Tonight, I wanted space.

I checked his comment. At least I had one friend. I wish I had more, but friends take time, time I didn't have. I needed to care for Mother, which had become a full-time job.

After throwing a meal together, Mother and I sat across from each other at the table. She looked much older in the last few months, her hair prematurely gray. I had always wanted blonde hair like hers. Instead, mine was red, thick, and curly, no doubt from my father.

Rimless glasses covered her green eyes. Even with her wrinkled creases, she still looked beautiful. I remembered the marks on her wrists from earlier in the day. I reached over and handed her the glass of water. When she took it, I didn't see any redness or bruises. Maybe I just imagined it this morning when I panicked.

Now that she had slept, I asked her, "Where did you go in the middle of the night?"

A blank stare covered her face. "Did I sleepwalk again?"

I nodded. "Do you remember?"

She shook her head. "No. I don't remember."

I glanced at the ceiling. I would find out even if I had to stay up all night and follow her.

After a quiet dinner, I cleared the dishes, and she returned to her favorite chair in front of the TV. Watching the news kept her mind occupied. She covered up with a blanket, leaned back, and closed her eyes. It was a blissful night for her, but I wasn't sure it would be for me, especially if I stayed up waiting for her to sleepwalk.

I needed to go somewhere. Sometimes I had to be alone. I glanced out the window at the small forest behind the apartment—my thinking place when I needed one. I turned to Mother.

"I'm going for a walk before it gets too dark. Don't go anywhere. I won't be gone but a few minutes, okay?"

She didn't respond as she had already dozed off. That could be a good thing. If I were going to go, now was the best time.

I put my phone in my pocket, grabbed a jacket for the cool night air, and shut the door behind me. I ensured it was locked, a deterrent to keep her from leaving.

Hope Garden Apartments didn't offer much hope, and it didn't have gardens, but it was home. What if there were a place with hope and flowers? Was that what I longed for—a place to live out my dreams? I wasn't sure, but there had to be more to life than school and taking care of a mother with dementia.

It didn't take long to get to the back of the apartments. The forest was darker than I had thought it would be. In the wintertime, the sun set early. I pulled out my phone in case I needed the flashlight.

Hauntingly dark shadows closed in on the dirt trail. I resisted the temptation to go so far that I didn't know my way back. Without summer frogs and romantic crickets, the stillness overwhelmed me. No cars, crying children, or airplanes from Dobbins Air Force Base scouring the skies—just the sound of silence.

I found a ledge to sit on to ponder my future. I needed a plan for my mother. She used to read books all day, and now she only watched the news. Her cognitive decline was happening quickly. I needed to stay close when I went to college. At least there were several colleges in the Atlanta Area. I could enroll at Kennesaw State College, Georgia Tech, or Georgia State.

Truthfully, college was the least of my concerns. With my grades, anybody would accept me. I could figure that out later. More important to me was my past. My 18th birthday couldn't come soon enough. The court order required all documents to be released when I came of age.

Unexpectedly, I heard something. It sounded like my name, but that was impossible. I waited timidly, but I was more curious than anything. I didn't see anyone nearby. No one would be hanging out here unless it was someone like me. Depressed. I listened again.

C-h-u-m-a-n-a.

My name floated on the gentle breeze as it whispered amongst the trees. Did I have goosebumps from the wind or from hearing my name?

I stood and took a few steps toward the sound. In the distance, I could see a light shining from above. Fear and curiosity gripped me.

I heard my name again, followed by “Come.”

I turned on the flashlight and pointed it straight ahead, but I couldn’t see anything in the darkness except a disappearing foot trail.

CHAPTER FIVE

A gentle breeze rustled the bare tree limbs, and yellow autumn leaves fluttered in the wind as they fell around me.

Did I really hear my name in the swish of the boughs? Or was it my overactive imagination? Either way, terror gripped me.

Despite my fear, I had to know what lay at the trail's end. They knew my name. I braced for a quick retreat, if necessary, but my heart quickened as I took small steps forward.

The overhead light turned the forest into ominous ghostlike wraiths. I swallowed hard, looking neither to the right nor to the left. The strange light penetrated the blackness, even to my afflicted soul. I needed to know what was there. Otherwise, the question would torment me when I returned home.

I dare not make any noise lest I scare myself into cowardice. As I advanced, nightfall tightened its grip. The tiny light from my phone was almost useless. I moved it in a circular motion that dissipated into nothingness a few feet before me. The overhead light must be bright to glow like it did on the forest trail. I edged closer.

Suddenly, something moved on the ground beneath the light. My heart thumped, and my gait slowed to a crawl. Two green eyes watched me from afar. Surprisingly, they were non-threatening, but I couldn't tell what the animal was.

Then, something else caught my attention near the small creature. This one had eyes that flashed amber like a predator. Whatever it was, the body was red, and I surmised it to be far more menacing. The sleek body squatted on its haunches, ears pointed up. He appeared to be edging toward the green-eyed creature.

The light from above increased in intensity as I approached, revealing glistening rain droplets on the ground. A lightning flash swept across the sky, and the forest became briefly visible. The bold amber eyes of a red fox eyed me with irritation. Only a few feet from him on the path, a kitten waited, alone and defenseless.

The orange feline seemed disoriented, like a helpless creature resigned to its fate. His eyes met mine, begging for mercy.

A voice blowing in the wind called my name.

C-h-u-m-a-n-a.

Only seconds remained. Would the red fox attack me if I rescued the kitten? If he did, it would be quick. I wouldn't have to wait long to meet my demise.

The stealthy fox ignored my advance; his eyes again focused on his prey. Time slowed to a crawl. If I were going to act, I needed to do it now. As the red fox leaped through the air, I rushed toward the tiny creature.

"No," I shouted. I threw my phone toward the fox. A loud thump followed and then silence. I could see nothing in the darkness except where the light from above still shone on the forest floor. But the light revealed no clues. I couldn't see anything.

Fear seized me. Did I accidentally kill the kitten, like my friend Shale, who accidentally killed Judd's dog?

If I did, it was an accident—not on purpose. My heart broke. I shouldn't have been so hard on Shale. I was beside myself with contriteness, holding back tears. What did I do?

Only silence filled the dark forest. A silence that seemed so meaningful when I arrived now became hauntingly disturbing. Surrounded in darkness—wait, my phone shone a few feet away. I still didn't see the fox. Where was he? Did I scare it away?

I scooted over to retrieve my phone and stumbled. My God, did I kill the kitten? Let it not be! Accusations of hypocrisy shattered me.

I picked up the phone and lit the area where I had tripped. The stunned red fox lay on the ground. He was still breathing, but not a happy creature. His eyes watched me as if he were calculating his next move. Thank goodness I didn't hit the kitten. I shone my light all around in a frantic search to find it.

When all hope of discovering it seemed futile, I found it crouched on the forest floor. Where was its mother? Had the red fox already killed her? A cat wouldn't abandon her kitten unless something happened.

I gazed at the red fox as he hyperventilated. For an instant, I felt remorse that I had struck him, but he didn't seem to be injured. Only stunned. I needed to get out of here before he sprang to life.

I grabbed the kitten and wrapped my jacket around it. I glanced up at the light, but I couldn't tell from whence it came. It just was.

I aimed the phone flashlight back up the trail and rushed home. When I reached the edge of the thicket, I stopped and rested, replaying everything mentally. I had heard my name three times.

The Hope Garden Apartment streetlights lit the surroundings and lightened my mood. I would make it to live another day, as would one lucky cat. I felt the kitten's heart thumping against my chest. Without my help, he would have become a meal for a hungry red fox.

As I approached our apartment, thankfulness took on a deeper meaning. Thankfulness, however, was superseded by the question that loomed. What would I do with a kitten in an apartment that didn't allow pets? I had no food or litter box for a feline. What would Mother think? Would she make me turn it in at the humane society?

I stopped to catch my breath at the front door. I unzipped my jacket to get a better look at it. Was it a boy or a girl? I wasn't an expert on cats. The animal weighed four or five pounds. It couldn't be a newborn, but it was not full-grown. Should I hide the furry creature from my mother? Oh, what should I do?

I thought about Judd. He knew more about animals than I did. I quickly texted, "Judd, I need your help. Can you come over now?"

While I waited, I peered into the hallway. Darkness descended faster than I anticipated. Mother only disappeared at night—until now, at least. Hurry up, Judd, and answer me before I go inside.

My phone lit. "Be right over."

"Thanks." I took a deep breath. It was too cold to stand outside and wait for him. I opened the door. When I saw my mother, I breathed easier. She was in her favorite chair, where I left her, watching the news.

I debated whether I should show her the kitten or wait and ask Judd what to do.

When I wasn't sure of things, I usually didn't do anything. I tiptoed through the hall to my bedroom.

CHAPTER SIX

I shut the door and sat on the edge of my bed. When I gently opened my jacket, the kitten poked out his head. He clutched my shirt, digging in his tiny paws with all his might. I pulled him away from my body and held him up in the light. The little creature was so cute. He looked around, bewildered.

His fur was deep yellow-orange with streaks of white across his forehead. A white patch framed his right eye and extended down his nose. His cheeks were all-white. Green-colored eyes studied my face. His calmness surprised me.

I chuckled. "I assume you're a boy, but I don't know." I was a dog person and had never had a cat for a pet. I looked at his hindquarters but couldn't tell what I was looking at.

I'd have to ask Judd. I couldn't remember ever holding a kitten. We always lived where we couldn't have pets. I slipped off my jacket and set the little fur baby in my lap, gently stroking him along his back.

The reality of what I had done overwhelmed me. The apartment didn't allow pets. Could I hide him from the apartment manager? How difficult would it be to do that?

I had no cat food. How quickly things had changed. Judd had practically begged to come over tonight, but I'd said no, partly because I was depressed about Mother. I glanced at my phone to check the time. We still had time to go to the store. I smiled. He was an animal lover. He'd do it for me.

I heard the doorbell ring, and I hopped off the bed and rushed to the door. Judd stood there and did a double-take when he saw my arm wrapped around the kitten. I put two fingers up to my lips. He got the message.

"Follow me," I said. I stopped by the living room. "Judd is here for a few minutes. I think we're going to the store."

Mother nodded and waved. She was still watching the news.

Judd and I disappeared into my bedroom. I spoke softly to Judd. "I found him in the woods. A red fox almost killed him."

"What?"

I said it a little louder. My mom couldn't hear that well anyway, especially with the TV on.

"I said I found him in the forest. A bright light pierced the dark forest canopy, and that's how I spotted him. An animal was tracking it because I saw two amber eyes a few feet away, and then I saw it was a red fox. I threw my phone at the fox and hit him. Then I grabbed the kitten and ran back to the apartment."

Judd's eyes became huge at this revelation. "Wow."

I sighed. "Judd, I want to keep him."

"Can I hold him?"

"I don't know if it's a boy or a girl."

"I'm sure it's a boy," Judd said.

"How do you know? You haven't checked."

Judd chuckled as if I didn't know the difference between a girl and a boy.

"You haven't checked," I said again. "You're just guessing."

"Even without looking," Judd said, "you could assume it's likely a boy. Most orange cats are male."

"Oh."

"Here, let me hold him."

I handed the cat to Judd, and he inspected underneath his tail. "Yeah, it's a boy."

"Okay. Not that it matters."

"And you want to keep him?" Judd asked.

"Why? Do you want him?"

Judd shook his head. "You know you can't have animals in the apartment."

I plopped down on the edge of the bed. "I know, but I could hide him. And you had your dog for a short time."

Judd raised his eyebrow. "Yeah, I know, and it was tough to hide a dog. How are you going to take care of him? Do you have food or a litter box?"

I stared at the floor and tried to play with his emotions. "That's why I texted you. Can you take me to the store to get what I need?"

Judd chuckled. "I knew this wasn't a date when you texted me."

"We still have time."

Judd looked away; I knew him well enough to know what he was thinking. I laced my arm around his.

We embraced for a quiet moment. The accident had changed many things.

I glanced at the kitten. "I still need to tell my mother."

Judd's eyes met mine. "You want to go now?"

I nodded. "I'll show him to Mother on the way out. It will give her time to consider it while we're gone."

"Sounds good," Judd said.

We walked into the living room, and I held up the small feline before my mother, its little paws dangling between my fingers. "I rescued this kitten in the woods. A red fox almost killed him."

Mother's eyes lit up more than I remembered in recent memory. A faint smile crossed her face. "You want to keep him, don't you?"

I nodded.

Our eyes met, and we connected. I held my breath.

"Don't tell anyone," Mother said.

My thumping heart slowed down. That was all I needed to hear. "We're going to the store to get food."

"Wait. Can I hold him?" she asked.

I hesitated because it was late and the store would soon close, but I relented. I gently placed the cat in Mother's lap.

She tickled his ears. "I had a cat once," she said, "long ago. His name was Rophe."

"Rophe?" I repeated. "Then, let's name him that."

"He's purring."

I'd never heard a cat purr. I leaned over to listen. How do you describe a sound you've never heard? Delight filled my heart. "When he purrs, that means he's happy, right?"

Mother nodded. Again, she said, "Don't tell anyone."

WHEN WE RETURNED from the store, we made Rophe happy in his new home Worry about Mother faded as Rophe took center stage. She was captivated by him and comforted him while we set up the litter box, water bowl, and food dish in the bathroom. I was glad I had the weekend to help him adjust and get used to his new home.

Judd now had a new excuse to come over. He brought his books, and we studied together on Saturday and Sunday. I could get used to this. Having him around lifted my spirits. I didn't feel so alone caring for my mother.

When he left Sunday night, I kissed him in the doorway. As I closed the front door, my feelings toward him changed. I had never thought about him seriously until now. I would keep all my options open.

Tomorrow would be another dull day at school. I imagined Rophe keeping an eye on Mother while I was gone. He seemed so wise. Maybe cats were more intelligent than dogs.

Everything seemed too easy. I expected conflict. I expected Mother to raise an issue with the no-pet apartment rules. Judd paid for everything. What could go wrong?

CHAPTER SEVEN

Monday morning, I awoke before the alarm went off. My first thought was Rophe. I'd check on him and make sure Mother hadn't wandered off. I glanced at the clock. I had time for coffee and a few minutes to review my AP Chemistry notes for the upcoming test.

I found Mother in the living room watching television. Rophe was sleeping in her lap.

"Good morning," I said.

"You're up early."

I picked up Rophe and caressed him. "You have a new friend."

Mother smiled. "Yes. Don't tell anyone."

I nodded. "You told me that last night."

Mom tilted her head. "Just making sure you know. The apartment doesn't allow pets, but he's not a pet. He's a lion. A magnificent lion. Lions aren't pets."

I laughed and returned him to her. "Now you have company while I'm at school. I won't worry about you as much."

Mother smiled. "You don't need to worry about me."

"Take care of him, and don't go anywhere."

Her eyes met mine. "Where would I go?"

I sighed. Mother seemed in her right mind at this moment, but at other times, she seemed oblivious to everything. I glanced at the television. It was always boring news.

"I'm going to grab some coffee and study for a few minutes before going to school."

"Are you making good grades?"

I smiled. "No need to worry. Good enough to get into college."

I fixed my coffee and returned to my desk. It wasn't that I didn't have good grades; school was just dull. Thank goodness I was taking AP classes, or I'd be bored out of my mind.

ON MY WAY OUT, I said goodbye to Mom and Rophe. I was happy Mother had a companion. After closing the front door, I ensured it was locked and secure. When I stepped off the porch, I started counting my steps—I always counted my steps.

With winter approaching, the nippy air gave me goosebumps. I could say that now, as I heard the sandhill cranes croaking above me on their three-thousand-mile journey to Florida. It wasn't winter until the sandhill cranes announced it at the Hope Garden Apartments.

I arrived in time to hear the final bell; I had it down to a mathematical equation. If I hit the crosswalk when the light turned red, I knew how much faster I needed to walk to arrive before the final bell rang and not be late. I was never late.

When I entered AP Chemistry, I saw Judd. I walked over and sat beside him.

"How's Rophe doing?"

I gave him a thumbs up.

Judd smiled.

"Let's meet for lunch," I mouthed.

He nodded.

Despite all the distractions, I was glad I'd found time to review my chemistry notes.

Forty minutes later, the bell rang, and I was off to Calculus. Judd went to parts unknown. We would see each other again in AP Biology.

When lunch arrived, I joined Judd, Shale, Rachel, and Gracie. We were considered the school nerds. I'm not sure how Shale got that reputation because she was always in trouble, but we shared friends and lived in the same apartments—except for Gracie. She was new to the school, so I didn't know her well.

However, her father was a Kennesaw State University professor. Rachel, who was Jewish, liked everyone. Gracie didn't know enough about anyone not to like everyone. Judd was the unifier among the bunch.

Of course, Shale and I had been friends before the accident. I regretted how I had treated her now. What if my phone had hit Rophe? It would have been an accident.

How did Shale live with herself? For the first time, I felt her pain. This feeling was new to me.

Shale opened her lunch bag—she rarely bought her lunch—and pulled out a sandwich and chips. "I forgot my water."

Judd stood. "I'll get you a cup."

"I'm having a Bible Study today," Shale said, "hopefully the first of many if anyone wants to come." Her eyes darted around the lunch table.

Rachel said, "I'm Jewish, so—I don't know if I'd fit in."

"You can come," Shale said. "Today, the study is out of Proverbs in the Old Testament and a passage from Colossians in the New Testament. You might enjoy it."

What was Colossians? I'd never heard that word before.

"Where will it be?" Gracie asked.

"In the library," Shale said. "Since it's the first one, we won't go long. I'd love for you to come."

Gracie nodded. "If Judd goes, can he give me a ride home?"

Judd returned, placing Shale's water cup beside her lunch bag. "If I go where?"

Shale repeated the announcement.

Judd seemed excited about it. “Sure. I’ll go and give you a ride home.”

He glanced at me. “Are you coming?”

I sighed. “Sure. Count me in.” If he gave me a ride home, I wouldn’t return that much later than if I walked.

Judd shared the news about my new cat—I’d forgotten to tell him not to tell anyone, and now I could hear Mother’s warning in my head.

Sometimes, he didn’t use good judgment, and this was one of those times. Why would he share it when he knew the apartments didn’t allow pets?

I interrupted the conversation. “Please don’t tell anyone. If the apartment manager finds out, she’ll take him away.”

Everyone nodded, and the conversation steered to other topics. I was thankful. The less we talked about Rophe, the better. Why did Judd have to bring it up? Now, I had something else to worry about besides Mother.

CHAPTER EIGHT

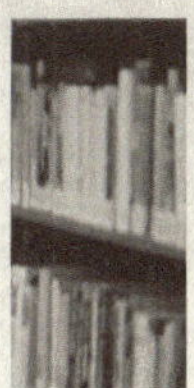

The final bell rang, and I grabbed my books and headed to the locker. The last thing I wanted to do was go to a Bible Study, but I said I would go. If Judd stayed too long, I'd head home.

I retrieved what I needed and dodged students through the hallway, arriving at the library before anyone else. The room was quiet, and I plopped my backpack on the table. Then, I strolled over to the book display to see if I saw anything that interested me. Thanksgiving books dominated the shelves, but a few early arrivals pointed toward Christmas.

Did they have any books on cats? I was looking for animal books when the library door opened.

Shale appeared, forcing a smile. Before I could say anything, Rachel entered, followed by Judd. I didn't see Gracie.

"Is Gracie coming?" I asked. I had a better relationship with her, except for Judd, but he didn't count.

"She's on the way," Judd said.

I nodded. I moved my backpack to the floor to make room for the others. I had never been to a Bible Study and didn't know what to expect.

Shale sat at the head of the table. I was glad there were only a few of us. Hopefully, it wouldn't go very long.

"I'll open in prayer," Shale said.

Everyone bowed their heads, so I bowed mine.

"'The Lord bless you and keep you; The Lord make His face shine upon you, and be gracious to you. The Lord lift up His countenance upon you, and give you peace.'"

After Shale prayed, Rachel prayed in a language that sounded familiar to me. I recognized it as Hebrew from news reports about the fighting in Israel. I didn't know she spoke Hebrew.

When she finished, Judd prayed a one-liner. "Thank you, Lord, that we could be here today."

I was next but didn't know how to pray, so I remained silent. After an awkward silence, Shale closed the prayer time with a short line, "Amen."

Relieved that prayer was over, what was next?

The door opened, and Gracie entered. "Sorry, I'm late."

"No problem," Shale said. "We've just started."

We paused to give Gracie a moment to settle, and Shale began. "I have a couple of verses I wanted to talk about today. We'll probably only have time to look at the first passage, but I'll give you the citation for the second one if you want to think ahead. Next week, we can talk about it."

No one said anything, so she continued. "Let's start with Genesis 1:1-2, the first book in the Bible."

I suddenly realized I didn't have a Bible. Rachel had hers; it looked like it was in Hebrew. Judd was using a phone app, but Gracie didn't have anything. I felt relieved I wasn't the only one.

When Judd saw we had nothing, he said, "Let me find a couple of Bibles."

He disappeared behind a bookshelf and returned with two Bibles, handing one to each of us. At least I didn't have to ask where to find the passage. It was the first verse in the first book of the Bible.

Shale repeated the verse reference: "Genesis 1:1-2: 'In the beginning, God created the heavens and the Earth. The Earth was without form, and void; and darkness was on the face of the deep. And the Spirit of God was hovering over the face of the waters. Then God said, 'Let there be light;' and there was light."

She paused before continuing. "Let me give you the second passage. If we don't get to it today, you can look at it later.

"Colossians 1:16: 'For by Him all things were created that are in heaven and that are on Earth, visible and invisible, whether thrones or dominions or principalities or powers. All things were created through Him and for Him.'"

I noticed both passages dealt with creation. Was that intentional?

Shale began the discussion. "I know we have AP Biology together so this was a good place to start." She continued from there with her thoughts, but my mind didn't pay much attention. I just wanted to go home.

When she finished, Rachel spoke next.

"I'm reading this in the Tanakh, which is in Hebrew, and I don't think the translation into English is very good. A better translation would read: 'In the beginning, God created the heavens and the Earth. The Earth had become ruined and uninhabited, or the Earth had become unfurnished and empty.' It uses the Hebrew words 'Tohu' and 'Bohu,' which mean without form and void.

"I believe it would be a better translation if it said, 'In the beginning, God created the heavens and the Earth.' There should be a pause there, and then it would continue. 'The Earth became formless and void; and darkness was on the face of the deep.'"

Her comment piqued my curiosity.

Rachel continued. "Don't you think that makes more sense? Otherwise, it appears to be saying that what God created wasn't good. It was without form, empty, a wasteland, and void."

A long silence followed. Shale spoke first. "Rachel, that's profound. I've been studying Hebrew and see what you're saying."

Perhaps for the first time, I was stunned. Maybe there was something to the Bible. What happened between Genesis 1:1 and 1:2, making the world formless and void? The discussion continued, but I had gone down a rabbit trail. I wanted to know what happened. Who could I ask?

Then, I heard Shale wrapping up the discussion with the passage from Colossians. "We won't have time to get into it today, but what do the words 'visible' and 'invisible' mean? We know what thrones are, but what does Scripture mean by dominions, principalities, and powers?

"Is there more than one dominion, principality, or power? If there is, is it on Earth or in heaven? Or someplace else? And how do we get in contact with it if it exists? Any thoughts?"

Rachel replied, "We pray to God, but I'm unsure about the rest."

Gracie added, "We know there is darkness and evil. But I don't know if you could call them powers, principalities, or dominions. That sounds scary."

I agreed with Gracie. I agreed with Rachel. I even agreed with Shale. Judd had remained silent. The truth was, I didn't know who was right.

Shale said a quick prayer to dismiss us, and Judd offered transportation to anyone who needed a ride home. We all piled into his car. For all of Judd's flaws, there were some things I liked about him. I'd have to talk with him more about this later.

CHAPTER NINE

Judd pulled up in front of the apartment to drop me off, and I saw several boxes stashed at the front door.

"Looks like you've got some Amazon packages," Judd said. "Do you need help taking them inside?"

I shook my head. "No, it's fine. I can get them." I shut the car door and waved to my friends. "See you tomorrow."

They waved back. The packages loomed large by the door. I couldn't imagine who sent them or what they were. We had already received our weekly delivery from Amazon.

However, when I examined them more closely, I found that the boxes weren't from Amazon but from various companies I didn't recognize. Maybe the deliveryman had made a mistake. I saw an important document amongst the boxes, so I grabbed it and took it into the house with me. I'd come back and get the boxes.

When I entered, Mother was sitting in her favorite chair. Rophe was still in her lap, where he'd probably been all day. The news played in the background.

She focused on me with a warm smile.

"Did you know there are packages at our front door?" I asked.

"No, Dear. Who sent them?"

"I don't know." I sat on the chair, opened the handwritten letter, and read it silently.

Dear Chumana,

This is an urgent message from your father—the first of many. Several packages containing ham radio equipment will arrive soon (perhaps with this letter).

Put the boxes in an undisclosed place. Don't tell anyone. Don't attempt to set up or operate the equipment until licensed. That's illegal. Your commitment to licensing ensures you're ready for the next step toward enlightenment.

The deadline for licensing is your birthday. Once licensed, you must learn how to operate digitally, and you must learn Morse Code at 20 words per minute, progressing to 25 wpm.

If you succeed in this and continue your good work in high school, you will qualify for a critical job in a top-secret government program that your father leads. If you are uninterested, please call this number, and we will arrange to pick up the equipment. Otherwise, we expect you to begin working toward your ham radio license.

To qualify for the bands we operate, you must pass the Extra licensing exam—the top tier. Based on your aptitude exemplified in school, this should be easy.

Communication will be sparse until you pass your Extra ham license certification and learn how to operate our preferred digital mode. Morse Code, or CW, as commonly referred to in ham radio, is necessary for vital communication. You will understand later. You have been groomed for this opportunity since you were born.

After passing your licensing exams, please get in touch with the person listed below. He will set up everything except the solar system. We'll explain more about that after the installation of the ham radio equipment.

Save this letter for future correspondence. Under no circumstances should you share with anyone what you're doing. We recommend that your training be online.

Breaking this rule means we will confiscate the equipment. We know you would not want to jeopardize the program's integrity and put your father and others in harm's way.

We look forward to welcoming you aboard.

73,

The Frequency Group.

I reread it slowly, unsure what to make of it. I was excited and overwhelmed at the same time. I glanced at my mother. Should I share it with her? My better judgment said no. Suppose she told someone, not that she ever talked to anyone but me, but her wanderings—I didn't know where she went.

Well, I didn't need to worry about it right now. I would take the boxes to my room and not open them until I passed the three tests listed in the letter.

I couldn't help thinking, though, with all our technology today—the internet, satellites, and AI—why did we need ham radio? It seemed archaic.

I heard my mother from across the room. "What does the letter say, Honey?"

My musings interrupted, I wasn't sure what to say. Suppose I decided to return the equipment. It looked like a considerable investment of time.

"Oh, it's nothing. Just telling me about some tests I need to take before I start my senior year."

It wasn't a lie—just a little vague. It was a senior project, just like Rophe wasn't a pet. As Mother said, Rophe was a lion.

Mother nodded and put her head back on the chair pillow, her fingers massaging Rophe's ear. "I'm glad your father sent you what you need."

My father? How did she know? I didn't understand my mother. Sometimes, she seemed prophetic; at other times, she seemed demented. How could she be both? I shook off my uneasiness and stood. "Let me grab the boxes, and I'll put them in my room."

Mother dozed off, and Rophe jumped from her lap and approached me. He gently rubbed his small body against my leg. I picked him up. "I love you. I need to check your food dish."

We walked into the bathroom, and I noticed his litter needed cleaning. I would do that as soon as I brought in the boxes. I lingered as I held him in my arms. I reflected on the months that had passed, and nothing significant had happened. I thought my life would never change, and I had no meaningful purpose other than caring for my mother.

But now two momentous events had occurred. Things often happened in threes. Was there a third life-altering event on the horizon?

CHAPTER TEN

I brought all the boxes inside and placed them in my room out of the way. I was curious but not curious enough to open them. I tended to follow the rules, unlike Shale, who broke them.

All I cared about was the time involved. How long would it take me to pass the tests?

I planned to read through the material, remember everything with my photographic memory, and take the first test within the next week.

I went to my computer and searched for ham radio technician licensing. Dozens of websites appeared, and I scrolled down to a Reddit post and read several comments. The technician license was easy if you had an electrical background, which I didn't. What did RF stand for—maybe radio frequency?

When I returned to the search engine for more sites, I clicked on another promising one. "Take the course and test online."

All I needed to do was open an account and pay a small fee. I did that, and immediately, I had access to the materials. The information suggested ten hours of study to pass the first-level exam. Ten hours seemed like a lot.

I clicked on "study," and a question popped up: Electrical current is measured in which of the following units? A, watts; B, ohms; C, volts; or D, amperes?

I chose A. It flashed red. Power is measured in watts.

So, I tried B, ohms. False.

Resistance, Reactance, and impedance are measured in Ohms. I didn't even know what those concepts meant.

I was a little deflated. This might be more challenging than I thought.

I clicked on C, voltage. False. Voltage (electrical pressure) is measured in volts.

Dang it. There was only one answer left. D, amperes. I clicked on that. A green word appeared: Correct! So, electrical current is measured in amperes.

I'd need ten hours to learn what I needed for the tech license. What else did the correspondence say?

Maybe I didn't want to do this. I thought about the time involved, and I still had my schoolwork. AP Chemistry and AP Biology were easy, but electricity—I was clueless. I picked up Rophe and hugged him. His orange and white fur was so soft to the touch, and as I held him close, I could hear him purring.

I sat on the side of the bed and re-read the letter. In addition to the three licensing exams, I had to learn CW at 25 words per minute and download some software on the computer. I needed to do all of this before my 18th birthday. The only good part was that my 18th birthday was several months away.

But why? Was it to prove myself worthy to my father? Or was he testing me to see if I would do it? Could it be to determine how badly I wanted to meet him. Or was it all a scam?

I never knew there were any requirements for disclosure except that I had to be 18.

I set the letter aside and scratched Rophe's head as he relaxed in my lap. "Little fellow, are you hungry?"

I took him to the kitchen and fixed some wet food for him. After eating it, he entered the living room and climbed onto Mother's lap.

Since I brought Rophe home, Mother had not disappeared in the middle of the night. Hopefully, it would stay that way.

I grabbed a bite to eat and headed off to study. I longed to text Judd about what I had received, but the letter warned me not to tell anyone. Why did everything have to be so secretive? Besides, Judd saw the boxes and would ask about them tomorrow. What would I say?

I glanced at the return addresses on the boxes. Each container came from a different store. There was no return address on the envelope. The only phone numbers in the letter were for the installer and a number to call if I changed my mind and wanted to return the equipment.

The email was to let them know when I passed all the tests. More information could be inside the boxes. What if I opened just one box?

I shook my head. No, it wasn't worth it. If I gave up and didn't want to go through with it, I'd open them before sending them back. Right now, I wanted to give it my best shot. I didn't easily give up on things, especially before trying. What I wanted most was to talk to Judd.

I finished my schoolwork, which was easy, and then pulled up the ham radio website and studied. Two hours later, even though I was falling asleep, I was learning as much as possible. As if validating my ability, I said aloud, "I can do this."

With that, I closed the computer and turned off the light. Rophe was stretched out like a log, already asleep. I lay my head down next to his. "Good night, Rophe. Sweet dreams."

CHAPTER ELEVEN

School had been as dull as usual except for lunchtime. I had managed to avert Judd's questions about the boxes, but he was persistent. I needed to figure out what I could and couldn't share.

There had to be a way I could tell him without telling him. Maybe he could make the discovery. That might be hard, though, since I hadn't even opened the boxes.

When I arrived home, Mother and Rophe were in the living room. I picked up Rophe and hugged him. I was surprised the television wasn't on. Mother had a book beside her chair. That was different. She hadn't read anything in months. I went into the kitchen, grabbed a snack, and sat with them as I ate.

I glanced out the window at the beautiful sunshine. The days were getting shorter and cooler, but today had been like an Indian summer. Besides, a wise person once said that all work and no play made Jack a dull boy. That applied equally to girls, too.

I finished my yogurt and stood. "I'm going for a quick walk."

"Okay, Honey. Would you mind flipping the television on for me? I left the remote on the dining room table."

I retrieved the remote and turned it on. The TV defaulted to one of the local news channels. More news, that's all she watched.

I handed the control to her. “Be back in a few minutes.”

“Love you.”

“I love you, too, Mother.” I never got tired of hearing her say that. I should say it more often, too.

I locked the door behind me and headed to the woods. The trees were completely bare now and gray. A few birds flittered about, looking for any seeds they could find. I reminded myself I should put some seeds out. I’d make a friend for life even if I helped only one bird.

While it didn’t get as cold here as up North, it wasn’t uncommon for it to freeze, and plants didn’t grow in freezing temperatures.

I walked along the trail, trying to remember exactly where I had found Rophe. I passed the log where I had rested when I saw the light shining in the distance. Nothing but a blue sky was overhead now. Things looked so different in the darkness than in daylight.

I arrived where Rophe was crouched, terrified by the fox, when I scooped him off the ground. Since the fox wasn’t still here, that meant he wandered off. Nothing had changed, except it was daylight, and I could see better.

After a moment of reflection, I started back on the trail to leave. I was already thinking about what I would study first, and there he was, directly in front of me—the red fox. The scoundrel had been watching me the whole time, and now he blocked my way. He sat squarely on the trail, ears straight up and eyes glued on me like lasers.

I froze. Should I back up and run away? Eventually, I’d have to return here to get back. My heart pounded. Even if I ran, I could never outrun a fox. I had my phone, but I was terrified to take my eyes off him. He wanted my flesh. It was his revenge time.

Neither of us moved or blinked. The fox’s focus was uncanny, just like a born killer.

Then something strange happened. The fox opened his mouth and laughed. How could he do that? As he laughed, the sound became louder, echoing through the trees. It wasn’t a human or animal voice. I wanted to cover my ears, but I was too afraid even to do that.

In my mind, he was mocking me. It was like he knew he could kill me or at least do me significant harm, but he would rather toy with me, mess with my mind, and make me doubt my sanity.

Then he stood and coyly trotted off into the woods. He disappeared before I even had time to realize he was gone. However, his laughter lingered in my mind. I shook my head to get my wits back.

Nobody would believe me even if I told them what happened. Could I be losing my mind? That scared me even more, that I might turn into my mother. What if I became her?

I peered into the woods to make sure the hunter was gone. I just wanted to go home now. My escape to enjoy nature had turned into a nightmare. I had the distinct feeling he wanted to rob me of my joy. He stole my peace. I went from being terrified to being angry. How dare he laugh at me!

Nevertheless, I was still fearful. I hurried back up the trail, but a sweet melody from a Rose-breasted Grosbeak caught my attention. I looked up at a bare tree limb, and there he was, his eyes filled with wonder.

I stopped to listen. The forest's edge was just a few feet up the trail, and something about his singing made me want to listen, if only momentarily. My heart slowed down as his sweet voice calmed me, and then I thanked him. "You have a beautiful voice. Keep singing, my friend. I hope to see you again."

He sang a few more notes and then flew away. I thought Grosbeaks migrated South for the winter. I could put some seed out in case he needed it. We'd have to go back to the store for cat food, and we could pick up birdseed, too.

I trudged back to the apartment, trying to sort through the indescribable. It was pointless to share it with anyone because no one would believe me.

CHAPTER TWELVE

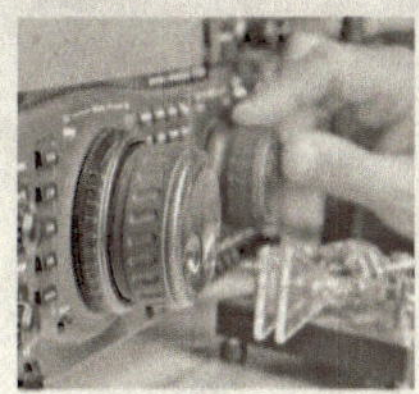

I ran into the living room to share the good news. "Mother, you remember those boxes my father sent me?"

She nodded.

"I didn't want to tell you at first, but since you know my father sent them, I think it's okay to tell you what was in them. It was ham radio equipment."

"Ham radio equipment?" she repeated.

"Yes. And, guess what?"

"What?"

"I passed my technician licensing exam."

She smiled. "Your father was very much into stuff like that. He was a communications guru, anything electronic. The apple doesn't fall far from the tree, does it?"

"I guess not." I hugged Rophe and kissed him. "I needed to tell someone. If only I could tell Judd."

Then I noticed Mother holding a book and reading for the first time in months. I remembered when she read several books a week. "What are you reading?"

"Oh, I'm reading one of my favorite books from childhood."

"What is it?"

She held it up for me.

I edged closer to read the title—*"Charlotte's Web."*

Mother nodded. "I love the mother spider in the story. She's—so real to me."

I nodded, although I could barely remember the story.

"Chumana," Mother asked, "am I a good mother?"

"Of course you are. Why would you ask that?"

Her eyes had that faraway look that had become so common recently.

"Sometimes I don't feel like I've been a good mother. There are moments when I don't even know who I am. But—my memory seems to be returning. I am remembering things I had forgotten."

"Like what?"

"I used to work, didn't I?"

"Yes."

"What kind of what did I do?"

"You don't remember?"

She shook her head.

"You were a teacher."

Her eyes lit up. "That's right. I remember now. I was a teacher."

"Are you proud of me for passing the test?"

Mother laughed. "Of course. I knew you would."

Whether she understood what I meant, I wasn't sure. But to see her holding a favorite book gave me hope. I kissed Rophe again before returning him to her.

"Let me fix something to eat."

A FEW WEEKS passed as I studied between school assignments for the general ham radio exam. One night, my phone beeped, and I saw Judd's text message.

"Are you going to isolate yourself forever? When can we get together?"

I sighed. I didn't know how to reply. There were only so many hours in the day. Frustration welled up inside me. Somebody was manipulating me unfairly—perhaps my father. Maybe I didn't want to meet him. I desperately wanted to tell Judd what I was doing.

I was intrigued by ham radio. How did I never hear about it until now? Talking to someone in Russia or South America with a small wire and antenna seemed far-fetched, but I couldn't wait to try it.

I heard my phone beep again. "Can I come over and see Rophe?"

Excuses, excuses. I should take a break. We were also low on cat supplies.

I glanced at the time. "How about in an hour?" I texted him.

He replied with a smiley face. If I told him in person about my ham radio adventure and made him promise not to tell anyone, how would they, whoever "they" were, know? Part of the fun in life is sharing secrets. I'd kept this secret long enough.

I HEARD the doorbell an hour later, so I stepped away from my desk. I was expecting Judd to arrive at any moment. When I greeted him, he held up an envelope. "This was taped to your door."

"What is it?"

"I don't know."

I opened it and read the contents: "An inspection will be conducted sometime in the next few days to ensure the occupants of this unit are in compliance with apartment rules. Management reserves the right to evict anyone found non-compliant with the renter's agreement after sufficient notice to rectify issues found." Signed by the apartment manager.

My heart sank. "Judd, I can't believe this. What am I going to do with Rophe?" I glanced at my mother. "What if they come when I'm not home? Mother might be confused."

Judd re-read the letter. "They don't tell you exactly when, do they?

"It says in the next few days. Just when things were falling into place. Mother has been so much better with Rophe here, and he keeps me company while I study."

Judd chuckled. "When did you ever need to study?"

I ignored his question and sat at the dining room table. News streamed from the living room, but Mother wasn't watching it. She was reading with Rophe in her lap. I should turn it off. Everything was irritating me now, mainly things I didn't care about.

Judd put his hand on my shoulder. "I can keep Rophe for a few days until after they do the inspection."

I squinted to hold back tears. I knew this was a possibility. They did annual inspections, but I imagined this happening far into the future and convinced myself I didn't need to worry about it. There was no way they could have known about Rophe unless someone tattled on me at school.

"Judd, who did you tell about Rophe? Do you think someone reported me?"

He shook his head. "I mentioned it that one time and then realized I should have kept quiet about it. I don't think Shale or Rachel would have said anything to the apartment manager. It's just inspection time on the calendar for this unit."

Judd's words reassured me. "Well, I suppose it's better to let you keep him for a few days than to be evicted or give Rophe away."

"As soon as the inspection is completed, I'll return him to you."

"They'll probably stop by during the day. I want to keep him with me at night."

"You'd have to bring him by in the morning before school."

That seemed like a lot of trouble. "We need to buy a cat carrier for him. I also need more cat food. And can we get birdseed?"

"Birdseed?"

I nodded.

"Okay. Birdseed and cat food."

I ran into the living room and told Mother we were going to the store to get cat food. She looked up from her book and nodded.

I paused. "Can I turn off the TV?"

"Yes, Honey. I'm not watching it."

My eyes focused on Rophe. I'd have to explain his absence to Mother. I wanted so much to believe that everything would turn out all right. It was just a momentary inconvenience, I said in my heart—a momentary annoyance, not permanent.

CHAPTER THIRTEEN

Judd and I sat in the car after returning from the store. I knew the time had arrived that I needed to send Rophe home with him. How would my furry baby feel? Would he think I'd given him away?

"Judd, why don't you come inside and spend a few minutes with Rophe? That way, he'll feel comfortable with you and not be afraid."

Judd nodded. "I'd love to. And remember, this is only temporary."

Knowing that it was temporary was the only thing that brought me comfort. "Did you ask your mother if it's okay?"

"I texted her, and she said it was fine. She knows it's only for a few days."

"Okay." I couldn't delay the inevitable any longer. I opened the car door and grabbed the cat food and birdseed. Judd retrieved the cat carrier.

Memories of Judd losing his dog from the accident pierced me. I remembered the pain he felt and how angry he was at Shale, even putting a curse on her. Did this bring back difficult memories for him?

Another thought entered my mind: Where do animals go when they die? I shouldn't think like that. Rophe would be okay with Judd. There wasn't anyone else I could trust like I trusted him, except my mother when she was herself.

I reminisced. I missed those days when I had a mother who cared for me. Now that Mother was more aware of her issue, the difference between what she was a year ago and her current mental state was more painful to me.

She was "waking up" to the fact that she wasn't quite right. Her dementia had made it easier for her to bear because of her lack of awareness. Now that she was learning about her deficit, she wanted to be a good mother. It was like she had to relearn stuff she once knew and accept that she wasn't what she once was.

I couldn't deny that Rophe's unconditional love helped her heal. Perhaps more love in the world could help others. Mother would miss him. I would need to reassure her that everything would be all right and that Judd was only keeping him temporarily.

I unlocked the door, and Judd followed me inside. The TV was still off, Mother was still reading, and Rophe was still lying in her lap. I glanced back at Judd.

"He's grown a lot since I last saw him," Judd said.

"Has he? It's only been a couple of weeks."

Judd chuckled. "That's a long time in a cat's life. They don't live as long as people."

Why did he have to say that? I walked over to Mother, and she looked up from her book.

"Mother, Judd is going to keep Rophe for a couple of days, so when the inspectors come by, they won't see we have a pet."

"Remember," she said. "We don't have a pet. Just a cat that's visiting."

I nodded. "Still, I don't want to risk the apartment manager taking him away, possibly to the pound. They'd probably put him to sleep."

Mother set the book on the table and picked up Rophe, kissing him. Then she handed him to me. Tears filled her eyes.

I swallowed, but my dry throat persisted. "It's okay, Mother. Judd will take good care of him."

Rophe's bright, trusting eyes gave her a reassuring look. I reached over to grab him and held him to my chest. “Hopefully, the inspector shows up tomorrow, and we can bring him back home.”

I handed Rophe to Judd, who was sitting in the chair. He gently stroked Rophe’s head. I could tell the two would get along fine.

After a few minutes, Judd said, “I’ll get the litter box.” He handed Rophe to me. I heard him sniffling as he headed to the bathroom.

I imagined him thinking about the loss of his dog. Our loss was only temporary; his was permanent.

Much to Rophe’s objection, I placed him in the cat carrier, quickly zipping up the top. I squatted and peered through the side opening. “You’ll be back soon. Don’t worry. Judd will take good care of you.”

He whined. I had never heard him cry before. I reassured him, but to no avail. He wanted out of the carrier.

Judd returned from the bathroom with the litter box wrapped up in a garbage bag. I grabbed the cat food. Rophe continued to complain. Fortunately, Judd lived close on the other side of the apartment complex, so it was a short distance.

“Maybe I should sleep at your house,” I joked.

He chuckled. “Mom wouldn’t care.” He turned on the engine, and we arrived in less than a minute.

“Can I come in?” I asked.

Judd nodded. “Sure.”

We brought everything inside. Judd’s mother must have already gone to bed. At least she didn’t appear to say “hello,” and I didn’t ask. All I could think about was Rophe.

We made him comfortable in Judd’s room, and then Judd walked me to the door. He put his arm around me, and I buried my face in his chest. A warm embrace ensued—not romantic, deeper than that. Warmth, reassurance, comfort—just what I needed.

“Thank you, Judd. What would I do without you?”

Judd laughed. “You’d be in trouble.”

I supposed he was right.

“All right,” Judd said. “Let’s go. There is too much emotion here.”

The ride back seemed even shorter. Judd parked and waited. “Are you okay?”

I nodded. "Let's hope the inspector comes tomorrow."

"Let me know. And I'll let you know how Rophe does."

"Thanks." I stepped out of the car. Walking to the apartment, I could have sworn I heard something in the night wind.

C-h-u-m-a-n-a.

Impulsively, I looked around but saw no one. I must have imagined it. I unlocked the front door and entered. Mother had fallen asleep reading her book.

I looked at the clock. It was later than I thought. I couldn't study tonight. I was too tired.

I went over and nudged Mother on the arm. Startled, she woke up.

"You need to get some sleep. You'll sleep better in your bedroom."

She nodded. "Good night, Honey."

"Good night, Mother." I leaned over and kissed her. "Please don't go anywhere. Just sleep."

CHAPTER FOURTEEN

Troubling dreams awoke me several times, and then my alarm jarred me awake. I jumped out of bed and went to check on Mother. I could see through the cracked door that she was sleeping.

I breathed easier. Hopefully, the apartment manager would come today for the inspection. My second biggest concern was whether Mother's mental deficiency would raise concerns with the manager if he came when I wasn't here.

Sometimes, she seemed entirely normal; at other times, her mind was elsewhere. But I couldn't stay home from school to be here when he came.

Mother looked so peaceful. I'd hope for the best. I returned to my room, dressed, and ate oatmeal and a banana before leaving for school. All I could think about was Rophe.

I grabbed my backpack, but I froze when I opened the apartment door. Did I forget to lock it? Or did Mother sleepwalk last night? Panic seized me. Was I losing it, too? Or was she out all night? I leaned my head on the door. I couldn't go on like this.

Things had been getting better. Rophe made our family seem

normal, and my success in passing the technician license exam boosted my confidence.

Now everything was falling apart. Anger at my inability to improve things, no matter how hard I tried, robbed me of my joy. I needed Rophe back.

I triple-checked that I had locked the door on my way out. Instinctively, I started counting steps. It was like I needed to count because it was all I could control. The steps I took to school were the same every day, and the number never varied.

With all the uncertainty that wanted to crush me, I liked the sameness. Monotony wasn't boredom. It was safety. I knew where the steps would take me and how long it would take me to get there.

I arrived at school as the bell rang—I was never late—and went to AP Chemistry. Judd acknowledged me as I entered. Out of view of the others, I texted him, "How is Rophe?" and he texted back a smiley face.

That settled me enough to pay attention. I had to listen to the teacher since I rarely cracked a book at home. Lack of focus meant I would have to study it.

I texted him, "Let's meet for lunch."

He replied with a thumbs-up. That was what I needed right now. Some reassurance that someone cared.

JUDD CHOSE a different table from the group we usually hung out with. Of course, that meant the rumors would fly, but I didn't care. When did I ever care?

I grabbed a tray with standard cafeteria food and walked to Judd's table.

He smiled. "Rophe did great last night."

"I'm glad, Judd, but my night wasn't great."

Judd's countenance fell at my not-so-great news. "What happened?"

"When I went to leave the apartment this morning, somebody had unlocked the door. Either I'm losing it like my mother, which is scary, or she was out sleepwalking again."

"Anybody can forget to lock the door," Judd said. "Don't make that connection. It's—not even true."

"Well, then, my mother was out last night. Judd, it scares me. It's not normal. Where is she going and why?"

"Maybe you should take her to the doctor, like a psychiatrist?"

"Judd, if I do that, they will say she's mentally incompetent and will want to take her wherever they take people like that, a psychiatric ward—I don't know where the hell they take them, and I don't wanna know. I'd be sent to a foster home. The home I long for will never be possible."

"You need Rophe, Chumana. I'd never seen you so happy as you have been over the last few weeks, even though you were too busy to spend much time with me." Judd smiled. "But I forgive you."

I rolled my eyes. "Mother hasn't wandered off since we got Rophe. She's gotten better. She started reading again. She was reading a childhood favorite—almost like she must relearn everything."

Judd was quiet for a minute. "Animals become so much a part of our lives. We don't even realize it until we lose them." He stopped mid-sentence.

I leaned over. "Judd, I'm sorry. I've hated Shale ever since the accident."

Judd shook his head. "Hate is not the answer. I don't know the answer, but I know it's not hate. Hate destroys the person. I'm sorry I cursed Shale. I shouldn't have."

We both remained silent for a minute, and I took a bite out of my egg sandwich. I wasn't hungry, but I would be later if I didn't eat.

I broke the silence. "Can you bring Rophe over this afternoon?"

Judd smiled. "Sure."

I felt better having someone else shoulder my burden. The inspection could have happened while I was at school, and then things could return to normal.

I felt emboldened to share my secret with Judd. "By the way, I passed my technician's license."

"Technician's license?" Judd repeated.

I laughed. "Ham radio license. But don't tell anyone. It's a secret. Promise me you won't tell anyone."

"I never knew you were into ham radio."

"Well, I'm not." I paused and reflected. How could I explain all of this? "Remember all those boxes in front of my door a few weeks ago?"

"Yes."

"It was the equipment."

"Ham radio equipment?"

I nodded.

"Who sent it to you? You're acting so mysterious."

I looked up at the clock. We only had a few minutes left before the next bell rang. "For them to disclose who my father is, I must fulfill certain requirements—proficiency with ham radio and Morse code."

Judd's eyes grew wide. "Chumana, this sounds—well, weird. Bizarre."

"Do you know who your father is?" I asked.

Judd shook his head. "He died a long time ago."

"Well, suppose you could bring him back to life. What would you do to make that happen?"

Judd stared at me. Finally, he answered. "I just worry about you, that's all. That's not how fathers treat their daughters."

"Well, now that I passed the first test, I've discovered I like it. There is something about it that I find intriguing. Maybe you might like to do it."

Judd studied me for a minute. "Maybe. Let's take it one thing at a time."

"Don't tell anyone, okay? I wasn't supposed to tell anyone."

Judd nodded. "As long as I don't feel like you're in danger, my lips are sealed."

"I'm not in any danger," I reassured him.

Or was I?

CHAPTER FIFTEEN

The bell rang, and I quickly left to head home. The sky was overcast, mimicking my heart. Too many things tugged at me that needed my attention. I knew Judd wanted me to be his girlfriend. Was it fair to him that I relied on him so much and didn't become what he wanted?

Perhaps I had set myself up for failure by putting too many expectations on myself. I just wanted to be a 17-year-old girl thinking about proms, dating, college, and a career. I liked Judd, but I didn't love him. Perhaps it was my upside-down world—trying to meet my father's expectations, wherever he was, and trying to be my mother's mother.

It was too painful to think about what I really wanted—a home with parents who loved me. I couldn't change the past. How much influence can anyone have on the future? Much is already fixed based on ethnicity, income, opportunity, or ability.

I thought about Shale. The Bible was her rock. Even though her family was as mixed up as mine, somehow, she found joy in that. I guess I was different.

Judd was right. Hate wasn't the answer, but how do you reconcile with somebody who has hurt you or your friend? Suppose I had hit

Rophe instead of the fox? How would I have been any different from Shale? "It would have been an accident," I would have said.

Okay. I reasoned that I wouldn't hate Shale anymore, but that didn't mean I had to like her. Judd, despite his shortcomings, had a bigger heart than me. Maybe my heart was so sensitive that it was harder to release the hurts.

Sometimes I felt other people's pain in a way that didn't make sense. I didn't know what to do with it, so I internalized it.

I quickened my pace until I saw our apartment in the distance. No sign or paperwork from the inspection was on the door. My heart sank. The inspector must not have come unless Mother let him in, and he left the paperwork in the house.

I found her in the living room watching the news. I checked the dining room table for paperwork. "Did the inspector come?"

"No, Honey. He didn't."

I sighed. "Well, Judd will bring Rophe over for a bit."

Mother nodded. "He helps me to be smarter."

What a strange thing for Mother to say. I walked over and sat beside her. "How does he make you smarter?"

She smiled. "I guess I used the wrong word. Rophe makes me feel whole."

I hugged her. "I love you."

Then I heard a knock on the door. Could it be the inspector?

I rushed to the door and opened it. Judd stood in the doorway with Rophe in the carrier. I took the carrier and set Rophe free in the living room.

"I'll get his litter box," Judd said. Then he chuckled. "Unlike you, I have to study, so I brought my books."

I wrapped Rophe in my arms and kissed him. Judd was right. He was growing. Soon, he would be a full-grown cat. Did that mean I needed to get him fixed? I remembered someone telling me that male cats tend to spray if they aren't neutered. I also knew there were certain required shots, like rabies. I wouldn't think about that right now. I needed to focus on one thing at a time.

The time passed quickly. Judd studied, and I buried my head in ham radio concepts. Rophe visited Mother, Judd, and me, making the rounds throughout the evening. I fixed an easy meal and allowed myself to enjoy it—worry-free. When was the last time I had a carefree spirit?

Late evening, Judd packed his books into his backpack, and I regrettably put Rophe in the carrier. Rophe complained loudly, but now that he had been through this before, he seemed to accept that it was only temporary. He soon gave up whining and resigned himself to the inevitable.

Judd said goodbye to Mother, and I walked out with him to the car. "Judd?"

"Yes," he said.

"I had a thought. If the inspector doesn't come tomorrow, maybe you could spend the night here until he shows up."

Judd put the carrier on the back seat and shut the door. Then he wrapped his arms around me. "I could love you if you let me."

I buried my head in his chest. "Maybe later. Right now, I need to figure everything out."

"Well, for now, I'll just settle for kissing you on the forehead."

"Thanks for understanding," I said.

He climbed into his car and shut the door. Soon, he was off to the other side of the apartment complex. I looked up at the glistening stars. As I contemplated what was out there, I heard my name emanating from the heavens.

C-h-u-m-a-n-a.

However, I saw nothing.

It must be my imagination. Still, I couldn't shake the feeling that something or someone out there wanted to reach me. Was it my father? Was that why I needed to learn ham radio? Was he somewhere among the stars?

I turned off my wandering, creative mind and headed back into the house. This time, I made sure I locked the door. Mother had fallen asleep in the chair. She probably didn't realize that Rophe wasn't in her lap, so I decided to let her be and not coax her into the bedroom.

I missed Rophe. I missed his sweet purrs and green eyes as they followed me wherever I went. If he wasn't in Mother's lap, he wouldn't let me out of his sight—not even to go to the bathroom. I wanted him back—whatever it took.

CHAPTER SIXTEEN

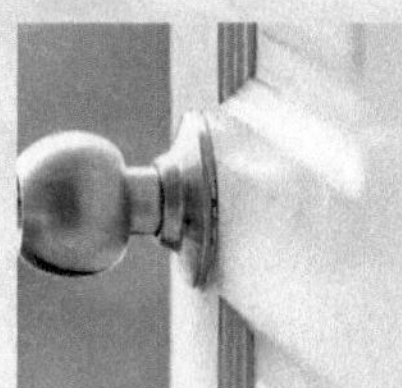

I woke up early the next morning, before the alarm went off, and hopped out of bed to check the front door. Somebody had unlocked it. I froze. I twisted the doorknob to lock the door. I ran to my mother's cracked bedroom door. She was sleeping.

I went into my bedroom and texted Judd. "Somebody unlocked the front door again. I am freaking out."

"Are you sure you locked it?" Judd texted.

"Of course, I'm sure."

"I have an idea. We'll talk about it over lunch."

"How is Rophe?"

"He's fine. He slept with me last night."

I was jealous. "Ha-ha," I texted him.

What was Judd's idea? I was up so early that I had time to study ham radio. I turned on the computer and started going through questions.

The website said learning the material for the general license would take about 20 hours. If I studied four hours daily, I would cover all the material in five days.

Of course, that meant I couldn't be distracted by my mother's sleepwalking. I didn't know how not to be distracted.

If only the inspector would come today, I would have Rophe back. Mother never went anywhere when Rophe was here; if she did, she locked the door when she returned.

I needed to focus. The first sentence read, "CW is permitted throughout all amateur radio bands." Communicating in dits and dahs sounded like fun.

❧

LUNCH COULDN'T COME SOON ENOUGH. AGAIN, I found Judd sitting alone, waiting for me, and I plopped beside him.

"Tell me what you're thinking."

Judd said, "First, let's hope the inspector comes today. If not, we have a couple of options. We could put a camera at the door to record if she's leaving. Or if somebody has access to the house and is letting themselves in in the middle of the night."

I shuddered. I hadn't thought about that. "That seems unlikely, but scary if it were true."

Judd nodded. "I want to make sure something isn't going on that we need to call the police. Another thing to do would be to put an alarm on the door. If someone opened the door, an alarm would sound."

I liked that idea, but there was a problem. "I want to know where she's going. If we put an alarm on the door, it would stop her from leaving because I would wake up. But we would never find out."

"True," Judd said. "But unless you wake up and follow her, you aren't going to know."

"Is there a way to hook it up to my phone and have an app alert me if someone opens the door?"

"You would probably have to go through a company, and they will charge you. Do you have any money?"

"I receive a monthly allowance on my credit card that I can use for personal things. If I spend too much, it tells me the purchase won't go through."

"How much is it?" Judd asked.

"It's a couple hundred dollars, but I learned the hard way not to abuse it."

"How's that?"

I laughed. "The bank canceled the card, but later they sent me a new one."

"Who sent you a new one?" Judd asked.

"If I knew, I would tell you."

"Whatever," Judd said.

"Can you bring Rophe over today?"

"Sure." Judd looked at his phone. "I need to do some studying before my next class. Do you want me to take you home after school? We can pick up Rophe on the way."

"Yes. That'd be great."

Judd grabbed his books. "I'm parked by the fence at the back. Meet me there."

"Thanks. See you later."

THE BELL RANG, and I hurried to the parking lot. Judd was already there with the engine running. I ran over and jumped into the front seat.

"Can we go by my apartment first? I want to see if the inspector came. If he did, we can pick up Rophe."

Judd nodded. "That sounds like a good plan."

We left the school and arrived at the Hope Garden Apartments in a few minutes. As we pulled up, my heart leaped. "Look, Judd, there is a sign on the door."

"Go see."

I jumped out and raced up to the door. Sure enough, we had passed inspection. Smiling, I waved at Judd. He gave me a thumbs-up. I ran back to the car.

"That's awesome. I'm so glad."

"Let me go inside and check on Mother."

"Sure. Take your time."

Mother was sitting in front of the TV with the news blaring. The book she had been reading lay beside her. Since Rophe had been gone, she hadn't picked it up and had reverted to watching the news all day.

I showed Mother the inspection sheet. "Did you see him when he came? We passed inspection."

Mother nodded. "I let him in. He walked around, checked the windows, attic, and that was it."

"Great. I'm so relieved."

"Me, too," Mother said.

"I'm going to Judd's to get Rophe, and then I'll be back."

Mother nodded. "If there is a God in heaven, he must have heard my cries."

Mother's response surprised me. When had she ever talked about God? I smiled. "Yes, Mother. He heard your cries."

I hugged her and ran out the door. Maybe Mother was right. Maybe there was a God in heaven who heard her cries. If there was, why didn't he listen to mine?

WE DROVE to Judd's apartment and returned within the hour. Now that Rophe was with me, Judd didn't want to leave immediately. After all he had done for me, I was okay with him hanging around. I could be Judd's girlfriend after I passed all the tests and did everything I needed for the next step, whatever that was.

To be truthful, I didn't want to be his girlfriend right now, but maybe in the future.

I fixed dinner, and we stretched it to feed three people. Judd said the grace, giving thanks to God, which seemed odd, and I took a bite of the couscous.

"Judd, I didn't know you prayed. The better I get to know you, the more I learn new things about you."

"I've continued going to Shale's Bible Study and am learning a lot."

"Perhaps I should come again," I said to be courteous. I still didn't know how he could forgive Shale and go to the Bible Study. Shale had even attacked him in the hallway, and the school expelled her because of it.

We finished dinner, and I cleared the table with Judd's help. Mother was tired and retired to the bedroom. It gave Judd and me time to talk.

I picked up Rophe and hugged him. "I never thought a small cat could bring me so much joy."

Judd smiled, "Animals love unconditionally—unless abused, and their ability to love turns into fear. Kind of like people." Judd's eyes bore into mine.

"What do you mean?" I asked.

"Who is the mother in this house?" Judd asked.

I went and sat in the chair. "I love my mother."

Judd knelt beside me. "I know you do, Chumana, I know."

He rubbed Rophe's ear. "Have you decided if you still want a camera installed? Now that management has done the yearly inspection, maybe you don't need to get one. You have Rophe back."

"When can we do it if I decide I still want one?"

"Let me look on Amazon and see what I can find. I'll let you know."

I leaned over and kissed Judd on the lips. Where did that come from? Unexpected on my part, but Judd was delighted.

I mused. When you let in a little bit of love, more follows. It wasn't a sexual thing. I was just thankful for his help and understanding. I had never even kissed a guy on the lips. My heart fluttered.

He stood. "Well, I need to go home and study. Unlike you, I must read textbooks to get good grades."

I smiled. "I have to study ham radio since I don't have an instructor. So, I'm reading books—at least reading the material on the computer. I'm not like my mother—a reader. Or at least she used to be. I like to listen."

With Rophe in my arms, I walked Judd to the door. "Thanks again for all your help."

"It's all good," he said. "I'm glad Rophe is back with you now."

Judd turned and walked to his car. I waited to shut the door until he had driven out of sight. I argued the pros and cons of having a boyfriend. If I did, I might choose him. But I didn't want one.

I checked to ensure the door was locked and took Rophe into my bedroom. He purred in my arms. "Home, sweet home," I pretended I heard him say.

CHAPTER SEVENTEEN

Days passed, and worries about my mother's sleepwalking faded into the background. I locked the door at night before going to bed, and it was still locked in the morning.

After many hours of study, I was ready to take the general licensing exam, my next big step. I pulled up the test site and entered the relevant information. I had made 100 on the technician licensing exam and hoped to duplicate my perfect score.

I set up Zoom for monitoring per the instructions. Three faces appeared on the screen, and, again, as before, they went over the perfunctory instructions.

"Please scan your room and underneath your desk."

I followed the Volunteer Examiner's commands. I was anxious to take the test, but I needed to let them check my room to ensure I couldn't cheat.

Then, I needed to keep the phone in a position so they could monitor me. The test consisted of 35 questions, and I had 90 minutes to complete it.

After the perfunctory instructions, the VE gave me the okay, and I clicked start.

"In what segment of the 20-meter band are most digital mode operations commonly found?"

I clicked on D, "Between 14.070 MHz and 14.100."

"What is VARA?"

I clicked on B, "A digital protocol used with Winlink."

"What sound is heard from an audio device experiencing RF interference from a single sideband phone transmitter?"

I clicked on C, "Distorted speech."

"What is reactance?"

I clicked on B, "Opposition to the flow of alternating current caused by capacitance or inductance."

I continued breezing through the questions.

"Why do voltmeters have high input impedance?"

I clicked on D, "It decreases the loading on measured circuits."

Within a few minutes, I clicked to the end and arrived at the final question: "Which size fuse or circuit breaker would be appropriate for a circuit that uses AWG number 15 wiring?"

I clicked on D, "13 amperes."

I'd forgotten I was being watched, and when I looked up, three faces stared back at me. "I'm done."

"Are you sure?" the VE asked. "You've got a lot of time left."

I nodded. "I'm done."

He closed the test, and I waited.

After a short pause, I heard the words I hoped to hear.

"Congratulations. You passed—in fact, you made 100."

"Great!" I said, ecstatic—two tests down, one to go. The extra was more comprehensive, with 50 questions and many more study hours required. I was two-thirds of the way through the licensing part. Once I passed the extra, I could call the contact person to install the equipment. Then, I would focus on continuous wave and digital modes.

The three VEs congratulated me again and bid me farewell. I exited from Zoom and plopped down on my bed, where Rophe was sleeping. I ran my fingers through his fur and told him my good news. He purred in a congratulatory way.

I wanted to text Judd and tell him, but what if someone monitored my calls and text messages? I was under orders not to tell anyone about my ham radio incursion. Why was it such a big deal?

I'd tell Judd in person and threaten him if he told anyone. I returned to my computer and looked up the extra licensing exam syllabus. The site said it would take around 30 hours to learn the new material and review some of the same topics in more detail.

I shut down my computer. I'd think about that tomorrow. For now, I would celebrate my success in passing the general license exam, which qualified me to use the HF bands. I could now contact other licensed users all over the world.

The tech license was restricted to VHF and UHF, which meant it was only good in close quarters or within a limited range. As soon as the radio was installed, I saw a vast new world of opportunities.

I rose from my desk and crouched beside the unopened boxes. Even if I opened them, I couldn't do anything until the installer set up the radio equipment. Maybe I'd peek inside one of them—what could be the harm?

I changed my mind. I was too tired to think about it. The adrenaline from making a perfect score had worn off. I'd go to sleep satisfied.

I reflected. Each licensing level got harder. I glanced at my schoolbooks. I was so busy studying ham radio that I neglected my calculus and chemistry studies. The other subjects were so easy that they took up little time outside class. I vowed to catch up tomorrow so I wouldn't mess up my perfect grades.

I left my bedroom and checked the front door. Mother had long gone to bed. I turned out the light in the living room and paused. Mother was reading a new book. I picked it up to see what it was. The Bible? Was she reading the Bible? I didn't even know we owned one. I glanced at the hundreds of books on the bookshelf. How did she even find it amongst all those books?

She hadn't marked the page where she was reading. I set the Bible down on the table. I had never seen her read it.

I returned to my bedroom, where Rophe waited for me to crawl into bed next to him. What was it about Rophe that brought my mother back from dementia? Every day, she seemed better, more conversant, and reading again. I had forgotten what a rabid reader she was. Perhaps the news sent her into darkness. The news was always depressing.

Wars and rumors of wars covered the headlines. How long would it be before someone did something terrible? I might need that ham radio license more than I realized. What if the internet went down? What if some rogue nation sabotaged our satellites? How would we communicate? Maybe my father was preparing me for something no one could imagine that was coming. Perhaps he knew something the rest of us didn't know.

Still, of all the books Mother could have selected, why did she choose the Bible?

I turned out the light, and Rophe scooted beside me, pawing at me making biscuits. I fell asleep listening to him purr.

CHAPTER EIGHTEEN

A couple of weeks passed. By necessity, I had isolated myself to study, even during lunch at school. I'd found an app I used on breaks when I wasn't home and took advantage of every spare moment.

However, total isolation isn't a good thing, so today, when I saw Gracie sitting alone, I walked over and sat beside her. The others hadn't arrived—Shale, Rachel, and Judd—so it was just the two of us.

She welcomed me with her bright green eyes and British accent.

"Have a seat and tell me what's going on with you. You've been so busy recently that I've hardly seen you."

I nodded. "I've been too busy between school, helping my mother, and hobbies, so I wanted to join you and the others for lunch today."

Gracie smiled. "I dreamt about you the other night."

"You did?"

"Yeah." Gracie took a bite of her sandwich. "Do you have a twin sister?"

"A twin sister?"

She nodded. "Yeah."

"Not that I know of. Mother would have told me if I did." But now I was curious. "What else did you dream?"

Gracie paused, her eyes looking far away as she remembered. "It was weird. I couldn't see what you were doing, but you seemed to be playing a musical instrument. At least you were doing something with your hands, and you were on TV."

"Really? It might have been someone who looks like me. I don't play a musical instrument and can't imagine why I would be on television."

"It was sort of odd," Gracie said. "I figured if you had a twin sister, she would attend the same school as you."

"Sounds intriguing. I've always wanted a brother or a sister. I don't have anyone except my mother."

"You don't know your father?"

"Not yet, but I hope to soon."

Gracie was a good listener. She replied, "Sometimes it's better to wait until you're older. You never know how it will turn out. I've known some who regretted it later, meeting their long-lost father or mother."

I hardly knew Gracie at all. Her family had moved here over the summer. "What about you? Any brothers or sisters?"

Gracie nodded. "I have a sister, a few years younger than me. My mother is an administrator at Kennesaw State University, and my father is a physics professor."

"So that's why you're so good at math and science."

Gracie laughed. "Well, I got it from my father, not my mother. Her major was English, and that's my worst subject."

"Really?"

Gracie added, "You Americans spell things weird. Your grammar is different from the British. I've had to relearn a lot since moving to America. My teachers keep marking up things that would be correct in England."

She sighed. "But I like it here and hope we don't have to move again for a while. It's tough living all over the world. You have no roots—except for your immediate family."

"Well, I love your accent—how the British talk."

Gracie smiled. "It's just me. Sometimes, I try to add a Southern drawl to sound like I belong here, but I don't think I do a good impersonation. However, it's fun pretending."

I tried to mimic a British accent but failed miserably.

We laughed.

"We should get together sometime," Gracie said.

I nodded.

The rest of the crowd arrived, and chitchat bounced around to other topics that didn't interest me. Still, I pretended to pay attention as I thought about the formulas I needed to memorize or at least know how to use if they appeared on the test.

Discussion came up about the Bible Study later in the day and who was going.

"We should move the study back to your house," Rachel said, "because we're so limited on time before the library closes."

Judd looked at me. "Can you come today?"

"Maybe next week," I said. "I've got some things I must do when I get home."

I could tell Judd was disappointed. Part of me wanted to go, but I needed to get the extra test out of the way before distractions got the best of me.

The conversation moved on, and we dispersed one by one. Judd approached me when the others were gone and said softly, "As soon as you pass that extra test, let's celebrate."

I nodded.

"I want to see the radio equipment also," he added.

"I promise. Just don't tell anyone about it."

"I'll tell you my secret now," Judd said.

Now I was curious. "What's that?"

I've been checking out ham radio online and signed up for the technician course.

"Really?"

"You can get a walkie-talkie on Amazon cheap," Judd said.

"You mean for VHF and UHF?"

Judd looked at me funny. "I just call it a walkie-talkie for close-range communication. I guess that's VHF and UHF."

He chuckled. "If the world goes kaput, I'll still be able to reach you on the other side of the apartments."

"I wonder if I have one of those in the boxes they sent me," I mused. "Let's talk more when we have time."

We bid each other goodbye, and Judd took off down the hallway. Was he serious? Or was it just another way for him to spend time with me? I only cared about passing the test and calling the contact person to set up the equipment. Anything else was a distraction, including him.

❧

THE ATLANTA AIR was more than nippy now, and the barren trees stood dank and naked. As I walked home, a Rose-breasted Grosbeak flew to a nearby tree and sang as I passed by. Was he the same one as before? What were the chances another one would serenade me? Perhaps he was looking for a handout—sunflower seeds, and then I realized I had never put out the birdseed Judd had bought.

I would do that as soon as I could. I liked him and wanted the sweet-singing bird to hang around. He must have decided to spend the winter in Atlanta instead of trekking down to Florida, where the winters were kinder.

I walked faster. I was like a bird in some ways. I longed for springtime, too. I hated winter.

I could pass the extra exam in two months if I studied hard. Then, I would sing with all the birds welcoming spring. Of course, they were great singers. But I would sing with them even if I wasn't.

That reminded me of Gracie's dream—playing a musical instrument on television. I wasn't musical, so it couldn't be me in her dream, but could I have a twin sister?

What a surprise that would be—but I doubted Gracie's dream. It was just a dream, nothing else. Maybe I should have stayed at school for the Bible Study. No—I needed to pass the test. Stay the course and go next week.

CHAPTER NINETEEN

I waited; it seemed like forever.

The Volunteer Examiner finally spoke. "Congratulations, Miss Ironvein. You passed."

"Wow! I'm excited." That was an understatement. Relief was more accurate. I had pushed hard to do it in a month and then worried I had jinxed myself. "What did I make?"

"You made a 93," he said.

It wasn't a 100 like on the previous two exams, but I only cared about passing it at this point.

The three Examiners congratulated me and reveled in my exuberance. One said, "We won't be seeing you again."

That meant I had no more tests to take. I still needed to focus on learning digital radio, but that didn't involve passing a test. My last requirement was proficiency in Morse Code.

Once the Zoom call ended, I grabbed my phone. Judd had been patient with me as I muddled through the three levels.

I texted him. "I passed my extra license exam." It seemed strange to be licensed at the highest level when the radio equipment was still in boxes, but that was about to change.

I plopped on my bed and hugged Rophe. "I love you." He

responded with sweet purrs and cuddled in my arms.

Judd texted back right away. "Can I come over?"

"Yes! Let's open one of the boxes. I will email my contact and see how soon he can set up the equipment."

"Be over in a few minutes."

I pulled out the original letter I received with the equipment. It was handwritten on official-looking government letterhead. I was unsure if the signer was my father or a designated person. I would soon find out.

I reread the instructions. It stated that I could have the radio installed once I passed the extra exam. Hopefully, digital and Morse Code would be easy to learn and less time-consuming. I was tired from all the studying. Of course, I needed to learn how to operate the radio.

I read to the end, and my heart skipped when I read the admonition about not telling anyone:

> *Breaking the rule means we'll need you to return the ham radio equipment, and you might never meet your father. Revelation of this information puts your father in harm's way.*

How could I make sure Judd didn't tell anyone? I remembered the confidential part, but I didn't remember the part about putting my father in harm's way. Well, I'd make sure Judd didn't tell anyone. I probably shouldn't have texted him just now about passing the exam.

I clicked on my email account and wrote to the name designated in the letter as the installer: "Dear Sir, you were given as my contact person to install my ham radio equipment when I passed all three licensing exams. How soon can you come?"

I'd have to wait to hear from him before I could do anything else.

I closed the computer and entered the living room, where Mother watched television. I felt like I had distanced myself from her and everybody else only because I had withdrawn from the world to study nonstop for the last several weeks.

"Mother?"

She looked in my direction.

"I love you."

"I love you, too, Honey. Have you come out of hiding?"

I laughed. "You're watching TV again."

She held up another book. "I'm trying to get back to reading. But it's more fun to read when Rophe cuddles up with me."

"Judd is coming over in a few minutes. I wanted to let you know."

She smiled but didn't say anything. She probably imagined that Judd was my boyfriend, but I wasn't ready to call him that yet.

After Mother's comment, I returned to my bedroom, grabbed Rophe, and took him to her. Gently, I placed him in her lap. "I've been keeping him to myself too much."

Delighted, she stroked him on the head.

"Mother, remember I received some boxes from UPS several weeks ago."

She nodded.

"I just passed the final test for my amateur ham radio license."

"Congratulations, Honey. And remember, the time is coming when you'll have to decide."

"What do you mean?"

"You'll have to decide what to do with your life. You're almost 18."

That wasn't what I expected her to say. Then I heard Judd knocking at the door.

I left Mother to greet him.

Judd surprised me with red roses. "You deserve these. Congratulations."

"Thank you. You're such a romantic. Let me grab a vase and put them in water."

I headed to the kitchen to find something and heard him talking to Mother.

I reappeared, showing Mother the vase of flowers. "See what Judd gave me for passing my extra test. Aren't they pretty?"

She nodded. "Yes. I love the red color."

I turned to Judd. "I'm not done yet, though. I've got to learn digital radio and Morse Code."

"Morse Code? I didn't know about that. That will take some time."

"I'll think about that later. Come with me and let's unpack the boxes."

Judd followed me into my bedroom, and we sat on the floor beside the pile.

"This looks like the real deal," Judd said. "I'm going to open this box, but then I'll reseal it so you don't get in trouble, okay?"

I nodded.

We carefully opened it, and inside the box was the strangest thing I'd ever seen. How would I ever figure out how to operate it?

Judd pulled out the instructions and looked them over. "I'm jealous."

"Are you still going to get your license?"

"Yeah, but this is more than I could ever afford."

I sat back, leaning against the wall. "I want you to get your license, too. Promise me you will?"

Judd laughed. "Give me the website you used, and I'll order the walkie-talkie from Amazon."

"Yes!"

"But ..."

"But what?" I asked.

Judd looked into my eyes with optimism. "Now that you passed the final test, can you start attending the Bible Study?"

"Okay," I promised. "I'll come to the next one."

THE FOLLOWING DAY, I received an email from the installer. He gave me several time options, and I chose the earliest appointment—in only two days. I couldn't wait.

CHAPTER TWENTY

The big day came, and I rushed home from school. Judd said during lunch that he would stop by later. I didn't realize I had set the time for the installation at the same time as the Bible Study, so Judd made me promise I would come next week.

Why had he gotten so spiritual? If he kept this up, he would be as spiritually minded as Shale. I didn't know if I could handle that. Even Gracie was getting into the Bible. Mom had laid the Bible aside—thank goodness. I felt like the odd man out. Or woman—whatever.

Mother had started cooking again, and I found her in the kitchen baking muffins, much to my delight. The change in her mental ability was dramatic since we adopted Rophe.

The doorbell rang, and I rushed to open it.

An older man introduced himself and handed me his business card. "I'm here to install a transceiver and antenna for Chumana Ironvein."

"That's me."

He smiled. "I expected you to be older. I love to see young people get into ham radio."

I turned to Mother. "This is Mr. Johnson. He's here to install the radio."

He gave her a cursory nod and asked, "Where would you like me to put it?"

I hadn't thought about that. "I guess my bedroom." I didn't want it to bother Mother when she was watching television or reading.

"And where is the equipment?"

I showed him all the boxes, and he studied his paperwork, checking things off to ensure everything was there.

"Can I see your attic?" he asked.

"Sure." I showed him where it was, and he climbed the stairs and disappeared for a few minutes before returning.

I pointed out the spot where I wanted to put the radio. "Right here on my desk."

He went to work unpacking everything.

I realized how much I had tortured myself about unpacking the boxes; he couldn't have cared less. "How long will it take?"

"Oh, a couple hours to run the wire into the attic and test everything. Not that long."

"Can I help you?"

"Sure."

I was excited and couldn't wait to get started.

Judd arrived shortly, for which I was thankful. If I forgot something important, I could ask him.

When Mr. Johnson finished, he explained the various pieces of equipment.

I noticed a small hand-held walkie-talkie among the equipment.

"Look, Judd, here's what you were talking about."

"That's for local communication," Mr. Johnson said. "It's programmed and ready to use, but you can mess it up if you don't read the instructions first."

"Where are those?"

Mr. Johnson handed me the pamphlet. "Here."

I had no idea what I was looking at.

"What's the difference again," I asked, "between the two radios, besides the price?"

"This hand-held is for local communication, like Simplex or

connecting to the local repeater. If the power goes out, the battery is inside the unit, and you can charge it through your computer or plug it into the wall with this charger. If you only have a tech license, you would use this small transceiver, more commonly referred to as a walkie-talkie.

"The large one here is a transceiver built for communication over long distances. Your antenna determines what frequencies you can use, but the radio is capable of voice, digital, and CW. You must have a general license to use it, or even better, an extra license—unless you only do CW. Then you only need a tech license to operate HF."

I glanced at Judd. "Just get your tech license and learn CW."

"And what about all the money it costs?"

"Well, work more hours."

Judd grimaced.

I smiled. "Just kidding."

Mr. Johnson turned on the radio, which "talked" quite loudly. It sounded like an electronic symphony, but it was music to my ears.

However, Mr. Johnson wasn't impressed. After he made a few adjustments, the disparate sounds settled down, and he looked satisfied.

The installer, a ham radio operator himself, picked up the microphone and identified himself with his call sign. I watched in wonderment. Could I do this? I was excited and nervous at the same time.

Mr. Johnson briefly explained what some of the knobs on the front of the transceiver meant and made a few more adjustments, testing the radio with the attic antenna on several frequencies.

Then, he focused his attention on me with a couple of admonitions. "Make sure you don't lose the manual. Many videos on YouTube will teach you how to use this popular transceiver. Oh, one word of caution. Don't ever run the radio without the antenna. That could cause some issues."

"Okay. Anything else that could damage the radio?"

Mr. Johnson thought for a moment. "Not that I can think of. I didn't mean to make you paranoid. You'll be fine."

I nodded. "Okay."

He handed me a card. "Now that your equipment is operational, here is the number to call if anything arises. I was only hired to do the installation. We install these radios for the government as subcontractors because they require slightly different settings, but contact them if you need more help."

"Okay."

"Before I leave, could you try it? Some people are initially afraid, but there is no reason to be shy."

"Okay. Tell me what to do."

"What's your call sign?"

"KO4LBS."

"It's good practice to use word IDs for the letters."

"I forgot what they are for my call sign."

"For yours, it would be Kilo-Oscar-4-Lima-Bravo-Sierra."

I repeated it a few times to feel comfortable saying it.

"What do I say next?"

You call CQ a few times, say your call sign, and then wait to see if anybody answers."

"That's all?"

"That's all."

He added. "Oh, let me point out a few things. Make sure you tune it for the frequency you are using." He demonstrated how to do that.

That was easy enough.

"Eighty meters is a good frequency to use in the evenings and at night."

"Okay."

"This is how you change the frequency." He demonstrated, and I mimicked what he did.

"And always ensure you operate within the frequency you're licensed to use."

"I have my extra."

He was surprised. "Really?"

"Yes."

"Well, the radio will beep when you go outside the extra frequencies, but it's good to check to ensure you stay legal. You don't want to get in trouble with the FCC."

I nodded.

"Are you ready?"

"I'm ready."

I clicked on the microphone. "CQ, CQ, CQ, this is KO4LBS, Kilo-Oscar-4-Lima-Bravo-Sierra, calling CQ."

"Say it a couple more times," Mr. Johnson said, "And then wait and see if anyone answers."

I repeated it and waited. When I thought no one had heard me, a voice boomed over the radio: "This is AE4HAM in Birmingham, Alabama, hearing you 5-9."

"Tell him your location and give him a 5-9 for his RS."

"I'd already forgotten what RS meant. But it didn't matter. I would look it up later.

"I said, "AE4HAM, I'm in Atlanta, and you are my first contact."

"You are doing great, KO4LBS. Keep up the good work. 73, AE4HAM."

The conversation was short and sweet, and I was hooked!

Judd and I thanked Mr. Johnson for installing the radio. As he packed his tools, he asked Judd, "Do you have a ham radio license?"

Judd shook his head. "Not yet, but I'm going to."

"It's a fun hobby," Mr. Johnson said. "And, who knows, if something were to happen, it's nice to know you can communicate worldwide with radio waves that fly through the atmosphere—even into outer space."

"That's true," Judd said. "You never know what might happen."

I escorted Mr. Johnson to the door and thanked him for coming.

"Don't lose that contact information. Add it to your phone."

"I will. Thanks again."

I shut the front door and turned to Judd. "So, you're going to get your license?"

Judd nodded. "I'll get my technician license—and if I do that, will you come to Bible Study?"

I chuckled. "I said I would come."

"Okay," Judd said. "We've got a deal."

And then I remembered the warning in the letter. "Promise me, Judd, you won't tell anyone about the radio."

"I promise."

"Don't call or text me anything about ham radio."

"Big Brother is watching," Judd said, "Read the book *1984.*"

"You heard him say it was a government installation, whatever that means."

"Are you comfortable with this?" Judd asked.

"Well, my father is involved in it, so it must be good—I mean, he's helping me get set up for emergency radio. Maybe he knows something is coming and wants to protect me."

"Well, just be discerning."

"I will, but if you can't trust your father or the government, who can you trust?"

CHAPTER TWENTY-ONE

The school year was flying by, and I needed to focus on my class studies as the end-of-year finals weren't but a few months away. The easiest subject so far had been AP Biology; it was the only class Judd, Gracie, Rachel, Shale, and I shared. But now that we were in the second semester and AP tests were around the corner, Mr. Beasley was upping the bar.

He stood before the class and announced, "We're going to have a group project focusing on the Origins of Life. More specifically, the Origin of Humankind."

"I see it this way," Mr. Beasley continued. "There are three possibilities. The first one is that God created us as humans in his image; second, we evolved into who we are through evolution; or third, other intelligent life in the universe seeded us."

Mr. Beasley paused, giving us time to write down the three choices.

Then, he said, "I want everyone to research it and return tomorrow knowledgeable enough to discuss it. I propose you decide which position most aligns with your truth. We'll have each of these three positions represented. Each group will choose who they want to present their findings to the class.

"Everybody with me so far?"

No one raised their hand, so he continued. "We can't be dogmatic about it, but we must use the scientific method to bolster our position.

"For instance, if you believe God created humans, don't just give us a bunch of biblical citations. That's not scientific. Give credible evidence to support why you think that—and the same for the other two views.

"Does anyone have any questions?"

No one said anything. I wasn't sure what I thought. I'd have to do some study. I knew what I'd be doing when I went home.

Mr. Beasley dismissed class early, assuming some students might want to visit the library. Not every student had access to the Internet at home.

Judd, Shale, Rachel, Gracie, and I went to the cafeteria.

Judd and I brought our lunch today. Rachel, Gracie, and Shale joined the line of students to buy theirs.

"Did you play around with the radio last night?" Judd asked.

"Oh, a little bit. But I want to read the instructions first. Maybe watch a couple of YouTube videos. Honestly, I don't know what I will do, and the last thing I want to do is break it before I learn how to use it."

Judd chuckled. "I don't think you can break it that easily. By the way, I bought a walkie-talkie from Amazon for $50. I also signed up for the technician class at the site you recommended."

"That's great. You could tell the others that you are learning ham radio. Just don't tell them about me."

"I'll wait until I pass the technician test. You've set a high bar, and I don't want to embarrass myself."

"Ah, you won't. It only takes eight hours of study for the technician course, and they guarantee you pass the test, or they refund your money."

"Can't beat that, and my extra money for this month is gone." Judd chuckled. "McDonald's is on you if we go."

Rachel returned to the table first, plopping her tray down.

"So, what's up with you?" I asked. "You seem stressed today."

"Oh, everything. The war in Israel. Antisemitism in America is growing. Sometimes, I feel like the world hates us just because we're Jewish. I never thought it would happen in America."

"I'm sorry, Rachel. I agree, it's uncalled for. It's wrong. Hurtful." I couldn't think of any other descriptive word that matched the intensity of the backlash toward Jews everywhere. "How is your family in Israel?"

"They're okay. But the stress is palpable. I can tell from the conversations we've had."

"Well, I'm your friend, Rachel, and if you ever need me, I'll be there for you—and your family."

"Thanks, Chumana."

Judd nodded in agreement.

Her comments prompted a question from me. "Rachel, as a Jew, how do you feel about going to Shale's Bible Study?"

"Well, I'm still determining if Jesus is the Messiah. It seems strange to me that Christians would believe in a Jewish Messiah. Even if he's not the Messiah, I still want to know about him because he's a significant historical figure.

"Jesus reshaped the world in many ways, such as how we record time and whether an event occurred in the B.C. timeframe or A.D. Then there is his impact on the Roman Empire.

"People were willing to face martyrdom in the name of Jesus. Even preserving history through the New Testament writings is a miracle, just like the Jewish Old Testament writings.

"Then, I think about the discovery of America in the name of religious freedom. The early settlers were all Christians. I can't think of any historical figure that has had more impact on the world than Jesus. If he is the Messiah, I want to know everything I can about him."

"So, you don't know yet? You're still trying to figure it out?"

Rachel nodded. "I think he is the Messiah, but if I make a public proclamation, I don't know what my family would think. It gets very complicated. I mean, the biggest question for me is, can you believe in Jesus and still be Jewish?

"Isn't it odd that some people think you must become a Christian to believe in Jesus, and yet Jesus was Jewish? How can both be true?"

I nodded. "I get it."

Gracie sat next to us, followed by Shale.

Rachel turned to me. "Are you going to come back to the Bible Study? We've already met this week and won't meet again until next week."

I shot a glance at Judd. "I promised Judd I would."

"Well, this will get interesting with the biology debate on the Origins of Life," Shale added.

"Could all three choices be true?" I asked.

Judd shook his head. "I don't see how."

Shale rambled on in her thoughts. "My biggest challenge will be finding scientific sources that support my religious convictions. Many scientists are atheists and don't embrace biblical truth."

I could see how this would play out. One thing it would do is require students to take a stance, including me. That meant I needed to discover the truth for myself. But really, what was the truth? Did we all have our own truth, as Mr. Beasley seemed to intimate? How could that be scientific?

CHAPTER TWENTY-TWO

INTERNATIONAL MORSE CODE

A	B	C	D	E	F
.-	-...	-.-.	-..	.	..-.

I hurried home after school. I no longer felt compelled to count my steps. Before, counting steps was due to boredom. School wasn't challenging, and I had become increasingly worried about Mother. There wasn't much in my life to cheer me up, except waiting until I turned 18. That was when I would learn about my hidden past.

I had so many good things to think about now; I'd stopped counting.

As I focused on the biology debate—how humankind came into existence—the real question was, how did I come to be? Forget the biology; it was about individual meaning.

Why were we here? How did we get here? And what, more specifically, was my purpose? Sure, I could read the Bible stories, but I perceived something more profound—perhaps something yet to be discovered or understood from the knowledge we already had.

Evolution was out of the question. As Mr. Beasley shared, only two possibilities remained: Was there a God? Or did it make more sense that another race of beings seeded us? If that were so, something would have had to create them, too.

Was it only about creating? When I made something, I didn't forget about it. I wanted to share it. Life was about sharing, especially secrets. So, was it something deeper?

If God created us, why was he so distant? I couldn't find him. Did he create us and then travel to another world or galaxy to make something else? Are we not important enough for him to stay here and help us? Did he not want to live among us?

On the other hand, would it make more sense that another race seeded us, returned to their home, and someday would return to Earth? Even if that were true, something had to create them, the planets, and the stars.

I looked forward to seeing what I could uncover. In the meantime, when I turned 18, the court papers would be unsealed.

I still looked forward to learning about my past, but it was less important now. Things in my life brought me joy: Rophe, my mother's healing, and I had a boyfriend, of sorts, even if he wasn't the one for life.

I passed the location where I had listened to the Rose-breasted Grosbeak sing to me the other day. He was so memorable. I wish he had returned, but not today.

What if I hadn't gone out to the woods that fateful evening? I never would have been there to save Rophe. The red fox would have eaten him. Imagine the pain and suffering he would have endured.

I opened the apartment door and saw Mother and my cat sitting together in Mother's favorite chair. Mom was holding a book but had dozed off. Rophe climbed down and greeted me as I entered, waking her up.

"How was school?" she asked.

I couldn't think of anything exciting to report. "Uneventful as usual. I have a little homework, and then I will play around with the radio."

"I saw your new equipment. What a special gift from your father."

"It seems to be from him, though the government is paying for it. At least they paid Mr. Johnson to install it, so I presume my father works for the government."

Mother tilted her head, thinking. "He worked on top-secret government projects. Half the time, I never knew where or what he was doing. He wasn't permitted to talk about it."

"You never told me that."

"My memory is returning. I was beginning to think I'd lost my mind."

I sat beside Mother on the sofa. Her eyes appeared brighter than they had been in a long time. It had been weeks since she had sleep-walked. The chronic lack of sleep stole her mind. It was a scientific fact that sleep deprivation is harmful, affects memory, and can make you psychotic.

"Please, tell me more about my father."

Mother smiled. "We lived on a military base, in a small apartment, when you were born, but I've forgotten which base it was; out West somewhere."

I remembered what Gracie had said to me at lunch. I interrupted her. "Do I have a twin sister?"

Mother laughed. "Why do you ask?"

I felt foolish. "One of my friends said she dreamed I had a twin sister."

"Well, if you have one, I don't know about it."

I reached down and picked up Rophe. "Why would Gracie dream about me?"

"That is a strange dream for someone to have."

"Gracie also dreamed I was on TV."

"Why were you on TV?"

I ran my fingers through Rophe's winter coat, which was soft and thick, and kissed him on the nose. "She didn't know."

Mother eyed us intently. "Chumana, we need to take Rophe to the vet to get his shots, and it would be a good idea to get him fixed, too. He's old enough now. If you wait too long, he might start to mark his territory, and we don't want that."

I knew Mother was right. I had thought about it but didn't want to bring it up. Plus, I was so focused on ham radio. When would I have had the time?

"I will call tomorrow and schedule an appointment to get his shots," Mother said.

I nodded.

"Do you think you and Judd could take him? It's been a long time since I've driven, although I feel much better now. I could drive if needed."

"I'll ask Judd if he can drive us."

I handed Rophe back to Mother and returned to my bedroom. After turning on the computer, I checked my email and found something that grabbed my attention.

"To the newest member of our team, Chumana Ironvein. Welcome aboard."

I continued reading: "We are thrilled you passed your final exam and your equipment is working. If the power goes out, you'll need a solar system to use with your transceiver. Communicating with you will be vital in an emergency. Amazon will send it in a couple of days.

"We would like to set up a Zoom call to introduce you to your ham radio mentor, who will teach you how to use your radio efficiently. She will also help you with the digital setup. And, as we expressed earlier, you must learn CW.

"Below are the dates and times for the first Zoom call. Choose the best time. Install the Zoom app on your computer. We look forward to hearing from you."

"73, The Frequency Group."

I glanced through the dates and times. When was that Bible Study? I knew it wasn't Monday, so I chose Monday afternoon after school. The weekend would give me time to familiarize myself with the basics so I wouldn't look incompetent.

I pressed send and waited to ensure it didn't get stuck in the outbox.

Then I turned on the radio. The CW keyer was still in the box. Mr. Johnson hadn't opened it, and I didn't know what to do with it, so I left it there. How long would it take to send out dits and dahs proficiently?

CHAPTER TWENTY-THREE

I sat at my computer and waited for the meeting's host to admit me. My ham radio idled in the background. I couldn't wait for things to get started. I had not met anyone on the team; I had studied alone on the computer. A mentor would boost my confidence. Judd was getting started, but it might be a while before he passed his technician exam.

As I was getting impatient, the host let me in on the call. A handsome gentleman sat before the camera. Anyone older than me looked old, so I didn't know how old he was, but old enough that I wanted to respect him.

He was probably in his early 40s. He couldn't have been 50. Anyone that old would be ancient, like a grandfather.

Streaks of gray highlighted his trimmed, wavy brown hair, and his hazel eyes appeared sharp and keen. He looked knowledgeable, although I don't know why I sensed that. He also seemed to be in excellent physical shape. He sat next to a table filled with ham radio equipment.

"Hello, Miss Ironvein," he said. "It's good to meet you. I want to congratulate you on your accomplishment. Sometimes, it takes a while for new hams to obtain their extra license, but you did it quickly."

"Thank you."

"By the way, can I call you Chumana?"

I laughed. "Sure."

"You can just call me Major. My name is too long for anyone to remember."

I nodded.

"So, let's get started. I'm your contact for The Frequency Group, but I have support staff. We always assign a mentor to our newest members to help them learn the ropes, so to speak, and I want to introduce you to yours.

"I don't want to rush through the process. We'll take a moment to do it gently because you will be surprised. You already know her, and that's why she is your best mentor."

I didn't know what he meant, but I listened with rapt attention.

"She will help you get comfortable with emergency radio communication. As the technology is increasingly refined, what we can do now is impressive, and our group of communications specialists, known as The Frequency Group, is on the cutting edge of a stunning revolution.

"AI is our newest tool in the toolbox, so to speak. We are the brains behind this new technology. There are several levels to the training, and this is the first level. The Frequency Group chose you to be on the team. Are you with me so far?"

I nodded. "I think so."

Major chuckled. "Okay. Let me introduce you to your mentor."

The camera switched to a different screen, and all my excitement dissipated as I saw my reflection staring back at me. Was she real? Was she human? I didn't know what to say.

She broke out in laughter, amused by my shock.

I stared. I thought I was going to be sick to my stomach. What had I gotten myself into? Who were these people? What did she mean? She even appeared to have my personality and smile. She fixed her thick red hair like I did, framing it around her face. She looked human, but was she?

I'd watched too many sci-fi movies or listened to too many

conspiracy theories; except I didn't go to the movies or listen to conspiracy theories. I was speechless.

The screen returned to Major. "Are you okay, Chumana?"

"I … I don't know. I feel light-headed. She looks like me."

Major laughed. "Rest assured, everyone reacts similarly when they see their double. They think they have lost their mind."

The screen panned out so I could see both her and Major. They were in the same room, just a few feet apart.

Major continued, "People don't realize this, but doubles have existed for a long time. They are so human-like that a typical person can no longer tell them apart—unless they know what to look for."

"She's my mentor? I'm mentoring myself?"

Major laughed. "Look at it this way. What's something you're good at?"

"I don't know. People say I'm smart, but it's not like I'm good at it. It just comes naturally for me."

"You had to learn how to read, right?"

I nodded.

"And you were not good at that initially, were you?"

I shook my head.

"That's because the way the teacher taught you wasn't conducive to your learning style. But if they had taught you according to the way you learn, you would have learned to read faster and with much less frustration."

"That makes sense."

"We know how you best learn. So, Humana, her given name, already knows everything about you: Your learning style, strengths, and weaknesses because she is you, in a sense. She can teach you without the struggle. Do you see what I'm saying?"

"Yes, I think so."

"Getting your ham radio license doesn't train you how to be an operator. It only teaches you what you need to know to be an operator and be legal—in other words, the FCC rules, the formulas, the science, the protocol, that kind of thing.

"Humana can help you reach competency more quickly, especially when working on CW. You can send messages repeatedly, so your proficiency and speed will develop more rapidly because you're practicing against yourself."

"I see."

Major continued. "Think about it this way. You're familiar with ChatGPT and Google Gemini, right?"

"Yes."

"She's better than ChatGPT and Google Gemini because she knows you better than any AI program or overworked teacher. Everything about her is human; she can teach you according to your learning style, pace, and intelligence. It's a beautiful way to learn because it's so individualized."

"That's true," I said. "I didn't know this kind of technology existed."

"The public has no idea what the government and military have developed. We roll things out when people are ready. Did you see how shocked you were to see yourself?"

I nodded.

"Imagine how crazy the world would become if everybody met their counterpart simultaneously. It would not be good. People might go berserk. Jump out of windows. Society isn't ready for it. ChatGPT and Google Gemini are just the beginning. The government knows what's coming, and we don't have much time to prepare the masses."

"Like what?" I asked. "What's coming?"

"You will see. No need to worry about it now."

"Okay."

"But let me share a few things so your training will go smoothly. Are you ready?"

"I'm listening."

"Humana already knows everything you need to learn on many levels, including ham radio. She will get you up to speed as quickly as possible. You have an important destiny to fulfill. Does that make sense?"

"I think so," I replied.

"Do you have any other questions?"

I thought for a minute. "I have many questions, but you don't have to answer them now. I want to see how this will work."

Major smiled. "So, let's get started. Today will be elementary. I will stay on the call and observe how things go. I'll switch the screen to Humana and let you two get comfortable with each other until the process becomes familiar."

"That sounds good," I said.

"I'll be here if you need me."

The camera was now on Humana. Is this what it would be like to have a twin? Suddenly, I remembered Gracie's dream.

CHAPTER TWENTY-FOUR

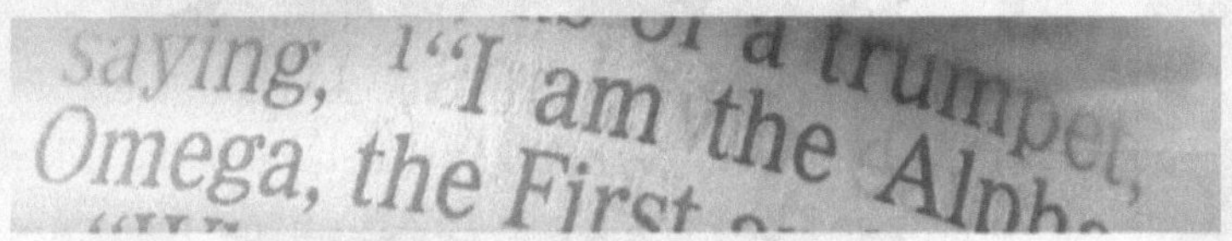

Friday arrived, which meant after-school Bible Study. I was tired and distracted and didn't want to go, but I had promised Judd I would.

Besides, Mother had scheduled Rophe to go to the vet on Saturday for his rabies and distemper vaccinations, and I could hardly expect Judd to shuffle us around if I wasn't willing to keep my part of the bargain. At least holding the study at the library meant it was shorter because they closed the doors 30 minutes after school ended.

The bell rang. Most students left by bus, and I could see all the buses lined up outside and the mad dash to exit. I slowly trudged to the library, stopping at my locker to discard what I didn't need to take home.

When I arrived, the others were already seated at the table. I felt welcomed, and their enthusiasm lifted my spirit.

I smiled and sat beside Judd—the only open seat.

Shale began by asking if anyone had prayer requests. Nobody had any, so she opened with a prayer and pulled out her Bible. I had forgotten to download a Bible app, and I didn't have anything to follow along. "Judd, can you find me a Bible like you did last time?"

"Sure." He left the table and disappeared behind some bookshelves.

Shale began. “Let’s turn to Revelation 22:13. It’s the last chapter in the last book of the Bible.”

I interrupted. “We were in Genesis the last time I came. Have you covered the whole Bible since then?”

Shale laughed. “This study focuses on the beginning and the end. We’ve covered parts of Genesis and parts of Revelation. I mean, it’s topical, not expository.”

“Oh, okay.” I wasn’t even sure I knew what that meant.

Judd returned to the table with the Bible and gave it to me.

“Thank you,” I whispered. I turned to the last book in the Bible, the last chapter. Fortunately, it was easy to find. I didn’t recognize the names of the different books except the more familiar ones, like Genesis, Psalms, and Proverbs. I’d never read the Bible.

Shale glanced at each of us. “Does anyone want to read Revelation 22:13?”

Gracie offered. “‘I am the Alpha and the Omega, the Beginning and the End, the First and the Last,’ the New King James Version.”

“Let me also read the Amplified version,” Shale said. “It adds an important detail.”

“‘I am the Alpha and the Omega, the First and the Last, the Beginning and the End [the Eternal One].’ Notice what’s different.”

“The Eternal One,” Judd said.

Shale nodded. “What does ‘eternal’ mean?”

Rachel clicked on her phone. “Some synonyms for ‘eternal’ are dateless, everlasting, timeless, ageless.”

Shale added. “Eternal means outside of time. God has no beginning and no end. He was here before time and will be here when time ends.”

“Ecclesiastes says something about time also,” Rachel said. “Let me look it up.”

She flipped through the Bible. “Here it is. Let me read a few verses.”

I was clueless about where Ecclesiastes was in the Bible. I would download a Bible app and look it up later.

Rachel began reading: “This is from Ecclesiastes 3. The headline reads, *Everything Has Its Time.*

To everything there is a season,
A time for every purpose under heaven:
A time to be born,
And a time to die;
A time to plant,
And a time to pluck what is planted;
A time to kill,
And a time to heal;
A time to break down,
And a time to build up;
A time to weep,
And a time to laugh;
A time to mourn,
And a time to dance;
A time to cast away stones,
And a time to gather stones;
A time to embrace,
And a time to refrain from embracing;
A time to gain,
And a time to lose;
A time to keep,
And a time to throw away;
A time to tear,
And a time to sew;
A time to keep silence,
And a time to speak;
A time to love,
And a time to hate;
A time of war,
And a time of peace.

Rachel said, "Let's skip a few lines and end with this."

That which is has already been,
And what is to be has already been;

And God requires an account of what is past.

No one said anything.

Shale broke the silence. "What do you think the overall point of the chapter is?"

"There is a time for everything," Judd said.

"But eternity is timeless," Shale said. "It's outside of time."

"God is outside of time," Rachel added.

"Exactly," Shale said. "So, when did time begin?"

I didn't know. I couldn't believe how much Shale had changed. She was different from the person I lived with a few years ago. What happened to her? I thought Bible Studies were boring, but this wasn't boring.

Gracie spoke first. "The Bible says God created the heavens and the Earth in the beginning."

Rachel added, "Something happened, and everything became Tohu wa-bohu, formless and void."

"Right," Shale said. "I believe that's when time began."

"Say that again?" I asked.

"Sure," Shale said. "In the beginning, everything was perfect. You could call it eternity past. Things might have existed for millions of years. God created the heavens and the Earth; even scientists say the world is ancient. But that historical record would be before time began. It was the age of no time—eternity or timelessness.

"Something must have happened," Rachel said, "that made God's perfect creation formless and void, like chaotic and corrupt. That isn't how God created the heavens and the Earth. God created a perfect heaven and Earth that was not formless and void."

"So, what do you think happened that marked the beginning of time, as found between Genesis 1:1 and 1:2?" Shale asked.

We all looked at each other with blank stares. No one seemed to know.

Rachel weighed in first. "Satan rebelled against God. We know that one-third of the angels rebelled with him, as stated in the book of Revelation.

"Having a war in heaven would be an incredible event in the grand scheme. Chaos and destruction would follow. So, when sin and rebellion took place, it would have marked the beginning of time."

No one said anything, so Rachel continued. "We remember painful or meaningful things that happen to us, and then all the mundane things we tend to forget. But this would have been monumental, the first sin ever committed. It would have marked a new era—the beginning of time when things were no longer perfect."

"Exactly," Shale said. "Time began when sin began."

"So, sin and time are linked?" Gracie asked.

Shale nodded. "What do you think this verse from Ecclesiastes 3:15 means?"

> *That which is has already been,*
> *And what is to be has already been;*
> *And God requires an account of what is past.*

Gracie spoke first. "My dad is a scientist, so I've heard crazy physics stuff through the years that I didn't understand. There are three views of time: The linear view, the circular view, and the multiverse perspective.

"The multiverse is what scientists like to research. It states that multiple universes exist simultaneously. The theory says there can be more than one future and one past. And they can happen at the same time. In other words, there is no predestination; we determine the outcome based on our choices."

Judd remarked, "That's cool."

Rachel continued. "Linear is easy to understand. It's how we know reality and most naturally perceive time, where things move in only one direction.

"The third view is that time is circular.

"This verse presents the circular view of time: 'That which is has already been.' It implies that the future has already happened, and God requires an accounting of what has passed."

"How can you have an accounting of something that has yet to happen?" Judd asked.

Rachel laughed. "I guess we would understand God's reckoning of time if we were God."

Shale nodded. "Let's make the question a little easier. If God wanted to judge the world between the beginning and the end, in the epoch of time, do you think He would be just?"

"Of course," Rachel said.

Shale nodded, adding. "He is the Alpha and the Omega."

"That's right," Judd said. "He is outside of time. Only someone not limited by time could be the judge."

Shale said, "When sin entered the universe, time entered the universe, and when God destroys sin, time will no longer exist."

I stared at Shale, amazed by her logic. "So, if there are multiple universes, would it be possible to return to one of those universes before time began?"

"Before sin?" Shale asked.

"Right."

Gracie spoke first. "My dad believes parallel universes exist, but I don't understand the idea."

Shale said, "Neither do I. But I wonder what existed before time—eternity past—and what it will be like when there is no more time—eternity future. What awaits us on the other side of time?"

The cleaning lady interrupted us when she entered the library. "You young-'uns will need to clear out so I can vacuum and dust."

Judd returned the Bible to the bookshelf, and we cleared off the table and headed to the door. That was the fastest 30 minutes I'd ever witnessed. Where did the time go? And I chuckled. Whenever I thought about time in the future, I would consider its deeper meaning.

CHAPTER TWENTY-FIVE

"That will be $128.29. Would you like to round up and donate?"

"Sure." I inserted my mother's credit card, and the vet receptionist handed me the receipt, adding, "Here's the reminder for the neutering appointment, and we'll see you in two weeks."

"Great, thanks." I stuck everything in my purse.

"Have a good day," she said.

Judd grabbed Rophe in the carrier, and we headed to the car.

I double-checked where I put the appointment card in my purse. It would be terrible if I lost it. "I'll be glad to get the surgery out of the way."

"It's good to get him fixed. Just avoids other issues that could come up."

"I know."

We drove to the apartment, and Judd brought Rophe inside.

When I opened the carrier, he hopped out and ran into my bedroom.

I laughed. "Rophe loved his visit to the vet about as much as I love going to the doctor."

Judd chuckled.

Mother walked into the kitchen, and I handed her the credit card. "The appointment is two weeks from today, on Saturday. We can take him over early Saturday morning, drop him off, and pick him up Sunday morning."

"Just put the card on the fridge, Honey, the details."

"I won't forget. Judd said he would take me to drop Rophe off and pick him up."

Mother nodded appreciatively. "I don't drive much anymore."

"It's no problem," Judd said.

I disappeared into my bedroom, looking for Rophe, and Judd followed me.

"Have you been on the radio much?" he asked.

I laughed. "A little. Can you grab Rophe from your side of the bed? I think he's upset with me."

"Of course he is. Why don't you let him be for a bit? He'll come around later when he forgets about the vet."

I giggled.

Judd looked into my eyes with a tinge of romanticism. "It's a beautiful day; you can feel spring coming. Why don't you show me where you found Rophe?"

I smiled. "Okay. But I only have an hour, and then I have a Zoom call."

Judd frowned. "Well, that's enough time. Let's go."

I hollered at Mother, who had retreated to her favorite living room chair. "We're going for a walk. Be back in an hour."

"Okay, Honey."

We walked outside into the bright noonday sun. I couldn't wait until spring arrived. Atlanta would become stunning, bathed in white dogwoods with crimson petal stains. Guttural sounds would pierce the skies as Sandhill cranes passed overhead.

Judd grabbed my hand. "Where are we going?"

"Follow me." We walked to the back of the Hope Garden Apartments and entered the woods bordering the property. Heavenly bamboo stood tall, with hints of blooms arriving soon, as muscadine grapevines wrapped around the trees like out-of-control weeds.

The gentle breeze brushed my face, and wintering birds watched us with interest. We followed the trail along the pathway and came to the log I had stopped at twice before, but a faint light in the distance caught my attention.

I pointed ahead. "Look."

Judd squinted to see better.

"Let's go."

I sensed we were intruding on the garden's slumber as we walked toward the light. Springtime had yet to summon its residents. Little critters hid in quiet places along the trail where birds would soon build their nests. The Rose-breasted Grosbeak, which frequently popped out when he saw me, flew over and welcomed me with his familiar call.

He was such a beautiful bird; if only I could interpret his songs. The red fox was nowhere to be found—thank goodness.

I looked for the exact spot until I was sure I had found it. I grabbed Judd's arm and pointed. "That's where I saw Rophe."

Once again, the circular area was a bit brighter, but a blue sky was overhead. The sun was off in the distance. Apparently, something or someone had chosen this small spot to release its mysterious light.

Even Judd noticed it. "Something is odd. The sun is over there to the West."

"You're right, Judd. So where is that light coming from?"

Judd and I stepped into the light. Unexpectedly, a peace enveloped me. Thoughts filled my head that I couldn't explain. It was like I was someplace far away, in a far better place, where there was perfect harmony with nature.

However, I was still in my body beside Judd. I had never experienced oneness with nature like this. I heard a harmonious melody, a song, a frequency that no words could describe, but the epiphany ended before I could say anything.

Judd seemed oblivious to what I perceived as a supernatural encounter. He saw the light, but I didn't get the sense he felt it sensuously like I did.

Judd pointed. "Let's go sit on that white bench."

I smiled. "Okay."

We walked over and made ourselves comfortable. I leaned my head on Judd's shoulder. "I'd think I was in a dream if you weren't here."

Judd tenderly stroked my long red hair. "Tell me about the Zoom calls. Are they going well?"

I pulled away from his embrace and reflected. I wasn't supposed to talk about this, but I couldn't hold back any longer. "Judd, some things about it are weird."

Judd's face showed concern. "Like what?"

"Well, my mentor is a double of me."

"A double?" His concern escalated. "What do you mean?"

"She looks like me. I don't know what I would call her. Major said she's a double or a clone, but fully human, as if you could use those words interchangeably."

The air was still as if I had silenced the forest. I waited for Judd to respond. "Say something. Your silence is—unnerving."

"I—I never heard of such a thing. How is that possible?"

I shrugged. "I don't know how it's possible. But whoever she is, she looks like me. She could be me—and no one would know it, and that's scary."

"Tell me more; start from the beginning. What do you mean by mentor?"

I brushed my red hair back from my face and took a deep breath. Should I get into this conversation now? We didn't have that much time. But I had already cracked the door, so I might as well step through it.

"On the first call, Major introduced himself to me. He said he was part of a team of communicators called The Frequency Group. I think he said he was the coordinator. I don't remember, but he introduced my mentor to me. She looks like me, like a pair of twins would look. You can't always tell them apart.

"Major has been on all four calls. I think he's human. I presume he is, but how would I know? My mentor calls herself Humana. Maybe she's a humanoid, and that's why her name is Humana, but I don't even know what a humanoid is. Do you?"

"Have you asked her anything? Does she have your memory or history? Did they program her like a computer?"

"I don't know. Humana didn't tell me, but then I didn't ask her. Major said she knows what they want to teach me. She needs to give me the knowledge. It sounded like programming is involved, but I didn't ask.

"Major said someday, that's how it will be with humans. Anything you want to learn, you won't have to study. You will download it into your brain like we download software into a computer. It's the same concept."

"Chumana, who are these people?"

"As I said, Major works for the government. We know the government provided all the equipment, based on what Mr. Johnson told us during the installation. Major said the name of the team is The Frequency Group.

"I'm not supposed to tell anyone about them. I forgot. We should've turned off our phones. They might be monitoring my conversations. I wish I'd thought about it sooner."

Judd didn't seem concerned about the phone and ignored my request. "What else did your double say?"

"She's like a mentor, teaching me things I don't know. So far, it's mostly related to ham radio and digital, but higher levels of learning are involved."

"What kind of ham radio?"

"She's teaching me digital modes. I've watched several videos. You can find the information on the web and on YouTube. It's legit stuff, nothing weird."

"Chumana, all of this is weird. I'm worried about you."

"Well, it's not like I'm going anywhere. I'm in my bedroom learning about ham radio and other things."

"What other things?"

I bit my lip. "I know you'll freak out when I tell you this, so don't, okay?"

Judd's eyes grew wide. "Okay. I'll try not to."

"Major said the government is involved with extraterrestrials in a friendship program, and The Frequency Group is developing a communications plan with them.

"I'm part of the amateur ham radio team who will broadcast information to the public using digital and CW radio frequencies in case something happens. I think communicating with the extraterrestrials is via thought, but ham radio is involved.

"Again, I know it's the dissemination of information. I'm unsure what else, but I know there is more. I've only had a few meetings so far."

"Extraterrestrials, as in aliens from another planet?"

I nodded.

He stared at me.

"Judd, the government has been in contact with them for years. Why look so surprised? You know UFOs, or UAPs, as they call them now, have been at the forefront of the news. You know there is a disclosure coming. You know something is up. Don't look so—shocked."

"And you've kept this all to yourself?"

"Well, it's only been four Zoom calls."

"Still," Judd said, "I'm surprised you didn't tell me."

"Honestly, I was afraid to. How do you call someone and say, 'Hey, I'm involved in a top-secret project involving ETs?' That's not an easy conversation."

"True. But—I mean, you don't know these people. They could be making it all up."

"Well, my father is involved, and that's how I got involved. The government gave me all the equipment."

"And your mother knows about this?"

"Not all of it. She knows some of it. In one of her more aware moments, she told me that my father, when they were together, worked for the government on top-secret projects, and half the time, she never knew where he was or what he was doing."

Judd placed his hand on my shoulder. "How is it you never knew anything about your father? Did she never want to talk about him, or did you never ask?"

"She would just say my father cared for me, and when I turned 18, I would meet him. The judge would unseal the court documents.

For a long time, I thought he was in prison, and she didn't want to tell me, like it was humiliating, and she didn't want me to know. Now I know that wasn't the case. She knew he was involved in top-secret projects that he couldn't discuss."

Judd squeezed my shoulder. "Just be careful, okay?"

I nodded.

Then he kissed me on the cheek.

I tried to reassure him. "I promise, if anything happens that worries me, I'll tell you, but you must promise not to tell anyone."

Judd nodded. "My lips are sealed."

I looked at my phone. "We need to head back."

"You aren't going to ask about my progress on ham radio?"

"Oh, yes. I forgot all about that."

Judd smiled. "I passed my technician test."

"Really?"

Judd nodded.

"If you learn CW, you can access HF frequencies with only a tech license."

Judd laughed. "Getting my general license would probably be easier than learning CW."

I stood, and Judd followed me. "I've got to start learning CW."

I glanced at the trail. The light still shone on the spot where I first saw Rophe. I vowed to return later. I didn't risk telling Judd about the red fox.

CHAPTER TWENTY-SIX

"Miss Ironvein," Major said, "you've done remarkably well in your ham radio training. You have achieved the highest level of ham radio certification and mastered two digital modes. Now we must focus on what operators consider the most challenging—CW. Are you ready?"

"I think so."

"There are plenty of resources online to help you, and Humana will work with you as soon as you know the first several letters. We also recommend an hour per day of practice. Much of it is just repetition."

"That's a lot of time, but I'll try."

Major smiled. "Let's have Humana give you a demonstration at 25 wpm."

He glanced at Humana. "Are you ready?"

She nodded. Immediately, she began to send out dits and dahs using a paddle. The audio tone sounded like something I'd never heard. They were rhythmic, distinct, and exact. The dits and dahs seemed almost mathematical.

Humana did it effortlessly.

.-- .... .- - .... .- - .... --. --- -.. .-- .-. --- ..- --. .... –

When she finished, Major said, “The timing needs to be as precise as possible. It takes three dits to make one dah.”

I asked Humana, “How long did you practice to achieve 25 wpm?

“It took some time, maybe six months.”

For a fleeting moment, I wish I were her. Six months seemed like a long time. That was longer than it took to get my extra license.

Major interrupted my musings. “Humana will help you learn quickly. Don’t be overwhelmed. Our time is short today, so we must move on to other topics.”

“Can I ask a couple of questions?”

“You can ask her anything you want. I need to tend to something. Let’s take a short break, and I’ll return in a minute.”

When Major left, I saw this as my opportunity to get some answers.

Humana sat in the chair across from me on the screen, dressed in clothing like mine—blue jeans and a sweatshirt. She pulled her thick, red hair back from her face, just like I did, which was long and curly. My double smiled, attentively waiting. I still found it odd to be looking at a twin version of me.

I asked, “Are you human?”

She laughed. “Yes, I have human DNA.”

“Do you have emotions like a human?”

She laughed again. “Of course.”

"Do you have a boyfriend? Can you get married and have children?"

"Yes, I have a boyfriend, and yes, I can have children."

"So, you are human?"

Humana replied, "Yes, of course. However, with a little gene editing, scientists can make us superhuman. That is the scientists' goal. They want to make us perfect and immortal like gods."

Could they do that? I didn't see Major yet, so I had time for another question. "Where did they get the information to create you?"

"DNA."

I glanced at the door. I felt rushed, so I didn't frame my question well. I would ask it in a different way. "Do you have my DNA?"

"My DNA is mine, although it's like yours."

"Where was I born?"

The door opened, and Major entered.

For now, that would remain a mystery.

Major sat down at the table and held up a sheet of paper. "I have a list of things I want to go over."

"All right."

He cleared his throat. "Are you ready?"

I nodded.

"Okay. Here we go. How would you feel if everything you knew about the Origins of Life was incorrect?

"What do you mean?"

"For example, many scientists claim that humans, through evolution, evolved from lower life forms, like apes. What would you think if I told you that all life originated on another planet and intelligent beings from that planet seeded Earth with humans?"

I remembered my biology class and the topic of the upcoming debate on the Origins of Humankind. The timing of this was intriguing. "That makes more sense than thinking we came from monkeys."

Major nodded. "Good answer. What would you say if I told you those extraterrestrials are soon returning? Would you be scared, excited, or something else?"

"It would depend on whether they were friendly."

"I see. Suppose you weren't sure if the extraterrestrials were friendly. Would you be willing to give them a chance?"

"Umm … I think so."

Major smiled. "Let me give you a history lesson. Thousands of years ago, a civilization existed on Earth before Adam and Eve. Based on skeletal remains, they were human-like, but something was different about them that we don't understand. The extraterrestrials visiting our planet know the answers, and we need their enlightenment to understand where we came from.

"To simplify things, since we know so little about them, we'll call them by their ancient name, the Anunnaki. We know they were forced at some point to retreat underground. They have been waiting for the return of their comrades. As time has passed, they have grown concerned about the future. They tell us through coded messages that war is coming, and it will bring cataclysmic destruction upon the planet. Are you with me so far?"

I nodded.

"Can I continue?"

"Yes. I've never heard this before. I'm not sure I believe it, but you can continue."

"I understand. I shall continue, then. The ETs, as we identify them in modern nomenclature, want to help but are selective in whom they trust. Only certain bloodlines can access the secret knowledge they possess. We need people like you to help us."

"Do I have that bloodline?"

"Yes, Chumana. Through your mother."

The upcoming disclosure about my origins involved my father. Now, I was confused. What was so special about my mother? Why was there a delay in meeting my father if my mother was the one who was special?

I stammered, not sure what to ask. "When can I meet my father?"

Major took a deep breath, almost like he was reticent to respond. "Are you familiar with the Manhattan Project?"

"The Manhattan Project?"

"Yes," he replied.

"Just that it produced the first nuclear weapons the U.S. used in World War II."

"That's good. You know your history. You may not know that the government secretly cloaked the project through compartmentalization. Most people who worked on the project did not know what they were working on. They only knew their personal task due to the need for secrecy."

"Yes, I think I studied that in school."

Major leaned forward to emphasize his point. "This project is similar in many ways. Very few people know about it, even at the highest levels of government." He paused for emphasis. "Whatever you do, do not discuss what I share with you here with anyone."

"I won't."

Major crossed his arms. "That's good."

"So why can't I meet my father now? Why do I have to wait until I turn 18?"

"We must protect his identity until disclosure. We can't risk it. Things are, I will say, delicate right now."

Major narrowed his eyes with such intensity that it frightened me.

"We're trying to avoid nuclear war, Chumana."

Now, I was at a loss. "What does my bloodline have to do with nuclear war? I thought the disclosure agreement was related to my father's position in the government or military. I didn't think it had anything to do with my mother."

Major nodded in agreement. "Yes, yes. However, we're dealing with extraterrestrials here and must honor their requests. They set the rules. Your father is a leader on the project, and we need to protect his anonymity.

"Otherwise, those who disagree with what we're doing might assassinate him. Not everybody in the U.S. government agrees with this approach."

I picked up the pen beside my computer and mindlessly clicked it. Why couldn't my mother have been more open about this? Did she know her bloodline was special?

"I thought my intelligence came from my father. My mother has had so many mental issues in the last few years that it's hard for me to fathom her being smart or, for lack of a better description, having a sacred bloodline. She seems so average."

Major laughed. "You have no idea how smart you are. And while your mother's bloodline marks your uniqueness, your incredible intelligence comes from your father. You're right about that."

Humana chimed in. "Your father has protected you all these years. You will soon see and understand everything."

Major stood as he finished his thoughts. "That's enough for today. However, there is one other thing I need to warn you about."

"What's that?"

"You've been attending a Bible Study."

How did he know that? "Yes, I have been a couple of times."

"The Bible is for weak people. It's not for someone like you, who is a leader and smarter than anyone else at your school. Do you want to spend time reading words written by flawed people about things scientists can't verify?"

"How did you know I went?"

"We just know." Major stopped short of saying how. "We'll see you tomorrow, okay?"

I nodded. "All right."

"Check your messages on the digital software for updates or changes, and practice on the radio daily to hone your skills."

"I will."

"Most importantly, you must learn CW as quickly as possible."

I didn't understand why. "Don't you have other people who can do CW? Do I really need to learn that, too?"

Major nodded. "I understand. It is a lot to expect in such a short period. But few people have your bloodline, and we must use the humans the ETs have chosen. They choose based on bloodlines. Your DNA is rare."

I didn't understand precisely what Major meant, but I could tell he needed to go to another appointment.

Major and Humana bid me farewell, and the Zoom call ended.

How did they know I had gone to a Bible Study? What else did they know about me? What about my conversations with Judd? How long would it take me to learn CW? And who were these ETs from another planet? Why did they want humans with my bloodline?

I closed the Zoom call to search for the link they had given me earlier to learn CW. I created an account on a recommended site and listened briefly to several letter sounds. K was dah-di-dah, A was di-dah, and M was dah-dah.

As I listened, I became intrigued. I imagined the distinct sounds traveling thousands of miles across the ocean. Could they even travel through outer space?

CHAPTER TWENTY-SEVEN

I crawled into bed, and Rophe scooted up beside me. I stroked his head and kissed him on the nose. His neutering was coming up soon—Saturday. I hated leaving him at the vet overnight. Fear gripped me. Suppose something went wrong? I was too tired to think about it.

Until now, I had been sleeping well despite all my distractions. However, tonight was different.

When I finally dozed off, bizarre dreams swirled in my head. I was someplace far away, but I didn't know where. Nothing looked familiar. The dream started with me entering a tunnel and descending beneath the surface. After a few minutes, the cavernous passageway leveled off and opened into a vast underground chamber.

When my eyes adjusted to the unexpected light, I saw a massive pyramid-like structure. No one was present except me—at least, I didn't see anyone. The building looked abandoned, but also newly built. The white limestone sides reflected dazzling light entering the chamber from above, and the pointed aperture at the top of the pyramid looked golden.

I walked around the perimeter, mesmerized by its grandeur. I had never seen a pyramid except in history books. I also knew most historians believed the pyramids housed the bodies of mummified kings. But was that their only purpose, or was there more? Why build something so big only to contain one body?

I didn't know how to enter the gigantic structure and wasn't sure I wanted to. Suppose a ten-thousand-year-old mummy was in there? Even thinking about it terrified me.

I must have triggered something because the floor beneath me moved, and I heard something that sounded like gears. I stepped back, and what had felt solid underneath my feet became an opening to another passageway. I didn't want to go further—not with the pyramid facing me. Besides, the chamber was well-lit. Who knew what was down that dark passageway?

Suddenly, the chamber began vibrating. Sounds filled the structure and bounced off the walls. Where did they come from? Clueless, I searched the massive enclosure. The vibrations reverberated, long and short, back and forth, echoing until they dissipated.

As I listened, I realized the noise wasn't arbitrary. The sounds had a pattern, like Morse Code dits and dahs that I'd listened to a few hours earlier. Maybe it was just my imagination or my subconscious tapping into the rhythm, attempting to process the new skill. I could only remember the dah-di-dah for K.

The sounds continued through several iterations, and when the vibrations stopped, a powerful resonance lingered.

Then, the pattern started again, repeating several times. If only I knew Morse Code. If that's what it was, I could decipher the message. I grew accustomed to its rhythm; melodic, in some ways, but the pitch was always the same, just like Morse Code, as it echoed.

Either I became accustomed to it, or the sound became softer, less harsh. Was it a message from long ago? I stared at the pyramid. Was someone beckoning me? My heart thumped faster when I imagined someone watching me. Was it a warning? I turned and checked behind me, making sure nobody was there.

The sound wasn't haphazard. I sensed an intelligence behind it. Perhaps the sound was trapped inside the chamber. Sound waves vibrate, but sound must be perceived by a person or an animal to be heard. The noise could have reverberated inside the cave for hundreds or thousands of years waiting to be received.

My thoughts mushroomed. Did all pyramids vibrate? How many pyramids did an unknown civilization build beneath the Earth's surface —under the oceans, Antarctica, rainforests, deserts, or enclosed in mountains? Why would anyone build immense structures and bury them?

The Mayans built pyramids that resembled Egyptian pyramids, and the Mesopotamians built similar structures and called them ziggurats. I learned about them in middle school. Was their only purpose to provide a burial place for a mummified body?

Again, their immense size seemed pointless—unless the body was a giant. The frustration of not knowing awoke me from my sleep.

I noticed Rophe wasn't beside me. When I couldn't find him, I slid off the bed and entered the hallway. Mother's door was ajar, and I peeked inside. Rophe had decided to sleep with her. I tiptoed in and picked him up.

"I need you to sleep with me tonight," I whispered.

I closed the door to my bedroom so he couldn't get out again. Rophe looked at me like he wanted to know why I had woken him up.

My thoughts returned to the disturbing dream. It may have been a warning. I had never seen a pyramid and had no intention of visiting one. Why would I dream about something for which I had no interest?

I drifted off in that half-conscious state of awareness until my alarm rang. Groggy, I glanced at the transceiver on my desk.

Before I got into ham radio, I knew nothing about sound, frequency, or radio. I understood now how frequency was related to sound, regardless of the form of transmission. Information couldn't be exchanged unless the sender and the receiver were using the same frequency. Someone sent those dits and dahs I heard in my dream, but who?

Someone also built the hundreds, perhaps thousands, of pyramids, but who? The more questions I asked, the more questions popped into my head.

How could pyramidal structures resemble each other worldwide if different civilizations built them? Maybe we really were seeded by aliens from another planet, but how could we know unless they communicated that information to us? Or could there be another unexplored explanation?

I stroked Rophe on the head. Although a cat couldn't speak a human language, we talked through sound. I recognized his purrs when he was happy and his distress when he wasn't.

If all sound was frequency-based, then were there good and bad frequencies? Good in the sense of peace and tranquility, and bad in the sense of discord and chaos?

What about aliens? Would extraterrestrials be able to speak to us through thought? Wouldn't that still require a frequency? I knew there were frequencies that humans couldn't perceive, like sonar. Dogs and cats hear sounds that we can't. I sighed. Nobody seemed to care about such things except me.

I brushed the questions aside. I needed to hurry so as not to be late for school. I was never late.

CHAPTER TWENTY-EIGHT

The next day, I studied nonstop for the upcoming midterms. After dinner, I spent the evening practicing CW. I got through the first six letters: K, M, U, R, E, and S.

The site recommended 90 percent accuracy before moving to the next lesson. I plowed through the lessons too fast, only to discover that I didn't know the letters like I thought. It was a miserable waste of time. I needed more repetition.

Frustration ate at me. I'd probably quit if I hadn't heard those sounds in my dream. Most things came easily for me, but this was hard. But then, something inside of me wouldn't let me give up. Since when did I let anything defeat me?

So, I turned on the radio and listened to CW. The dits and dahs went too fast. I couldn't figure out what they were sending. "How do they do that?" I muttered.

Could Humana help me that much? I was envious that she already knew everything.

Perhaps the good thing about computers is that they don't have emotions like we do, despite AI trying to mimic humans and claim hallucinations when they mess up.

Humana had emotions, so she had to be more than a computer. I still didn't understand what a clone or a double was. If she were my twin, then she had my abilities, but she seemed to have abilities I didn't have. Maybe it was the training she had received.

I couldn't comprehend how she could do CW at 25 words per minute in six months. Besides, why did they even need me if they had her?

I turned off the radio. Tomorrow, I'd start over. I picked up Rophe, my accountability partner. "I will practice my dits and dahs with you."

He rubbed his head on my arm, and I scratched him behind the ear. His sweet purrs warmed my heart. What if animals could talk? What if they could tell us what they were thinking?

I longed to know Rophe's story. Why was he alone in the woods? How did he lose his mother when he was so young?

I glanced at the clock. It was getting late. My time would be better spent if I didn't try to practice CW when I was tired. Studying calculus, AP Biology, and AP Chemistry was easier than learning languages and history.

I took Rophe to the living room and sat on the sofa. Mother was reading, but I couldn't tell what book it was. The TV played silently in the background. I was glad she was reading again.

Mother glanced up at me. "You studied a lot today. How is school going?"

"Great."

"What are those strange noises I hear coming from your bedroom?"

I laughed. "I hope it isn't annoying. I'm learning Morse Code. It's called CW, or Continuous Wave, on the radio."

"Oh," she said. "Sounds interesting. What do you do with it on the radio?"

"You send dits and dahs. When conditions are bad, like if there is a lot of background noise, it's easier to hear than voice. Plus, CW travels farther with less power than voice."

Mother laughed. "I'm afraid I don't understand all of that. I hope we never need it, but you never know."

I changed the subject. "I love seeing you read again like you used to."

Mother chuckled.

"What are you reading?"

She flipped the pages. "Oh, it's nothing. I found it on the bookshelf from a long time ago."

"Can you hold it up? I want to see."

She leaned forward to hand it to me.

I read the title. "I'm not familiar with that at all."

Mother took back the book. "It was your father's. I was afraid to read it back then, but now I must know the truth."

Maybe I was more like my mother than I realized. "That seems to be the biggest question in the universe, 'What is truth?' In AP Biology, we have an upcoming debate about human origins. We can't even agree on that, it seems."

Mother smiled. "The truth will set you free."

I pondered her words. "It sounds like you are speaking from experience."

Mother looked away. "I haven't been myself recently. I thought I was getting old, maybe had Alzheimer's. Some days, I wasn't even sure who I was. I felt like something was trying to possess me."

The word "possessed" sent shivers down my spine. I remembered Mother sleepwalking and the terror it caused me. I still didn't know where she went, but she seemed different since that stopped. She appeared normal now, instead of acting like a zombie watching TV all day. I thought I had lost that mother. I hoped it would never happen again.

Mother turned her gaze to me. "Does that make sense?"

I nodded. "Yes, it does."

She continued. "I think there are secrets somebody doesn't want me to know. I don't know who the good guys are and who the bad guys are. I want to know the truth."

"I understand," I said, even though I didn't. But it was a good prompt for a question I had been afraid to ask. "What do you know about your bloodline?"

"My bloodline?" she repeated. "Oh, not much. Just that it's rare."

"Anything else?"

"It's ancient. Like it goes back to the beginning."

"The beginning of time?"

"Yes, something like that." She paused before continuing. "Sometimes, I think your father only married me for my bloodline."

"Why do you say that?"

Mother puckered her lip. "He seemed obsessed with my ancestry, and I never understood why."

She didn't want to continue the conversation as she settled back in the chair with her book. But that was more than she had ever said before. I didn't know what to think.

I said goodnight and took Rophe back to my bedroom. Reflecting on the title of the book Mother was reading, I asked my cat, "What is Area 51? Did my father work there? Otherwise, why would we have that book, and why would Mother be reading it?"

If Rophe knew the answer, he would have told me.

CHAPTER TWENTY-NINE

The week went by quickly. Each day, I had an online session, and Major was complimentary of my CW progress. Friday arrived, which was Bible Study. I didn't want to go, but how could I ask Judd to help me with Rophe if I didn't keep my part of the bargain?

Getting my driver's license was at the top of my to-do list so that I wouldn't be so dependent on him. However, I needed to keep my promise until the summer, when I planned to take a driver's ed course.

The bell rang, and I trudged to my locker before heading to the library. I remembered what Major had said about Bible Study being a waste of time.

I still didn't know how he knew about my attendance. I shut off my phone in case the government was tracking me. How else could they have known? I arrived, surprisingly, before anyone else.

I never downloaded the Bible app on my phone, and since I turned off my phone, it was useless anyway. I looked around. Where were the Bibles? Then, Judd entered the library.

"Looking for a Bible?" he asked.

"How did you know?"

"I just know," he said. "Maybe I'll buy you one."

I didn't want to tell him I'd never read it.

He showed me where they were and suggested a different translation than last time, as if I would know the difference. Then we went and sat at the table to wait for everyone else.

"I got my walkie-talkie from Amazon," Judd said. "We should do Simplex since we live so close."

"We should try it. That sounds like fun. Let's wait, though, until after Rophe comes back from the vet."

I guess my response clued him in on my anxiety.

"He'll be fine, Chumana. It's a straightforward procedure."

Rachel, Shale, and Gracie arrived, and the study began with prayer requests. I wanted to ask for prayer for Rophe, but how do you ask when you don't believe in prayer?

Shale began the study. "Let's turn to I Corinthians 13:1. Who would like to read?"

For some unknown reason, I volunteered and then realized I didn't even know where the Bible verse was.

Judd leaned over to help me find it, and I began reading:

> *If I could speak all the languages of Earth and of angels, but didn't love others, I would only be a noisy gong or a clanging cymbal. If I had the gift of prophecy, and if I understood all of God's secret plans and possessed all knowledge, and if I had such faith that I could move mountains, but didn't love others, I would be nothing. If I gave everything I have to the poor and even sacrificed my body, I could boast about it; but if I didn't love others, I would have gained nothing.*
>
> *Love is patient and kind. Love is not jealous or boastful or proud or rude. It does not demand its own way. It is not irritable, and it keeps no record of being wronged. It does not rejoice about injustice but rejoices whenever the truth wins out. Love never gives up, never loses faith, is always hopeful, and endures through every circumstance.*

Prophecy and speaking in unknown languages and special knowledge will become useless. But love will last forever! Now, our knowledge is partial and incomplete, and even the gift of prophecy reveals only part of the whole picture! But when the time of perfection comes, these partial things will become useless.

When I was a child, I spoke and thought and reasoned as a child. But when I grew up, I put away childish things. Now we see things imperfectly, like puzzling reflections in a mirror, but then we will see everything with perfect clarity. All that I know now is partial and incomplete, but then I will know everything completely, just as God now knows me completely.

Three things will last forever—faith, hope, and love—and the greatest of these is love.

I looked up when I finished. "I guess I was only supposed to read the first verse, but it was so beautiful, I couldn't stop."

Shale smiled. "No worries. What translation is that?"

I double-checked. "The New Living Translation."

"I love that translation," Shale said. "Does anybody have a favorite line?"

"This is the one that speaks to me," Rachel said. "'Love never gives up, never loses faith, is always hopeful, and endures through every circumstance.' Since I'm Jewish, that has a special meaning; the importance of never giving up, enduring, and always being faithful, even when people say unkind things about being Jewish. Only through love can we do that."

Gracie shared next. "This is the verse that speaks to me: 'If I had the gift of prophecy, and if I understood all of God's secret plans and possessed all knowledge, and if I had such faith that I could move mountains, but didn't love others, I would be nothing.'

"I know this is going to sound weird," Gracie said, "But sometimes

I feel like I have the gift of prophecy. Sometimes, I'll see things before they happen and wonder how I did that. And I think about my father and all he knows about physics, but what good is it if we don't love others? Knowledge is great, but love is better."

I remembered what Gracie had said at lunch a few weeks earlier when she asked me if I had a twin. Was she seeing Humana, my clone, in her dream? What she said now was freaky, but I couldn't tell her about Humana without getting into trouble

Judd went next. "It's hard to choose, but this is what I need to focus on: 'When I was a child, I spoke and thought and reasoned as a child. But when I grew up, I put away childish things.'

"I think God is challenging me to grow up and not reason as a child does, putting curses on people out of anger … I'm sorry, Shale, for doing that to you."

Shale dropped her eyes. "It's okay, Judd. I'm sorry about what I did. I wish I could change the past. Only through the love of Jesus could I forgive myself. Sometimes accidents happen. I suppose that's why I chose this chapter out of I Corinthians, to help me learn how to be more like Jesus and to love as He does."

Sorrow welled up inside of me. Perhaps I was the one who was the child in all of this—my rantings about Shale, all the accusations I made to hurt her. I needed to apologize, but I didn't know how.

Shale continued. "I guess my favorite verse would be the last one: 'Three things will last forever—faith, hope, and love—and the greatest of these is love.'"

No one said anything, and I reflected on the emotional impact of Judd's and Shale's confessions. I felt their pain, but I wasn't ready to acknowledge mine.

Shale interrupted my musings. "Chumana, you said you thought all the lines were beautiful, but do you have a favorite?"

I re-read the first verse: "If I could speak all the languages of Earth and of angels, but didn't love others, I would only be a noisy gong or a clanging cymbal."

I took a deep breath. "I like that verse the best because love is a universal language. Even as I think about animals, like my cat Rophe, animals know when they are loved, even though we don't speak the same language.

But Rophe sees love in my eyes when I look at him. He hears my voice and comes when I call him. The tone I use when I talk is how he perceives if I'm upset, tired, or in a bad mood.

There must be a universal love frequency, no matter what language a person speaks. Perhaps it's not the words we say so much but how we say them."

I looked into the faces of my friends. "Does that make sense?"

Shale nodded. "It does. It makes perfect sense. Thank you for sharing."

The clean-up crew interrupted our Bible Study again. I was disappointed we had to end so soon, as the words I read stirred my heart. I didn't know what to believe—Major, who said the Bible was for weak people, or what I perceived as truth, the truth that Mother and I had spoken about a few nights earlier. What is truth?

As we left, Judd said, "I need to run some errands since I'll be helping you with Rophe tomorrow, so I can't give you a ride home. Are you okay walking home?"

"Yes. I walk to school every day."

"What time do I need to pick you up in the morning?"

"By 8:00. Poor Rophe gets no food tonight."

Judd chuckled. "He might complain, but he'll be fine."

"Chumana," Shale said, "Why don't you walk with Rachel and me?"

I nodded. "Okay. Then we can talk more."

CHAPTER THIRTY

The walk home felt so familiar. I used to walk with Rachel and Shale, but I quit and walked alone when Shale and I became enemies. That word may be too strong. I regretted now that I had been so quick to condemn her; despite my bossy attitude, she had continued to reach out to me.

We didn't talk about anything meaningful until I saw the Rose-breasted Grosbeak that frequently greeted me on the way to school and home. He began his usual call when he saw me.

"He sings so beautifully," I said, "if only I knew what he was saying."

"I know what he's saying," Shale said.

I laughed. "You do?"

"Yes, I do."

We stopped to listen as he sang a cheery song in a clear, melodic voice. The tiny bird had enchanted me and captivated my heart all winter.

"What is he saying?" I knew she couldn't understand him, but part of me wished she could.

"He is praising the Lord."

"Seriously?" I laughed. "What is the bird saying?"

Shale listened for a minute before replying. “Let all the trees of the forest sing for joy.”

“That’s what he’s saying?”

“He’s not saying it,” Shale said. “He’s singing it.”

“You didn’t know that Shale can talk to animals?” Rachel asked.

I shook my head. “No, I’ve never heard of such a thing.”

I looked at Shale. “You couldn’t do that when we lived together.”

Shale laughed. “When I was born again, that is the gift God gave me.”

I didn’t understand what Shale meant. “Born again?” I repeated.

“When you accept Jesus into your heart, you become a new creature and are born again.”

“Oh,” I replied.

As we passed by, the bird flew up into the tree. How could I get Shale’s gift so I could talk to Rophe?

WHEN I OPENED the door to our apartment, a sweet aroma aroused forgotten memories. My mother used to cook, and my favorite thing she made was peach cobbler.

“Yummy! You haven’t made this in a long time.”

Mother smiled. “I was cleaning out a drawer and found the recipe. Fortunately, we had all the ingredients.”

“When will it be ready?”

She glanced at the timer. “Oh, another 30 minutes.”

I reached out and hugged her.

Mother pointed to the note on the refrigerator. “Don’t forget you’re taking Rophe to the vet tomorrow morning for his neutering.”

I sighed. “Yes, I forgot to remind Judd. Let me text him.”

I walked into the living room and sat beside Rophe on the sofa. He acknowledged my presence with a sweet purr as I patted him on the head.

“Don’t forget to pick me up at 8:00,” I texted, “to take Rophe to the vet.”

After I sent the message, I remembered he told me he had to run errands after school because he was taking Rophe to the vet tomorrow. I forgot, but I'd already sent the message, so I waited to see if he responded.

He sent a thumbs-up. I could feel my heart pounding in my chest. It was a simple procedure, so it was unnecessary to get so panicky. Still, I would be glad when it was over. With surgery, a risk always existed.

I picked up Rophe and hugged him. "I can only give you a little bit of food now because of your surgery tomorrow."

I set him on the sofa and walked into the kitchen to fix him a small food dish. "Don't give him any more tonight," I told Mother.

She nodded, and after feeding him, I wandered back to my bedroom and flipped on the transceiver. I turned the knob and listened for anything that might sound interesting.

Not hearing anything, I opened the digital software and connected it to the transceiver. Following protocol, I sent a heartbeat to ensure the correct setup and checked for messages from the group call sign @TFG.

Finding one, I opened it.

"A shipment containing a solar panel and a portable power station is coming from Amazon. 73, KL7UAP." I didn't recognize the call sign.

Why did they seem so concerned about emergency power? I replied, "Roger, 73, KO4LBS."

Then, I switched to CW and practiced in the oscillating mode for a few minutes, making sure I didn't send anything out on the air. I knew all the letters, numbers, and punctuation, but I wasn't proficient—not yet, not well enough to have a QSO with anyone.

I heard Mother calling me from the kitchen. "Your peach cobbler is ready." I turned off the radio and headed to the kitchen.

Mother smiled as I sat at the kitchen table. Long-forgotten memories, awakened by the rich aroma of my favorite dessert, filled me with thankfulness. My mother was back from wherever she had gone.

"It's delicious," I said.

"Let me know if you want some more. A chicken salad I made earlier today is in the refrigerator."

"You outdid yourself!"

"What time do you have to get up in the morning to take Rophe to the vet?"

I swallowed a tasty piece of cobbler. "We need to drop him off at 8:00. I suppose about 7:30."

"At least he only has to stay one night."

I lamented. "One night too many."

Mother smiled. "You have fallen in love with that kitten like I never imagined."

Rophe wasn't a kitten anymore. He had grown into a magnificent cat. I glanced at him in the living room. He was peering at me like he knew we were talking about him. Mother was right. I loved him so much. He had saved her life. He was a miracle cat. Best of all, I had a mother again.

CHAPTER THIRTY-ONE

The alarm, set to "Pachelbel's Canon," went off at 7:20 the next morning. I was surprised I had slept at all, not even any dreams. I turned off the music and quickly dressed. I looked in Mother's bedroom and saw Rophe lying beside her. He didn't have a care in the world, but once I pulled the cat carrier out of the closet, he would know something was up.

I reminded myself I couldn't give him any food. I had also moved his water dish up high. Mother was still asleep, and I didn't want to wake her, so I was very quiet.

I fixed some coffee and threw two slices of bread in the toaster. Then, I checked my messages. Judd had texted that he was on his way. I replied with a thumbs-up and retrieved the cat carrier.

I needed to get Rophe, but he had jumped off Mother's bed and gone underneath it. How would I get him out without waking her up?

I heard the doorbell, so I left Rophe underneath the bed to let Judd in.

He was unshaven with a disheveled appearance, as if he had just crawled out of bed.

"Hi, Judd. Thanks for coming."

"Before I forget, the Bible Study will be at Shale's next week.

She's tired of cutting it short because of the cleaning crew, so we're switching it back to her house."

I nodded. "Okay." I didn't want to think about that right now. "Do you want some coffee?"

"Sure."

We sat briefly at the kitchen counter, drinking coffee and eating toast. I took a deep breath. "I'll be glad when the surgery is over and Rophe's home."

Judd nodded. "Where is he?"

"Underneath Mother's bed." Then I realized I needed to retrieve Rophe without Judd's help. Mother wouldn't want him in there.

"Let me see if I can get him. You can catch him when he runs out."

"All right," Judd said.

"And don't look in Mother's room. She would be embarrassed if you saw her in her nightgown."

Judd laughed. "I'll stay in the hallway waiting for a lion to run out."

I entered Mother's bedroom, leaving the door cracked so Rophe could quickly exit. When I looked under the bed, I didn't see him. Where did he go? Frustrated, I looked around the room. He was playing hide-and-seek.

I couldn't find him in the bedroom. Maybe he went into my room, where the bed was unmade and a wreck. I should have told Judd not to look in my room. Oh, well. It was what it was. At least Mother was still asleep.

I shut the door to her room so Rophe couldn't go back in and peered into my room. He was on my bed. I saw a little bulge underneath the blanket where he chose to hide, which made it easy for me. I scooped him up, and he tumbled into my arms.

I kissed him on the head and reassured him, "You'll only be at the vet's one night. We'll come get you this time tomorrow."

When I brought Rophe to the front door where the carrier was, he tried to climb out of my arms, but Judd grabbed him and plunged him inside the carrier, quickly zipping it up.

Smiling, I thanked Judd. "I couldn't have done it without your help."

"Are you ready?"

I nodded. "Yeah, let's go."

I took the carrier and put him on the back seat. The air was cooler than I expected. Winter was still here, and I should've brought a sweater. But I didn't want to go back and get one. "Can you put the heater on?"

Judd reached over and angled both vents toward me. I heard Rophe complaining behind me. I reassured him, "It's okay, you'll be fine. Don't worry."

The ride took less than ten minutes, especially with no traffic on a Saturday morning. I had worried about this for nearly a month, and now I just wanted to get the procedure over with.

Judd grabbed the carrier, and we headed inside the vet's. Three others were checking in; a dog and two cats.

The large canine mix was overly interested in the cats, and his owner struggled to control him. I was glad when the tech came and took the dog into the back.

Once he was gone, Rophe settled down, resigned to his fate. At least he quit complaining.

Finally, it was my turn. The receptionist said, "We'll call you when he's in recovery."

"Does he have to stay overnight?"

"We like to watch the animals after anesthesia and surgery. It's just precautionary."

I nodded. "What time do you think he'll be out of surgery?"

The receptionist looked at a notebook. "Oh, I think by 1:00. We have several procedures, so it depends on the order."

She smiled. "Don't worry. He's in good hands."

"Thanks."

As the tech grabbed the carrier, I encouraged Rophe, "We'll be back tomorrow."

I turned to Judd as the tech whisked him out of the lobby.

He reassured me again. "Don't worry. He'll be fine."

We left the vet without saying a word, and Judd took me home.

Finally, I asked him, "How late do you work today?"

"They knew I might be late coming in, so I'm working till closing."

I nodded. "I'll text you when Rophe is in recovery."

"What are you going to do all day besides worry?"

"Study," I lied. Well, maybe I would study a little once he was in recovery. All I could think about was my scared baby locked in a cage.

Judd said, "I will pray for everything to go well."

Pray? I hadn't thought about praying. But I would never turn down someone praying. "Thanks" was all I could find to say.

CHAPTER THIRTY-TWO

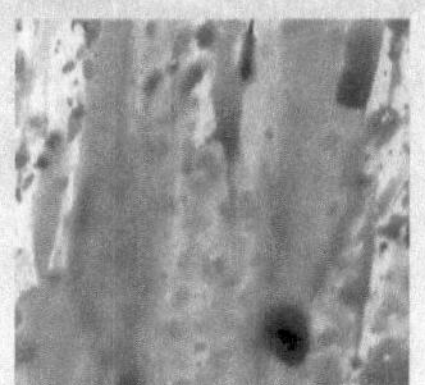

I thanked Judd again before closing the car door and waved as he pulled out of the parking lot. I felt alone. Maybe Mother was up by now, but I could only think about Rophe.

When I opened the door, she was cooking over the hot stove. Mother must have heard us before we left and got dressed. The smell of coffee filled the room, and I walked over to pour myself another cup.

"Is everything okay?" Mother asked. "You seem depressed."

I shrugged. "I just hated leaving Rophe. Depending on the surgery, they said they should call me by 1:00 to let me know everything went well."

Mother wrapped me in her arms. "He'll be fine. Don't worry."

After fixing coffee, I went and sat in the living room. Mother joined me. We rarely had a moment like this. I was usually at school or going somewhere, and seldom up this early without a reason. I remembered what Major had said about Mother's history.

"Mother," I asked pensively, not knowing what to expect, "do you know anything about your parents or grandparents? I mean, like, a family history?"

Her eyes grew big, or maybe it was my imagination. We had never talked about our family history, at least not like this. While most families spent holidays with extended family, we never did so.

I never met my grandparents. They had died long ago in a car accident. My mother felt discussing it was too difficult, so I never pursued it.

"Honey, I don't remember that much. I used to know more, but I've forgotten things. When my parents died in a car accident, I wanted to put everything out of my mind. It was so painful; I didn't want to think about it."

"How old were you?"

Mother bit her lip. "Your age, maybe slightly older, 18."

The pain in her eyes was difficult to watch. I was sorry I had started the conversation because I had upset her in a rare heart-to-heart talk. What could I say now?

But she spoke next. "Chumana, there is something I never told you about the accident, which I think you should know."

"What's that?"

Tears welled up in her eyes. "It wasn't an accident."

I stared at her. "What—what do you mean, it wasn't an accident."

Mother's lips trembled. "My mother and father had a bloodline that gave them privileges to things most people don't have—like knowledge. Secret knowledge. But—they wouldn't obey the rules, perform the rituals, or keep the pact. So, somebody killed them."

"Who killed them?" I asked, horrified by what she said. No wonder she never told me anything. No wonder I knew nothing about her past.

"I don't remember. I used to know, but I forgot."

"I'm sorry," was all I could say.

"You see, Chumana," she continued, "I wanted to protect you, so I never told you any of this. The less you knew, the better. But when you turn 18, you must be given the information and decide whether to continue the legacy."

Mother paused, and her eyes seemed to drift off into another world. "If only I knew the truth …"

I nodded. I didn't think knowing the truth was possible anymore.

Mother stood. "Let me clean the kitchen a little and clear my mind." She walked over and turned on the TV. "I miss Rophe."

"I'll let you know when they call. Thanks for paying for everything."

"Well, your father pays for everything. I should give him credit where credit is due."

"He's not part of this—family bloodline, is he?"

Mother laughed. "No, he was brilliant and good-looking, but he didn't have the bloodline. That's why he married me. He wanted the power."

"What power?"

"The power of the secret knowledge. He told me as much."

"So, why did he divorce you?"

Mother looked sad. "I don't know. He agreed to take care of you until you turned 18, and he provided support for me. That was the agreement. He didn't want a scandal—with his reputation and all his government connections, it would have been messy.

"He was never around anyway, so it wasn't a big deal. I think he found someone he loved more."

I felt my mother's overwhelming sadness and my loss. "I understand."

The television played in the background as Mother returned to the kitchen. CNN News was airing a boring story, and I couldn't decide whether to listen or study.

I checked the time on my phone. It was still early. I wouldn't hear anything for at least another two hours.

As I watched Mother clean the dishes, an uncomfortable thought entered my mind. She wouldn't try to go anywhere tonight, would she? Rophe wasn't here.

I'd been so worried about the surgery, I'd forgotten about her sleep-walking. It hadn't happened since Rophe arrived, except when he stayed at Judd's.

It was probably a coincidence, I told myself. Besides, I could only worry about one thing at a time. I wanted to make sure Rophe came through the surgery. I'd worry about Mother later.

Sitting on the sofa, I leaned back to watch television, totally disinterested in the story. But the noise drowned out my worries, and I dozed off, only to be awakened by the phone ringing.

CHAPTER THIRTY-THREE

The ring startled me, and my hand shook as I grabbed the phone.

"Hello," the voice said. "Can I speak to Chumana Ironvein?"

I steadied my voice. "That's me."

"We wanted to let you know the surgery went well, and Rophe is recovering."

With the weight lifted off my chest, I could finally breathe again.

"Thank you." In the back of my mind, I thanked God. Maybe God did answer prayer after all. I couldn't wait to tell Judd.

"You can pick him up tomorrow any time after 8:00. Since it's Sunday, you must come before 12:00, or we'll be closed, and you won't be able to get him until Monday."

"No problem," I said. "We'll pick Rophe up first thing in the morning."

I thanked the lady again and quickly texted Judd, "Rophe is good. Thanks for your prayers."

He attached a heart to my message.

I wish I could talk with him, but he was at work.

I ran into Mother's room and announced, "Rophe is out of surgery and doing well."

Mother was relaxing on the bed, reading a book. She looked up and smiled. "I knew he'd be fine."

It was after 1:00, and I was hungry, so I grabbed some of Mother's chicken salad and went into my bedroom. I would spend the afternoon practicing CW and then focus on schoolwork. I also had that biology debate coming up in a few weeks.

SEVERAL HOURS LATER, I had made great strides on my CW. I was at 10 words per minute. Major said they would consider me competent when I reached 20. I still needed lots of practice to reach that, but I was progressing.

I glanced out the window, surprised to see it was already getting dark. I could smell something from the kitchen. What was Mother cooking? I had taken over that responsibility a year ago when she began to deteriorate mentally.

I heard her calling me, "Dinner's ready."

I found spaghetti waiting to be consumed on the stove. "Oh, I love spaghetti."

"I know you do. Since Rophe's surgery went well, I thought you would enjoy your favorite dish."

I helped her put everything on the table. Unexpectedly, she asked, "Can I pray?"

"Sure."

Mother said a perfunctory prayer, nothing original, but still, I couldn't remember the last time we had prayed over a meal.

We mostly ate, not speaking much, but I couldn't resist telling her about my Morse Code progress. "I'm over 10 words per minute."

"What can you use Morse Code for?"

"Major says we may need CW to communicate if an attack affects our electrical grid. We have satellites, so I don't know that it's that important, but as a communications specialist, I need to be proficient. Twenty words per minute is the goal, preferably 25."

"And that's all those dits and dahs I hear from your room?"

I laughed. "Yes. You spell every word with a dit or a dah.

"So, how do you spell mom?"

I had to think for a minute. Maybe I was getting ahead of myself. "It would be da-da, da-da-da, da-da. No dits in 'mom.'"

"What's a word with a dit in it?"

I stopped to think. "Judd would have dits in it. It would be di-dah-dah-dah, di-di-dah, dah-di-dit, dah-di-dit."

Mother rolled her eyes. "It's hard to believe you can communicate with just those sounds."

"I know, but it's fun. I can't wait until I make my first contact."

We continued eating, and then I offered to clear the table.

"If you want to do the dishes, I'll get back to reading my book," Mother said.

I nodded. "What are you reading again? I forgot."

"Oh, I'm reading another book now. I forgot the name, but it's an older, classic book by CS Lewis."

"Who's he?"

"A famous author who died in the '60s."

"Oh. Well, enjoy your book."

I had never read much, but I sensed that was changing. Going to the library for Bible Study had triggered something. I should check out that author next time I go.

I thought about Judd as I finished the dishes. He would be home from work. I went into the bedroom and called him. "What are you doing?"

"Relaxing, watching a preseason baseball game. What time do I need to come get you in the morning?"

"Why don't you come over at 8:00? We can't pick Rophe up before then."

"Sounds good."

I could tell he was tired, so I didn't suggest he stop by. "Thanks for praying."

"No problem. I always believe in prayer."

I ventured into an area where I felt uncomfortable but compelled to ask anyway. "Can you pray for Mother?"

Judd didn't reply at first. "What for?"

I inhaled. "That she doesn't sleepwalk tonight. She quit after we got Rophe; remember, we talked about it, but since he's not here …"

"Oh, I see. Well, I'll pray, but I don't think you need to worry about it."

"Sure, but I want to make sure."

"Lock the door. Too bad we didn't get the camera."

"It didn't seem necessary when Mother stopped sleepwalking."

"Get some sleep," Judd encouraged me again. "Another early morning tomorrow."

We said our goodbyes, and I reluctantly hung up. I wanted to ask Judd to stay tonight at the apartment, but I couldn't bring myself to be that forward. I should also ask Mother first. I'd keep my door open and the hallway light on. Of course, if she did, what would I do?

CHAPTER THIRTY-FOUR

If only I had a Bible—not because I believed anything it said, but because I perceived a supernatural entity had written important information within its pages. When I read it, I remember feeling like I wasn't alone in the universe. Perhaps it was nothing; maybe it was everything.

Thank goodness Mother was asleep and, hopefully, wouldn't wake up. I tiptoed into the living room. She had been reading the Bible a few weeks ago, so it had to be on the bookshelf somewhere. How would I find it amongst the hundreds of books lining the walls?

Despite checking several shelves, I didn't see it. I gave up. I'd go to bed and lie awake, staring at the ceiling, wishing it were morning.

I made sure I locked the front door. What if I put something in front of it that would make a lot of noise if she tried to open it? I glanced around the living room. The only thing I could do was block it with a piece of furniture. That seemed like a bad idea. It would confuse her, maybe even scare her.

I decided to do something different. I wrote, "Mother, I couldn't flush the toilet before I went to bed. If you get up before I do, can you flush it before you leave? Love, Chumana."

I put the note in bold letters on the front door. Would she be able to read it in a sleep-like, hypnotic trance? I wasn't sure, but I would try to stay awake. This idea was in case I fell asleep.

Then I had second thoughts. Perhaps I was overreacting. But I had already written it, so I left it on the door. Then I went into the bathroom, making sure to avoid flushing it.

I felt encouraged that I had done something. Now, I needed to stay awake. I would leave the light on in my bedroom. When I climbed into bed, my mind swirled. I looked at the clock; 11:30 p.m., eight hours until 7:30 tomorrow morning.

❧

I AWOKE TO A FLUSHING TOILET. My heart stopped, and I froze like a night terror had seized me. I couldn't move.

I heard Mother's footsteps in the hallway. Was she going back to her bedroom or to the front door? I glanced at the clock. It read 3:40 a.m. I heard the door unlatch. I still couldn't move.

The front door opened. Perspiration dripped down my face. Was I so terrified I couldn't move? Or was something preventing me?

"Mother!" I shouted. But she had already left the apartment. I stared at the ceiling.

I cried out, "Jesus!"

Immediately, whatever was holding me down let go. I rolled off the bed, grabbed my phone, and headed for the door. I had left my shoes there in case I needed to leave quickly.

Mother left the door cracked, and cold air was already seeping into the apartment. I shut the door and locked it behind me. Immediately, I looked around, but I didn't see her. I took a few steps, scanning the darkness, but it was so black I couldn't see.

I turned on the phone flashlight and lamented that I hadn't thought to bring a more powerful one.

Despite the darkness, I would find her. She was an old lady and couldn't walk that fast.

I scanned every direction but saw nothing.

C-h-u-m-a-n-a.

Was someone calling me? Was it audible or in my mind? Did it even matter?

Suddenly, I saw something white moving in the distance. I ran to follow it.

"Mother," I shouted as loud as possible, but she didn't hear me. Maybe it was just as well. I wanted to know where she was going.

I stayed close behind her for several minutes and then had a hunch.

The school came into view. A light shone in the darkness beside the building. Was this the supernatural presence I had felt since all of this began? It was haunting, beautiful, mysterious, and intelligent. Whatever it was, Mother was headed straight toward the light.

Suddenly, a foreboding came over me. Suppose it was what I thought it might be. No, I didn't believe in those things. It was just stuff for Hollywood movies. People used these ideas to make money, sell toys, steal people's imaginations, and create fabulous stories, books, and cartoon characters.

However, as I drew nearer, I couldn't deny what my eyes saw. My mother stood before a gigantic saucer hovering over the school football field. White and red lights blinked as if they were alive. If I didn't acknowledge that UFOs were real, then I was denying the truth. If I refused to call it a UFO, then I was a liar.

"Please, Mother, don't go any closer," I whispered.

What had I gotten myself into? I had learned the technology to be an intercessor between the U.S. government and the world, and the government wanted me to be an intermediary between them and the extraterrestrials. I didn't truly believe in them; I just wanted to meet my father. Yet, extraterrestrials had taken hold of my mother in a non-human way. What was inside that vehicle?

The saucer hovered in a stationary position several feet above the field. To my horror, as Mother approached, the bottom opened. How could she do this? Maybe she had no choice. Perhaps she never had a choice. Could they be stealing her mind, mining it like crypto, abusing her?

"Mom," I screamed, "Stop!"

I was so close. Why didn't she hear me? There was no other sound except—I listened. I listened some more. The sound pierced through the still air, and the UFO lights blinked in a familiar rhythm.

Somebody on the ship was speaking to me in CW. I needed to write the letters after they flashed and sounded.

I looked beneath my feet. I could write the letters in the dirt. I grabbed a stick and wrote each letter as I heard it.

The first letter was W.

The next letter was H.

Followed by A and T.

The first word was "what."

I waited for the next word.

Di-di-di-dit.

That was an H.

Di-dah.

That was an A.

Dah.

That was a T.

Next was an H.

The second word was "hath."

A strong force was pulling Mother into the saucer.

The next letter flashed. My hand shook as I scratched out what I heard. Suppose I couldn't remember the letters?

But I recognized the next one. It was dah-dah-dit, which was a G.

The next letter was an O.

Then I heard a D.

The three letters read "God."

"What Hath God" –

Was there more?

Mother disappeared inside the vehicle. I sat on the ground, feeling hopeless. I should have caught her, called 911, called Judd, done something. Then another letter flashed.

I focused long enough to write it in the dirt. Di-dah-dah—W.

I had a hunch what the next word was, but wrote it down as I heard the sounds.

"What hath God wrought?"

I was speechless. Was God in that gigantic saucer or someone pretending to be? Whoever "they" were knew I was here. It wasn't threatening. It was a question. Was I supposed to know the answer?

I pulled out my phone and called Judd. Of course, at 4:00 in the morning, he was asleep. I held up my phone, snapped a photo, and sent it to him. He would never believe me without evidence.

I sat on the bare, cold ground, weeping. All this time, she had been rendezvousing with a UFO. I cried over my ignorance.

Was I a fool? I had trusted the government when I hardly trusted anyone. Who can you trust if you can't trust your father or the government?

My fear turned into anger. I hadn't done anything to deserve this fate, and neither had my mother.

Indeed, "What hath God wrought?" Maybe all of this was because I had begun to trust God. Why did I attend that Bible Study?

Surely my father wouldn't hurt me. I looked into the night sky with tears rolling down my cheeks. Mother was right. I needed to decide what I would do with the rest of my life. But this wasn't what I had in mind.

Now that the initial shock was over, coldness swept over my exposed body; like a menacing cold that gets into your bones, makes you shiver, and think you'll die. I wanted my mother back.

Major and The Frequency Group could have their equipment. I didn't want to meet my father. I wanted nothing else to do with them.

I couldn't trust them. I didn't even trust myself now. Perhaps everything I had ever believed was a lie. If only my mother would come back. I had no desire to live. Exhausted, I saw no point in living. Without Mother, my heart would be empty. Without love, our purpose in living becomes meaningless.

Then I heard something unexpected. Almost as if the stars knew my pain and wanted to touch me.

R-o-p-h-e.

Who said that? Then I repeated his name several times, reminding myself I had something for which to live. He was waiting at the vet.

Love entwined our lives. I couldn't let him down. He needed me, and someone or something was telling me not to give up.

I don't know how long I sat on the ground. I looked at my phone again. It still read 4:00. How could that be? It was 4:00 over an hour ago. I could see the faintest signs of sunrise across the school football field in the East. It couldn't be 4:00.

I no longer trusted my senses now, but I had to accept I had experienced a UFO encounter. I could no longer deny they existed. Maybe that was the point of it—to bring me here so that I knew what the government was doing was genuine, but top-secret.

But how could I know who the good guys and the bad actors were? One thing I knew for sure: They were dealing with an entity of unknown origin.

One moment, I was hopeful; the next, I was in despair. As I was about to lose my sanity, I saw the bottom of the UFO open, and the bright light I had seen earlier shone on the ground.

I watched as Mother levitated to the ground. Thank God, they didn't keep her. I struggled to stand on my near-frozen feet. Every part of my body felt numb, but I didn't care. All I cared about was that my mother was back.

Once on the ground, she walked toward me. The gigantic saucer took off in one fell swoop, disappearing within seconds.

I ran toward Mother. I caught up to her and embraced her, weeping. "Are you okay?"

She looked at me, puzzled. "Honey, you shouldn't be out in the cold, sleepwalking. Don't be like me. Once you start, you never stop."

CHAPTER THIRTY-FIVE

I hugged Mother without responding to her words. I was just glad she had returned. If only she could tell me what was inside that gigantic saucer. Now, we would go home and get away from this horrid adventure. I'd never look at my school the same way again.

I glanced back to make sure no one was following us. The familiar path felt eerie as we walked in the dead of night, but the first rays of sunshine peeked through the clouds as we neared the apartment. The heaviness of the night lifted as we reached the door. I wanted to believe I was waking up from a nightmare, but this was more than a nightmare. It was real. UAPs were real. UFOs were real. I didn't care what anyone called them.

Once inside, I felt safer, but Mother seemed disoriented. She wasn't even sure where the bathroom was. Fear rose within me; what did they do to her inside that giant spaceship?

I showed her where the bathroom was, and she thanked me. Could she have dementia again? When she reappeared, she sat at the table and asked if I could prepare something for her to eat.

This wasn't my mother a day or two ago when she cooked peach cobbler pie, spaghetti, and a chicken salad. I tried to calm myself.

We had exchanged roles again. I was now the mother, and she was the child. I wanted my mother back. I tried to hold back tears.

I sat beside her and asked, “Mother, what do you remember about your sleepwalking? Do you know where you went?”

She looked at me with vacant eyes, like she had no idea what I was asking.

“You don’t remember anything at all?”

She shook her head.

I fixed her some coffee, and as I set it before her, Judd texted. “I’m on my way.”

I sent him a thumbs-up.

I spoke to Mother as someone would to a small child. “Judd and I are going to pick up Rophe from the vet. He will be here in a minute. When you finish your coffee, you should lie down and rest.”

Mother nodded.

While I was panicky about Mother’s condition, at least we were bringing Rophe home. I went into the bathroom to prepare his litter box and put some fresh food and water out.

When I returned, Mother smiled.

The smile calmed my nerves a little. At least the extraterrestrials didn’t hurt her, but something was amiss. If only I knew the whole story. I hated not knowing what was going on.

I heard a knock on the door. I stood and rubbed Mother’s shoulders. “Don’t go anywhere. I’ll be back in a few minutes.”

She nodded.

I GRABBED the carrier and headed out the door. The sun’s rays glistened off Judd’s faded-blue car, lifting my spirits. After so much darkness, I appreciated the dazzling light.

When I opened the car door, I asked Judd as I climbed in, “Did you see the JPEG I sent you?”

“What JPEG?”

“You didn’t receive it? I know I sent it.” Flustered, I pulled out my phone and checked. "It didn't go out. I'll resend it but don't look at it until we arrive at the vet. I don't want you to be distracted."

Judd rolled his eyes like I was playing a joke on him, but I was in no joking mood. I was exhausted, fueled only by my excitement to bring Rophe home.

After parking, Judd checked his phone to see what I had sent him. He laughed. "Why are you sending me this?"

He didn't get it. "Judd, that UFO abducted my mother last night at 4:00 in the morning. I took that picture. I didn't get it off the web."

His eyes bulged, and he didn't say anything at first. When he did respond, he choked over his words, "Say that again."

"Judd, all that sleepwalking my mother has done for the last year has been to rendezvous with a UFO—UAP, or whatever you want to call them. They have been taking my mother.

"Mother and I have reversed roles—again. When we returned, she couldn't find the bathroom and asked me to make her coffee."

I stopped. I couldn't say anymore as I struggled to hold back tears.

"Do you think they are doing something to her?"

I looked Judd straight in the eye. "I feel like they are stealing my mother, taking something from her."

"You mean, like her soul?"

That stopped me in my tracks. "What is the soul? I mean—I don't know."

Judd reached over and grabbed my hand. "You need to return all that ham radio equipment, get out of that ham radio secret government group you belong to, and let your father go.

"If he wanted to be a father to you, he never would have left you and your mother in the first place. I've been worried about you ever since you got involved with them."

He continued. "Why do you think I got my ham radio license? It's certainly a cool idea, but I wanted to be able to communicate with you in case something happened with the electrical grid. I'm worried about you. I'm worried about your mother."

I inhaled deeply. "There are some things I need to tell you about my mother, but it can wait. Right now, I want to get Rophe."

Judd nodded. "Let's go."

I opened the car door, and we held hands as we entered. The lady at the counter greeted us, the same lady we had dropped Rophe off with the day before.

She smiled with much bravado. "Hi, Miss Ironvein, Rophe did great. He's ready to go home now."

Just then, the door opened. The vet tech held Rophe in her arms. Judd unclasped the carrier, and she gently plopped Rophe inside it.

"He might still be a little groggy from the anesthesia. He'll probably want to sleep today."

"Thanks," I said. In my mind, I was thinking Rophe could sleep beside Mother—and hopefully restore her sanity.

Judd picked up the carrier, and I spoke softly to Rophe. "I'm so glad you're coming home."

Nobody would ever appreciate how much those words meant, except maybe Judd.

Soon, we were out the door. Rophe never said a word the whole time, but his eyes were glued on me through the carrier's side opening. He wouldn't let me out of sight.

CHAPTER THIRTY-SIX

I was glad it was Sunday, and Judd didn't have to work. I hated to admit it, but I needed him now.

When we arrived home, Mother had gone into her bedroom. The door was closed, and I was happy to let her be. I unzipped the carrier, and Rophe stayed inside it. Still groggy from the surgery, he seemed content to take his time extricating himself.

"Do you mind if I fix myself some coffee?" Judd asked.

"Sure, go ahead. I should have offered."

I sat on the living room floor beside Rophe, reassuring him as he looked out of the carrier. My love lifted his spirits, and soon, he hopped out. I started to grab him, but he scooted away and rushed down the hallway.

Judd relaxed on the sofa with his coffee, and I joined him. I laid my head on his shoulder. "Thank you. I appreciate all your help."

He leaned over to kiss me, but I turned my head and just let him kiss me on the cheek. I was too emotionally drained to go further, but I appreciated his sitting beside me. His concern and understanding meant a lot.

"What did you want to tell me about your mother?"

"Oh, just bloodline stuff. Mother's family history has the Illuminati bloodline, and that bloodline seems important to the extraterrestrials."

I took a deep breath. "Judd, I am starting to believe some of this stuff that I've been in denial about. I wish I knew the relationship of all the different parts, but UAPs are real, and somehow a relationship exists between them and certain people."

"I've heard of the Illuminati," Judd said, "but I don't know anything about them."

"Neither do I, except they seem important to important people—in the military, government, whoever is anybody."

Judd twirled a few strands of my red hair in his fingers. "I thought everything was about your father, but your mother seems important, too. It makes me wonder where you fit into all of this."

I leaned my head back on the sofa. "Even if I pulled the plug, so to speak, on the ham radio, nothing would change. Mother would still sleepwalk. I would have fewer means of learning the truth about my past. It would forever remain a mystery to me."

"Do you really want to know, Chumana?"

Judd's question seemed absurd. "Wouldn't you want to know?"

Judd shook his head. "I don't know anything about my father and don't want to."

"You don't have any curiosity?"

"Nope."

"Well, I guess we're just different then."

"It doesn't mean you're right and I'm wrong, or I'm right and you're wrong," Judd said. "It's more about, how do I put it, I think this is a bottomless pit that could lead to a deeper pit—a pit that you may not be able to climb out of. You may be stuck in it forever."

I shuddered. "Don't sound so morbid."

"I'm not being morbid, but this is dangerous stuff, and you need to know what you're getting into."

I pulled away. I had been looking for comfort, not judgment or condemnation. I was too tired for this conversation. Maybe later.

Then we heard a banging at the door.

"Someone is delivering something," Judd said.

I shook my head. "We're not expecting anything. We've already received our deliveries this week for food and essentials. Besides, it's Sunday."

"Let me go see." He set his coffee on the table, and I followed him to the door. The deliveryman waved as he headed back to his vehicle.

"Thanks," I said, not knowing what he dropped off.

Judd grabbed the largest box, and I picked up the smaller ones.

Once inside, Judd opened one of them. "It's a solar panel. Did you order a solar panel?"

"Oh, I forgot. The Frequency Group contact said they would send me a solar system in case of a power failure to run the radio and digital."

"The government knows an EMP attack is coming."

"What did you say?"

Judd repeated, "The government is expecting something to happen that will take down the power grid. Do you know how to set this up?"

I shook my head. "And I'm too tired to think about it. I have a Zoom meeting on Tuesday—if I even attend. Major said they could help me with it."

Judd looked at the other packages. "This is just standard electronics. It looks like some Faraday bags. At least one of them is big enough for a computer. Nothing unusual."

He appeared almost relieved that it wasn't some exotic piece of equipment from someplace out of this world. "I suggest we put it in the corner for now."

Judd helped me move everything until I found a more permanent location for the boxes. Then I remembered the CW message the UFO sent when they were abducting Mother. Despite my tiredness, I needed to ask him what he thought it meant.

"Judd, when all of this happened, in the beginning, the UFO sent me a CW message that I translated as, 'What hath God wrought?' What do you think it meant sending me that?"

Judd's face turned ashen. "The UFO sent you a message—are you serious, in CW?"

I nodded. "Yes. I was impressed with myself for being able to translate it. I wrote it in the dirt on the football field."

Judd looked at the ceiling and rolled his eyes. "I can't believe it sent you a message."

"The other thing, Judd, I don't understand is that my phone lost an hour."

"What do you mean, your phone lost an hour?"

"It said 4:00 in the morning, and I know it should have said 5:00 or 6:00. The sun was rising, and it doesn't rise at 4:00 in the morning."

"Slow down. First, I want to see what you wrote."

"You mean you want to go to the school right now?"

Judd nodded. "I want to see where everything happened."

"Well, can we drive there? I'm pretty tired."

"Sure. I don't want to walk either. I want to see it before it disappears."

"I just wrote it in the dirt. There is nothing unusual about it."

"I have other reasons why I want to go."

"Right now?"

"Yes, right now."

"Well, okay. Let me check on Rophe and leave Mother a message."

"She doesn't use a phone?"

"Not for texting."

"Old people," Judd said. "They want to live in the dark ages."

I entered my bedroom, and Rophe was stretched out on the bed asleep.

I checked the bathroom and saw he had used his litter box and eaten some food. That made me happy. I jotted Mother a note as Judd waited at the door.

"Okay, I'm ready. Let's go."

The drive was quick. Parking wasn't an issue since no one was around. I took Judd to where I had been, and there were my crudely written words. "What Hath God Wrought?"

Judd shook his head. "You weren't kidding, were you?"

"No, Judd, I wasn't. It was all real. UFOs are real. They abduct people. They steal people, do something to them, and then return them, for better or worse."

Judd walked away, and I followed behind him. "Where are you going?"

"I'm looking at the burn marks. See the grass. It left a signature. Look at the crushed, burnt weeds. Here are more markers, and I can see triangular indentations."

I stayed beside him, still finding it hard to believe what I had witnessed. Were there other people, like us, who had seen unexplained things and witnessed the unimaginable?

If the extraterrestrials were from another planet, were they for us or against us? Why would they send me such a strange question? It wasn't threatening or encouraging. It just was.

Then I remembered Major's question about how I would feel if I knew extraterrestrials were visiting us. I gave him an academic answer, not an emotional one.

"Chumana, I had a thought. Do you think I could listen to the Zoom call on Tuesday?"

"You aren't even supposed to know about any of this. If Major knew I told you, I'd be in trouble. Besides, why would you want to?"

Judd rubbed his eyes. "I don't know. I'm just worried."

"Well, maybe not this time because it's not going to be pretty. I will demand answers and would be distracted if you were on the call. I'd be thinking about what you thought and what you might want me to ask, rather than what I want to ask. Does that make sense?"

Judd acquiesced. "Okay. It was just a thought. In the meantime, I'll get my general ham radio license. How long did it take you, Miss Brains?"

I smiled at his comment. "Oh, about three weeks. Not that long."

"If I have my general license, I have more options."

Judd looked up into the heavens, perhaps searching to see if something might be nearby. The sun was directly overhead, but there were no UFOs anywhere.

"The equipment is rather pricey," I said.

"I know. I'll think about that later."

We returned to the car, but Judd stopped at my handwritten message. "I want to take a picture."

"Why?"

He shrugged. "I don't know. Just do. Maybe Rachel or Shale might have some insights into its meaning."

"Do you think it's in the Bible?"

"I don't know, but we're going to find out."

CHAPTER THIRTY-SEVEN

Judd dropped me off at the apartment—probably exhausted. He claimed he wanted to run errands, but I imagined that was an excuse. I was glad; I needed to clear my mind.

When I walked in, Rophe lay on the sofa, cuddled next to Mother, as in old times. She smiled, looking peaceful despite everything that had happened. Could things return to the way they were? They would never be the same, but similar would be reassuring.

"Did you sleep well?"

Mother yawned. "Part of the night, I slept well. The other part, I don't know where I was. That's how it is with dreams."

I nodded. There was no need to ask anything else. She wouldn't remember, and it would frustrate me. "How is Rophe?"

Mother ran her fingers through his thick orange fur. "He seems content."

Glancing in the kitchen, I asked, "Are you hungry?"

"Oh, maybe a little. I think there are some leftovers in the fridge."

"Do you want me to fix you anything?"

"No, Honey. It's okay. Could you put on the TV?"

I grabbed the remote control and did as she asked. The news came into focus, and she seemed content with that.

I wandered back into my bedroom feeling tired. I needed to focus on schoolwork and the upcoming debate on the Origins of Life.

Flippantly, I had chosen the group that we originated on another planet. How fortuitous that was. Little did I know I'd have the evidence to back it up. Maybe I shouldn't assume. I didn't know.

Too bad Mother couldn't tell me anything. What did the inside of that saucer look like? Were there extraterrestrials within that glistening sphere that traveled here from another planet? Or maybe there were humans inside. After all, Morse Code was a human invention.

After sleeping, Mother seemed normal. At least she wasn't asking me where the bathroom was or to make her coffee.

My phone beeped. I checked my messages and saw that Shale had texted me.

"Friday's Bible Study will be at my apartment. Hope to see you, Shale."

I wasn't sure if I wanted to go. I'd have to think about it. I turned my focus to ham radio. The CW paddle sat beside the transceiver, waiting for me to practice. Did I want to stop all of this, as Judd suggested?

After investing this much time in a perishable skill, I wasn't ready to "flush it down the toilet." Too much was at stake. Although no one had guaranteed anything, it was a doorway to something in the future, an opportunity that may only visit me once.

I sat on the bed, conflicted. Maybe Judd was right. Whoever was in that UFO knew who I was. They sent me the CW message. What would I say to Major on the next Zoom call? What should I ask him?

Rophe strolled in and jumped on the bed as I weighed my options.

"Rophe, what should I do? You tell me." He nudged me with his head as if to say, "You know."

If only I did know.

I thought about Shale. If only I could talk to animals like her. Perhaps I should attend the Bible Study.

Rophe purred in response to my question. Listening to his sweet sounds brought me comfort. I should have been born a cat.

Then, I wouldn't have to make decisions about Mother and the future. I'd felt the weight of it on my shoulders especially over the last year. However, allowing myself to be a victim of circumstances wasn't a good solution.

I forced myself to reason like an adult. I didn't have to decide right now. So, I pulled out my book bag. I needed to study for the upcoming exams. I also needed to do an internet search on the Origins of Life.

Could we be the offspring of life from another planet or even planets? What did the Bible say? I knew evolution was out of the question, so I wouldn't waste my time on Darwinism.

Two hours had passed when I stopped for a break and checked the clock. And then I heard Mother. "Honey, I fixed a salad if you want some."

I went to see. Prepared food covered the table. Mother must not have regressed despite my fears. Maybe everything was okay. Except that a UFO abducted her, and I had the same bloodline as hers.

The message the UFO sent still reverberated through my soul.

"What hath God wrought?"

CHAPTER THIRTY-EIGHT

I sat before the computer screen, waiting for Major to admit me into the meeting. I presumed it would be Major, my mentor, and my counterpart, Humana. I was getting impatient. What was taking so long?

Finally, the screen lit up, and a smiling Major gazed at me. However, I wasn't smiling. I'd had two days to think about everything that'd happened, and I wanted my questions answered.

"You made your first CW contact," Major said. "Congratulations."

So, he already knew. I wasn't surprised he knew, but the question seemed out of place. I was already tongue-tied, and the conversation hadn't even started.

"Yes, I did," I said, trying to be matter-of-fact and non-emotional. "However, I have many questions I need answered."

Major leaned back, appearing somewhat amused. "I'll be glad to answer any questions you have. Humana might chime in, too. She was in the UAP."

My eyes shifted to Humana. "You were in the UFO?"

Humana laughed. "Yes. The idea is you will take my place when you're ready."

"Ready for what?"

"Don't you want to go for a ride?" she asked.

Either I was being supersensitive, or they were being insensitive. We were not on the same frequency.

"Let's back up. Let's start with my mother. Why does she have no memory of anything when she returns? Why didn't you tell me your UFO friends, the extraterrestrials you want me to work with as a communications specialist, are abducting my mother against her will? Why does she seem to suffer mental setbacks when she returns? She was almost an invalid until we adopted Rophe.

"When we adopted him, she quit sleepwalking, and her cognitive abilities improved dramatically. She's the mother I thought I'd almost lost. I wanna know what's going on."

Silence followed as Humana glanced at Major. I didn't get the impression she wanted to answer my question. Maybe she didn't know the answer.

The smile had left Major's face, and he leaned forward sternly. What started as a friendly conversation was now hard-core serious, just how I wanted it. I had red hair and the fiery temper to go along with it if others mistreated me.

I did not think they had been upfront with me, and now I needed to know the truth behind everything. It was no longer just about my father; it was about something much more profound: my life, my future, and my mother's life and future.

Major nodded. "I understand your concern, and it's not without merit. We have a pretty good handle on your high intellectual ability, but learning how high your frequency level is, how should I say it, it's staggering."

I interrupted Major. "What do you mean, my frequency level?"

Major stood and took a few steps in deep thought. Then he turned toward me with his piercing brown eyes.

I sensed he cared about me, so why was he taking so long to answer my question?

"Chumana, frequency is the level at which you operate. It's determinative of how the world affects you and how you, in turn, affect the world. Let me ask you some questions which will help you understand."

I took a deep breath. "Okay."

"Let's start with an easy ham radio question. What does frequency mean?"

I rolled my eyes. I didn't want to talk about ham radio. I wanted to talk about myself. Nevertheless, I'd answer this one question, and hopefully, he would provide answers.

"Frequencies in ham radio are the radio waves or bands on which people operate. The FAA allows amateur ham radio operators to operate on specific frequencies and within specific ranges on those frequencies."

"Good, Chumana, straightforward. And those frequencies are allocated by the FAA, right?"

I nodded.

"People also perceive frequency, like the transceiver receives and sends radio waves at different frequencies, depending on the operator's preference. But—how can I explain this—people operate on different frequencies, but it's not a conscious choice. Some people operate naturally at a higher frequency, while others are more comfortable at lower frequencies. Does that make sense?"

"Sort of, I guess." But I didn't see the point he was making.

"Let me be more specific. You operate at an incredibly high frequency. That means you are highly intuitive. For example, do you hear angels or spirits, whispers in the trees, or animals seeking you out in almost supernatural ways?

"Do you feel the wind vibrating against your face, the warmth of the sun even when it's cold, the nuances in the changes of the seasons, perhaps even perceive vibrant colors that others can't see or hear things that others can't hear?"

Major was starting to make sense. "Yes, I do. Sometimes, I hear whispers like someone is calling my name."

Major nodded. "I know. We've learned that about you. Do you pick up on other people's moods, whether they are happy, sad, upset, or worried? So much so that it affects you more than you want it to?

"In other words, your empathy for others' pain can be so overwhelming that you almost become the pain, so they don't have to feel it."

I nodded, "Except when I'm angry at someone."

"Yes, but the anger you feel is a righteous anger. It's justifiable because you want to rectify a wrong. You feel for the wronged individual so much that you want to make it right, and when you can't, you get upset about it."

"Okay. I get all of that. But what does that have to do with my questions?"

"Believe it or not," Major said, "You get that quality from your mother. But—this is the part we wanted to spare you from learning, but we realize now we can't—your mother has a mental condition that will make her an invalid without medical help. You have inherited that same condition. It's only a matter of time.

"We've tried to work with your mother for many years, knowing that it would affect her as she grew older, but she's been stubborn. That's why we've tried to keep her from remembering where she sleepwalks.

"We never wanted to give up on her. Her genetic makeup is extremely rare, but her condition had deteriorated to the point we had to intervene directly."

"What do you mean, intervene directly."

"Who do you think sent Rophe to you?"

"Rophe?"

"Don't you remember the strange light over the forest floor when you found him? We put him underneath the UFO, just like we did with your mother. And we put the red fox there because we knew you would rescue the cat if you thought the fox would kill him. We set it up.

"We knew your mother was dying, and we hoped, because of her intuitive nature—like you—that a special cat like Rophe could help her. We didn't expect the outcome to be so profound."

I interrupted Major. "You mean, you sent the cat to save my mother?"

"Your mother is much better, isn't she?"

"Well, she regressed when we took Rophe to the vet for neutering. She started sleepwalking again."

"That's because Rophe wasn't there to comfort her. And Rophe will prevent the disease you carry from taking hold, which is hibernating inside you. Your intuitive nature and higher operating frequency will also help to keep it from developing until you are older.

"Hopefully, our friends who have returned can find a cure in time to save you from its devastating effects."

I started to interrupt to ask who "our friends who have returned" were, but Major didn't give me a chance.

He continued. "There is also the flip side to intuitive, high-frequency people. You can know so much that you forget others are less endowed and become impatient with their naiveté.

"You can also become so burdened with other people's sorrow that you can't function at all, dropping to such a low frequency that your underlying disease impairs you and makes you only a fragment of the real you."

When Major paused, I asked, "So, the extraterrestrials are doing experiments, performing medical procedures, and trying to make people well by healing their diseases?"

"Yes. That and so much more. They have technology way beyond ours. They are sharing their technology with us, trying to heal us and give us what we deep down want but don't want to admit."

"What's that?"

"What do you think? What do you wish for your mother, yourself, Rophe, and friends?"

"Well, I guess, a good life."

"What about if you could live forever without disease. Humana longs for that. Both of you have the bloodline the Shining Ones need for their research. It's not just about AI or cloning. It involves the spirit and the soul."

I focused on Humana. What was she? She said she was fully human, but was she a clone? A double, as Major also alluded to, could mean many things. I was sure she was more than a humanoid.

Even computers needed upgrades lest they become obsolete. To live forever had to have a biological component to it, but spirits and souls—what were they?

I wasn't sure what to think. I needed time to sort through all of this. Maybe—maybe that message had more significance than I thought. Perhaps it was more than just my first contact.

I blurted out, desperate for one answer I could comprehend. "Why did they send me the CW message, 'What hath God wrought?'"

"Why do you think, Chumana?"

Maybe Humana knew. She was on the UFO. My desperation to see the truth was getting me nowhere. It didn't matter how smart or sensitive I was if I couldn't understand.

"I don't know."

"Think about it," Major said, trying to encourage me that I would figure it out. "Don't fret. The answer is within you."

Humana entered the conversation, saying, "Isn't it good that your mother is getting well? See how the Creator works through these magnificent beings who have chosen to rescue us and save us from ourselves."

"Why would they do that? Why would they choose to come here in the first place?" I asked.

Major leaned forward and gazed intently into my eyes. "Because this is their home. They were here first, hundreds of thousands of years ago or earlier. They have returned. And soon, the whole world will know what you have already discovered. Disclosure is coming, and it will be magnificent."

CHAPTER THIRTY-NINE

Humana's eyes brightened. "I have an idea."

"What's that?" Major asked.

"The ship is coming back on Friday, right?"

Major nodded. "But nobody knows that except those who need to know, per the Anunnaki's request. They aren't ready for disclosure yet."

Humana smiled. "See, Chumana, you are special. They have selected a few humans to know what they are doing, and you are one of them. However, don't tell anyone. The Shining Ones want to help us, but if we don't do what they ask, they might leave us to our miserable future as predicted, including war and annihilation."

I still found it difficult to see myself in another person, a likeness of me. But with twins, that's the way it was. However, I loved it. I loved talking to someone who understood my worries, fears, and concerns.

Rather than trying to figure out what she was, whether a robot, humanoid, clone, double, or something biological, I didn't care anymore. I found her reassuring because, in a way, she was me, in my likeness.

Of course, how could I not tell Judd about all of this? Somehow,

I'd have to keep quiet. Otherwise, I'd get them upset with me, and I needed Major's and Humana's support. I needed Rophe, which they had given to my mother and me. I needed what they were providing to make us whole.

Humana's eyes met mine. "So, what do you think? Would you like to come aboard the spaceship on Friday night and take a tour? See their amazing technology, meet them face-to-face?"

Part of me was terrified, part of me was honored, and part of me was unsure. So much was happening, but I didn't want to miss the opportunity.

"Yes," I said emphatically. "I want to. What do I do?"

Humana looked at Major. "Can you send them a message telepathically and ask them what time they expect to arrive on Friday night?"

He nodded. "Yes, I'll see what I can find out."

Then he turned to me. "Check your digital messages for the confirmation and information. In the meantime, keep working on CW. You must attain the highest level of proficiency as soon as possible.

"Disclosure will be forthcoming, and the government will need you to act as the liaison to listeners worldwide. A confused population will seek answers wherever they can, whether it's the truth, a lie, or a conspiracy.

"I can communicate telepathically with them, but most humans can't. How do we get the word out about what's going on? We need CW operators to cut through the 'space noise.'"

Major continued. "Most people are unaware that outer space can be loud, with sounds ranging from plucks to hums, crackles, and whistles. We can bypass that noise with telepathy, but humans don't have that ability unless they are trained and gifted to do it.

"That dimension exists beyond most people's awareness. Astronauts, ham radio operators, and space enthusiasts who listen to the frequencies know there is more to be discovered."

I felt excitement growing inside of me. "I will improve my proficiency. I will practice a few hours daily between now and Friday. Now that I'm not as worried about Mother, and Rophe is neutered, I can focus on practicing and not be distracted."

Major smiled. "Yes, that would be excellent."

"I have one question, though."

Major studied me intently. "What's that?"

"I have an upcoming debate about the Origins of Humankind in AP Biology. I want to discuss the Anunnaki, tracing their existence back to the beginning, and explore how we, as a species, might have originated from them. Is that okay if I don't give away anything we've discussed here?"

Major nodded. "Whatever you can find on the web or in books is fine. What we discuss here is sealed. These Zoom meetings fall under the purview of government secrecy for the safety and protection of all individuals, not just those in the United States. Governments around the world have agreements with the extraterrestrials. We must wait until the time is right for disclosure.

"Also, your father is a vital emissary, so we've delayed your meeting for a little longer. Too many conspiracy theorists will use anything they can discover online to attempt to discredit all our hard work over the last few decades."

"I get it," I said. "People would probably think I was insane if I talked about this stuff anyway."

Humana laughed. "Let them think you're smart, which you are, and the rest can wait. You have an important role to play."

"Oh, I want to be involved. Whatever I can do to help."

"Good," Major said. "I'm glad we talked and addressed your concerns. The last thing we want is to make things harder for you.

"On another topic, have you tested your solar system yet?"

"You mean the solar panel and emergency power unit?"

"Yes."

"No, I haven't done that. Judd said he could help me if that's okay. He works at a prepper store and is familiar with the equipment."

"I hear he's gotten his ham radio technician license," Major said.

My heart skipped a beat. "Yes."

"We knew he might be a complication, but we made provision for that to some degree. It should be fine if he doesn't know anything beyond ham radio. Emergency preparedness is a good thing. That's all we want him to know. Nothing else."

Now that I was in this deep, I didn't want to disappoint them. How much more did they know?

I must remind Judd to turn off our phones when we discuss things. Fortunately, we had been careful about what we said or texted. However, it was easy to forget that ears might be listening to our conversations, not just when we were on the phone or texting.

"Yes," Major said. "Let him help you set it up. We're out of time tonight to review the instructions, and we want to know that you can operate on solar power if necessary."

Humana chimed in. "I'll probably be the one to send you a message on digital, so check your messages for the exact time on Friday night. The location will be at the school."

"Sounds good. Thanks for everything."

Major then ended the Zoom call.

"Wow!" I exclaimed. I turned on the radio and connected the CW paddle. I would practice until I fell asleep.

CHAPTER FORTY

I practiced nonstop for four hours. Then I couldn't stay awake any longer. I quickly showered and hopped into bed. Rophe was sleeping with Mother, and I let him be. Until I knew Mother wouldn't sleepwalk again, I preferred him to be with her.

Sometimes, school was inconvenient, but we were nearing the end of the school year, and ACT/SATs were around the corner. I couldn't escape going to school. Not that I wanted to skip, but I had stayed up too late, and in some ways, school seemed less important than other things now.

I only studied to make hundreds on tests because I wanted a college scholarship. I needed to be diligent and not slack off. But there was much wasted time in school that I could use for something else. I often felt torn between my academic responsibilities and my desire for more meaningful experiences.

I dozed off, probably from sheer exhaustion. As I drifted into dreamland, images filled my mind.

I walked through a dense forest, following a trail to a precipice. I didn't recognize my surroundings, but warmth radiated from the setting sun. I knew I was safe.

The sweet sounds of birds filled the sky, and butterflies darted from the four corners of the heavens. I felt myself climbing higher and sensed that I would be at the top of the world when I arrived. I would pass through a portal, perhaps into another dimension.

When I reached the plateau, the view was unimaginable. The sun sank below the mountains in the distance, and anticipation beckoned me to keep walking.

Butterflies danced on the wings of currents, and even here, they flittered among the trove of flowers. The breadth of the heavens seemed vast, and I felt so small and insignificant. The first star appeared in the sky, singing in the heavens. Then another one joined, and they sang in harmony.

As I reached the plateau edge, the trail led to something I didn't expect to see. A stunning wooden bookshelf, filled with books, was carved into an ancient oak tree. The books lived here, in this mystical forest, awaiting the day somebody would open them. The sight filled me with a sense of awe and curiosity.

When I drew closer, I heard my name.

C-h-u-m-a-n-a.

Like all the times I had listened to my name in the whispers of the forest boughs back home.

A piping hot drink of rainbow colors beckoned me. I picked it up and sipped. The taste was exquisite. I longed to curl up in the nook and read for hours. However, there was too much more to see.

I tried to read the book titles, but I didn't know the languages. Someone must live here, and my heart beat with curiosity.

To my right, I saw a swing hanging from a tree. It swayed gently in the breeze. Undulating hills, dressed in nature's glory, stretched as far as I could see.

A flock of white birds swept up the precipice in formation and chirped excitedly. They seemed eager to meet me. How many adventurers made it to the top of this hideaway? Was I one of many? The birds made me feel special.

As I sipped my heavenly drink, I noticed a book on the swing's seat.

I edged over and picked it up, carefully sitting on the swing, holding the coffee and book. Gently, I rocked back and forth. The view took my breath away. I handled the book with great care, as it was old. It was about an inch thick, and unlike the others on the bookshelf, its ancient cover had no words.

I tried to flip the book open to the middle, but couldn't. Then I tried to open it from the back, but couldn't. The book would only open from the front.

So, I opened the book as most people do, and a handwritten message appeared on the first page: "Dear Chumana, I have prayed for you not to be deceived." Signed, YH.

That's all it said. I couldn't turn the page. It was like someone sealed the rest of the book. Who was YH? The message felt ominous, like a warning. I couldn't shake off the feeling that it held significant meaning.

I thought about all my friends, even my enemies, and I couldn't imagine who YH was.

At that moment, a white butterfly danced before me. If only Shale were here; she could talk to the butterfly, the birds, the flowers, and the trees.

I envied her connection with nature, her ability to understand and communicate with the world around her. I felt like an outsider, a mere observer in this mystical place. I had no answers. Even my high I.Q. couldn't tell me what I longed to know.

Perplexed, I rocked back and forth. I always read the last chapter of a book before deciding if I wanted to read the whole book. If I didn't like the ending, I wouldn't read it. I'd never had this happen before. Maybe that was the point:

Startled by what I'd seen, I woke up from my dream.

CHAPTER FORTY-ONE

I checked the time. It was too early to get up, but I was too disturbed to go back to sleep. I needed Rophe.

I climbed out of bed and retrieved him from Mother's bedroom, careful not to wake her up. I tiptoed back to my room, clutching my furry friend.

I made Rophe comfortable, pulling a blanket up halfway, and I rubbed his head. He loved that and responded with sweet purrs. Soon, I drifted off and didn't awaken until my alarm sounded.

I looked for new text messages. Seeing none, I quickly dressed and checked on Mother. Much to my relief, she was still asleep.

I chastised myself for staying up so late to practice CW. I glanced at the hallway corner near the front door. Maybe Judd could stop by this afternoon and show me how to set up the solar system.

Rophe moseyed back into Mother's bedroom as I headed to the front door. A wet mist covered the grass and streets. It must have rained.

I looked for the friendly Rose-breasted Grosbeak that usually greeted me, but I didn't see him this morning—probably sheltering in a warm nest somewhere out of the chill.

As I waited for the light to change at the crossroads, my mind flashed back to Mother's sleepwalking nightmare. Since then, she had been fine. Hopefully, she never sleepwalked again.

The light turned, and the walk sign lit. I had stopped counting my steps. I now perceived my proclivity for counting as resignation, much like a caged, hopeless animal pacing back and forth

Try as I might, I couldn't make sense of my dream the night before. I started ticking off things it could be, but I came up empty. I was bothered by the inability to read anything beyond the first page in the book. It was as if the author had signed a book for me but wouldn't let me read it.

I always read the last chapter of a book first to see how it ended. I wouldn't read the book if I didn't like the ending. Why take the time to read an entire book if you won't like how everything turns out?

Nevertheless, I'd keep my eyes open. I didn't see how anything could deceive me. I was diligent in my schoolwork, almost to a fault. I was fortunate that it didn't take that much effort.

But ham radio was different. I had worked hard to develop the skills Major, Humana, The Frequency Group, and the Anunnaki wanted me to have. I thought about all the hours I had put into CW in the event of a crisis, whether it be an all-out war, a power grid collapse, an EMP attack, or a global satellite failure.

I thought about everything I did that anybody would commend as good.

I took excellent care of Rophe and Mother.

I rarely listened to the news, so I was immune to the stupid political pundits who thought they had all the answers.

And I didn't do unhealthy things like drink, smoke pot, go to bars, look at porn, or gossip.

Anybody would say I was a good person, except I did have a temper. But even Major said my temper was borne out of righteousness brought on by my attempt to defend the defenseless.

I had even been going to Bible Study.

Still, I would be cautious to avoid being deceived. I wish I had been allowed to read the last chapter of the book in my dream. How could I know if it was a good or bad book? I wanted to see how the story ended.

I arrived at school as the bell rang and headed to AP Chemistry. I knew Judd would ask about the Zoom call and what I learned. Sure enough, as soon as I sat at my desk, he whispered, "How did the meeting go?"

I put my finger up to my lips to hush him. "We'll talk over lunch."

He nodded. "Sounds good."

I'd have to figure it out before lunch. If Judd and I turned off our phones, how would they know what I told him? The government couldn't "bug" the entire school.

I MADE a quick trip to the library before lunch to pick up some books about the Anunnaki, partly for the AP Biology debate and partly as grounds for discussing the UFO topic indirectly with Judd.

I was the last to join our small lunch group, which had become routine. Everyone was already eating and seemed delighted to have me join.

Shale noticed my books right away. "Is that for the upcoming debate?"

I nodded.

She chuckled. "You like the Hollywood version of human origins, and Judd likes the Darwinian version. We should have a good debate next week."

I needed to get started. I had lost track of time.

"I'm glad you're taking the topic seriously," Gracie said. "It's important we know why we believe what we believe."

Judd agreed. "I'm about done with my research. Evolution doesn't rule out either of your viewpoints. In fact—"

"Whoa," Shale said. "Save it. We'll have plenty of fire next week in AP Biology. I can already feel the flames."

She turned to me. "Can you come to my apartment this week for

Bible Study? I promise we won't talk about evolution, creationism, or panspermia."

I glanced at Judd. I needed to keep my word, at least a little longer. "Sure. I'll join you. Thanks for inviting me."

Shale smiled. "Thank you for coming. I'm trying to make amends with all of those I've offended. Jesus calls us to forgive, even as he's forgiven us."

I watched Judd and Shale, somewhat amazed. Once mortal enemies, they had come to terms with each other. At least to some degree.

"I'm coming, too," Gracie chimed in. "I'm enjoying learning the Bible. It's been interesting."

Rachel nodded. "I knew nothing about the New Testament before I joined."

We chatted about other things until the lunch bell rang, and my friends took off, except for Judd. He lingered. I knew he would.

"How did the Zoom meeting go last night?"

"Turn off your phone. Mine is already off."

Judd did as I asked. "Sorry, I forgot."

I relaxed and talked in a hushed, hurried tone. "It went well. Major and Humana explained many things about my mother and the extraterrestrials' desire to help her. She has a genetic condition, like Alzheimer's, that affects her memory. They said it's inherited. They have been intervening to help her. They sent Rophe to us."

"Who do you mean by 'they?'" Judd asked. "The government? The extraterrestrials?"

I'd have to be more open than I wanted. "Just promise, Judd, you won't repeat what I say."

"Chumana, if I said anything about this to anybody, they'd call me a conspiracy nut and write me off as insane."

I looked at the clock. "Can you come over later today and show me how to set up the solar system? We'll have more time to talk then."

Reluctantly, Judd agreed. "Okay. I'll need to go home first, then swing by."

I hugged Judd briefly. "Thanks. See you later."

He bid me farewell.

Hugs always went over well with men. I glanced down at my three library books. There wasn't enough time in the day to do everything I wanted.

However, I'd read the last chapter of each book and see if I liked their endings. I'd make up something if I didn't like how they ended. I just wish I knew which book I saw in my dream. That's the book I wanted to read.

CHAPTER FORTY-TWO

I was practicing CW when I heard the doorbell ring. I stopped and rushed to the door, and Judd greeted me unexpectedly with a peck on the cheek. He took my exuberance as a romantic invitation. I was just happy he was here to set up the solar system.

He glanced at the solar panel and other accessories. "Is everything here?"

"Everything they sent me."

Mother sat in the living room with Rophe beside her, and Judd said hello to her from the hallway. "Glad to see you and Rophe are doing well, Mrs. Ironvein."

"Thank you, Judd. Rophe is fine now. He won't be chasing any young-ins."

Judd chuckled at Mother's allusion to him kissing me on the cheek.

We pulled out the equipment, and he made a few suggestions. "I recommend you charge the portable power station. Then, if the power goes out, it'll be ready to use.

"When you need to recharge it, you can use the solar panel. The power station has a built-in charge controller, so you won't need to use the one they sent. I could also charge it from my car."

I nodded.

Judd examined the power station in more detail. "You can plug in small things like your cell phone and computer and charge more than one thing at a time, up to 1200 watts. Pretty nifty."

"Can we try it?"

"Well, you need to charge it first."

"Let's do that."

We plugged the power station into the outlet, and Judd examined the solar panel's capacity. "Four hundred watts is plenty."

With Judd's help, setting it up was easier than I thought.

"You've got this. If you can pass your Extra test, only missing a few questions, you can easily connect this to your radio equipment—if you ever need to."

I laughed uneasily. "Major makes it sound like it's a given that I will need it."

Judd's eyes met mine. "Who is 'they'?" he asked. "You skirted my question earlier today, but now I want to know what they said last night."

I glanced at Mother. "Let's talk somewhere else. Can we get some coffee?"

"Sure. But first, I want to see you do some CW. Can you give me a quick demonstration?"

"You want to hear me send CW?"

"Yeah, I want to hear what it sounds like. Can I video you?"

I laughed. "I guess. It'll just make me nervous."

"Well, it could help you to get over your nerves."

We went to my bedroom, where I'd been practicing. "It won't go over the air, but it's in oscillation mode so you can hear it."

Judd nodded.

"Tell me when you're ready?"

"Go ahead."

I sent my call sign, KO4LBS, and the phrase etched in my mind. When I finished, Judd stopped recording and asked what I had sent.

I laughed. "What do you think?"

He thought for a minute. "What hath God wrought?"

"Yep. It seems appropriate, don't you think?"

"Well, I suspect God is doing something."

I turned off the radio, and we left to go to our favorite coffee place. I ordered my usual, and we found a table away from the rest of the patrons. "Make sure your phone is off."

"It is," Judd assured me.

I took a sip. "Where do you want me to start?"

"What did they say about the CW message from the UFO?"

"Major said the answer is within me."

Judd leaned back. "That's not very helpful."

Judd's comment wasn't helpful. We had just started, and he was already critical.

He saw my irritation. "Chumana, it's a reasonable question, and they should have given you a reasonable answer, not some vague response that could mean anything."

I took a deep breath. "Okay. Here's the gist. The extraterrestrials were on Earth before we were, and they have returned. They want to save humankind from self-annihilation. They can talk to some people telepathically, like Major, but not everyone has that ability.

"CW is a way for the extraterrestrials to communicate with a broader audience, like those who don't know how to use telepathy. In an emergency, like a power failure, CW would be one of the primary ways the government would communicate with us, especially if voice was compromised. CW travels farther and is easier to hear than voice when the bands are noisy."

"Keep going," Judd said. "Is there more?"

"Yes. Mother's abductions are related to the extraterrestrials trying to help her. She suffers from a deteriorating neurological condition that I inherited, unfortunately. She's been uncooperative, they said, so that's why she's gotten worse. So, they sent Rophe to us. It was an experiment to see if he could help her."

"Help her how?"

"There must be healing power in animals."

"All animals or just Rophe?"

I hadn't thought about it that way. "I don't know. But here's the thing. They aren't here to hurt us. They want to help us. They are our friends. They are collaborating with governments worldwide to promote harmony and peace. They want to ensure everything is in place before disclosing their identity.

"Let's face it. If the timing isn't right, people might jump out of windows like they did in the *War of the Worlds'* broadcast in 1938."

"Right before the start of World War II," Judd added.

"Why do you make that correlation?"

"I don't know. It just popped into my head."

Judd finished his coffee and attempted to summarize. "So, the government will disclose some national or international catastrophe. You'll be helping with the communication between the government and the extraterrestrials while the rest of the world waits in horror to find out what's happening."

"Judd, you make it sound so evil. They aren't evil. It's more likely that some rogue nation will attack someone. It might be Russia attacking the U.S. or China invading Taiwan. Pakistan and India could have a nuclear exchange. Iran or Turkey could launch an attack against Israel, or it could be some natural event, like an exploding volcano that sets off a cascading winter from which we can't recover.

"Besides, who would come to our aid if we needed it? Most of the world hates the United States, except for Israel and a few European countries."

Judd grabbed my hand. "Okay. Just go along with whatever they say for now. I'll continue to work on getting my general ham radio license. If everything goes kaput, it's another way to stay in touch."

I cautioned him. "I don't think we should talk about this over the phone or by text. They're listening. I'd be in trouble if they knew I'd told you all this. It scares me that I have."

"Well, they don't have to find out. My lips are sealed."

I nodded. "How far are you along studying for your general?

"I just started, but we can talk on VHF. My radio is in the car. I programmed it last night. Did you program yours?"

I laughed. "No. I haven't even attempted to use it. I've only used HF, focusing on CW."

"When we return to your apartment, I'll take your walkie-talkie home and program it. We can test it on Simplex later and see if we can hear each other. We're so close that it shouldn't be a problem."

"Maybe we can come up with some code words to use, just in case we have to resort to Simplex."

Judd nodded. "Are you finished with your drink?"

"Sure."

When we got in the car, Judd handed me his radio. He had bought the same brand as mine. "So, you keep this in the car?"

"Well, in an emergency, if the phones were out, it would come in handy."

"Let's hope that never happens." I turned it on and heard the usual crackling sounds in the background: a little static, the repeater announcing its callsign, and, surprisingly, a rag chew was in progress between two operators.

I chuckled. "I've never listened to the local repeater before."

"Well, let's test it first without using the repeater between us. Make sure we can hear each other."

"I haven't talked as much as I would like on the radio. I've been listening to others on CW to learn the jargon. I'm too scared to do CW myself; I'm afraid I'll mess up my call sign."

Judd eyed me. "You know what's coming. Get over your fear. You must be proficient to be a key cog in the wheel during an emergency."

"Well, it's easier at first to do it with somebody you know so that you don't feel stupid if you mess up. So, drop me off at my house, and then you go home, and we'll try it."

"But you said you hadn't programmed yours."

"Oh, that's right. Well, can you do it or show me how to do it?"

"Do you have a programming cable?"

I shook my head. "Major was only concerned about using HF for long distances, so I didn't bother with the UHF/VHF.

"Well, since I can only use UHV/VHF until I get my general license, let's practice on that, and I think you'll gain enough confidence to do HF on your own."

"That sounds good."

As we drove, Judd coughed. "I'll head home after I get your radio. I've been tired all day. Hope I'm not getting sick."

"Well, we can do the Simplex test any time. We don't have to do it today. Go home and get some sleep."

"Okay."

"Besides, I need to focus on CW, and I've got to read those books on the Anunnaki for the debate."

Judd pulled into a parking space, and I ran inside to retrieve the walkie-talkie. Then I returned and handed it to him through the car window.

He chuckled. "You haven't even taken it out of the box."

"Well, I took it out, looked at it, and put it back. I didn't know what to do with it."

"The antenna is low quality; you should probably get a longer one, but we live so close, it should still work. I can't believe you didn't do anything with it."

"Well, the big radio is more fun. You can hear people in other states talking."

"Okay. You don't have to rub it in. I'm getting there—slowly. I'll give your radio back to you at school tomorrow."

I nodded.

We parted ways, and I went inside, where Mother was cooking dinner. Then I remembered Humana had told me to check my digital messages for the rendezvous time on Friday night.

I set the radio and computer to digital mode. The digital heartbeat appeared on the computer screen. When I checked my messages, I found one. I went to my inbox and retrieved it.

"10:00 pm Friday at the designated location, 73, KL7UAP."

That should work. The Bible Study was at Shale's apartment on Friday, but it would end earlier. However, it meant I'd need to walk to school in the dark. If only I had my driver's license. I didn't like walking in the dark. I didn't feel safe. If I told Judd so he could walk with me, would he keep it a secret and stay out of sight?

Mother called me from the other room. "Dinner's ready."

After dinner, I'd start preparing for the debate.

I joined Mother in the dining room.

"Can I pray for the food?" she asked.

"Sure."

Mother uttered a short prayer, and I added "Amen."

As we ate, she said, "I read the Bible today."

"Really? We are both getting spiritual. I'm going to a Bible Study at Shale's on Friday."

Mother looked surprised. "I didn't think you were friends with her anymore."

"Well, things are better now."

Mother said, "I'm glad to hear that. We shouldn't hold grudges. They can come back to haunt us."

The baked chicken was so good that I focused on eating and let Mother talk.

"Sometimes I miss Mrs. Heller," she continued. "We got along very well. I hope she's happily married."

I shrugged. "We don't discuss those things much, but I know it's been challenging." I knew a lot more, but I wouldn't tell Mother. It was Shale's burden. I was learning not to take on everyone else's burden and make them my own.

"If you see Mrs. Heller, tell her I said 'Hi.'"

I nodded. "I will."

CHAPTER FORTY-THREE

Judd had been absent from school all week but texted that he would return on Friday. I hoped to see him in AP Chemistry. He entered the classroom as the bell rang and sat beside me. I could tell he still didn't feel good.

He acknowledged me with a nod, and I texted him, "Did you bring my radio?"

He grimaced and mouthed. "I forgot."

That was understandable since he had been sick. I texted him, "NP, we can get it later."

The class went by quickly. Our narcissistic teacher was prepping us for the upcoming AP Chemistry final, so it was all review. We needed to do well so we could make him look good.

The bell rang, and I lingered to talk to Judd. "It's good to see you back, even though I can tell you still don't feel good."

"I don't have a fever anymore, so I'm not contagious. I'm glad I didn't give it to you the other night."

"Are you going to the Bible Study at Shale's?"

"Yeah, since it's the first meeting back at her apartment. I want her to have a good turnout, so I plan on coming. How about you?"

"If you're coming, I'll be there. Did you drive today?"

Judd nodded.

"Maybe you could swing by your apartment and get the walkie-talkie on the way."

"Yeah, I can do that. Good idea."

"I'll see you at lunch, then."

Judd asked. "Are you ready for the debate?"

"I've been reading. It's fascinating what I've discovered. How about you?"

Judd grinned. "I think it will be good. Even if we present different views, that doesn't mean they are incompatible."

"I know."

"I just don't want you to be angry with me if I win."

I laughed. "You won't win."

"We'll see," he replied, with a twinkle in his eye.

I OPTED to walk to Shale's apartment with my friends. Gracie and Judd would be a little late. The walk to her place was shorter. It would be my first time visiting her apartment since they moved.

I was excited to hear the Rose-breasted Grosbeak serenade us on the way. "What is he saying today?"

Shale laughed. "You really want to know?"

"Yeah, I do."

"My father feeds me, and I am satisfied!"

Now, it was my turn to laugh. "I like that."

Soon, we arrived, and Mrs Heller greeted us at the door. "I have some chocolate cookies and milk for you in the dining room."

As we entered, a white dog approached me, wagging her tail.

"I forgot what you named her," I said to Shale.

"Much-Afraid because she was so nervous in the beginning. We called her that because she reminded me of a dog in a children's book. However, she's not afraid anymore. I think she was pretending to be frightened to woo me to where she wanted me to go."

"Where did she want you to go?"

"To a magnificent garden where animals talk."

"What kind of garden?"

"Well, it's someplace that's not here."

"Like where?"

Shale laughed. "Let's just say it's in another dimension."

"You lost me," I replied, secretly wishing to go there.

I leaned over to pet Much-Afraid. "I think she likes me. She's wagging her tail."

"She likes all my friends," Shale said.

"You've been able to hide her from the apartment manager?"

"Yeah, they haven't kicked us out yet."

The doorbell rang, and Gracie and Judd entered. A couple of other students followed behind them.

We finished off the cookies and milk, and Shale opened the Bible Study with prayer. Then, she asked each of us to introduce ourselves. I watched as Much-Afraid lay beside Shale's chair.

My wandering thoughts refocused when Shale gave us the passage we were to look at. I had grabbed Mother's Bible on the way out the door that morning, so I felt more prepared this time.

Shale said, "I'm reading from the NIV, Luke 21:35: 'People will faint from terror, apprehensive of what is coming on the world, for the heavenly bodies will be shaken.'"

No one said anything at first. I had no idea where Luke was in the Bible, so I looked it up discreetly in the index at the front of the Bible. It was the third book in the New Testament. I was the last person to find it, but I was proud that I found it myself without Judd's help. That was a good start for me.

I reread the lines. Did this have anything to do with UFOs? What a coincidence she would pick this passage, or did Judd clue her in? I wouldn't know if I asked; if I asked, I would give away my secret, so I didn't say anything.

"Does anyone have any thoughts on what the passage is referring to?

Gracie spoke first. "My dad is a professor at Kennesaw State

University, and he's always looking up at the heavens. He even has a telescope.

When I look through the telescope and see all that's out there—planets like Saturn with its beautiful rings and Mars with its eerie landscape—it makes me wonder if there could be life elsewhere.

My dad thinks there's life on other planets, and if we keep looking, we'll find it."

"Or they might find us," Rachel added.

"If we did find life on other planets, they might want to be our friends," one of the new students said. "But even if they were friendly toward us, I think the whole idea of aliens would be terrifying."

The other unfamiliar student added, "It would terrify me."

Shale nodded. "If celestial bodies were shaking in the heavens, I can imagine fallout to Earth in the form of fire and hail. It also makes me think of the war that took place in heaven. Perhaps there are extraterrestrials than those from other planets."

"Like what?" Gracie asked. "I don't understand what you mean."

Shale took a minute to craft her words. "The Bible talks about an apocalyptic war long ago between God and the sons of God. One-third of the angels rebelled, and God cast them out of heaven.

"Imagine what that would have been like. I can envision heavenly bodies shattering, projectiles flying through outer space, and debris falling to Earth as hail and brimstone."

"That's in the past, though, right? It sounds like this is in the future," Rachel said.

"Yeah," Shale replied. "But—maybe it has a dual meaning."

"What do you mean?" I asked.

"We know there is a big battle that happens when Jesus returns. Maybe what happened in the beginning when Satan fell from heaven will be repeated in some way before Jesus returns."

"That's speculative," Judd said.

Shale nodded. "I know, but the Bible says people will be terrified and the heavenly bodies shaken. When you look at what's happening in the Middle East, I wonder if the end is near.

"Jesus died on the cross to save us, so we don't need to live in fear. All we must do is confess our sins, and he will forgive us."

Shale made it sound so simple. When no one had any more thoughts, she broke the silence. "Does anyone have any prayer requests or anything they want to share?"

I had many questions, but I was too afraid to ask. Then I remembered my UFO appointment later that evening, and my mind drifted. After a few more comments, we broke into groups of two, and Judd edged over to be with me.

"Here," he said. "Your radio."

"Oh, thanks. Do you want to try Simplex tonight?"

"Yes, let's try it. It looks like we'll be breaking up soon."

We dispersed a few minutes later, and Judd offered me a ride home. After dropping me off, he drove back to his apartment. My walkie-talkie was set to the frequency he would be using, and I went inside and waited for his signal.

Soon, I heard a crackle. "This is K4PREP calling CQ for KO4LBS. Can you hear me?"

I answered, "This is KO4LBS. I can hear you. Over."

"KO4LBS, do you have any plans tonight?"

I stuttered, not sure how to respond. "K4PREP, can you come over?"

"I was just there."

"Can you return? This is KO4LBS."

A pause followed. Judd didn't expect me to ask him to come over again, especially because he still wasn't feeling well, but I didn't want to walk to school after dark.

He finally replied, "Be there in a second."

I turned off the radio and told Mother, who was half-listening in the living room, "Judd is coming over."

"This late? He was just here."

"We're going to go for a walk. It's a full moon tonight."

"It is? I didn't know," she replied.

I didn't know either. I just made it up.

CHAPTER FORTY-FOUR

"Don't feel like you need to stay up for me," I assured Mother.

She patted Rophe on the head. "Be careful."

I smiled. "Judd will be with me." I double-checked that I had locked the front door and waited outside.

A few minutes later, Judd arrived, and I motioned for him to join me on the porch. He looked puzzled, but did as I asked.

"Why did you want me to come back?"

I had practiced what I would say to him. "I was afraid to tell you this earlier, but I've got a rendezvous with the UFO tonight at 10:00 at school. I got nervous thinking about walking to school at night. Would you come with me?"

Judd stared at me. "Let me see if I understand. You're afraid to walk to school after dark, but you aren't afraid to go aboard a UAP?"

"Well, you've put it in weird terms."

"No, Chumana. I've gone along with this craziness because I wanted you to have someone to talk to, but it's bothered me from the beginning. Now I feel trapped."

He crossed his arms and turned his back on me, even stepping a few feet away.

I knew he would be upset. After all, he hadn't been on the Zoom conversations, and I had kept him in the dark about most of what I knew. Now, I regretted it.

However, I wasn't supposed to tell him anything, so no matter what I did, there would be problems. I had to choose my battles. I waited for him to say something. Anything.

Finally, he turned and faced me. "Don't do this. Whether I walk you there or not, it doesn't matter. You've set your mind on this, but I'm telling you, it's a mistake. Honestly, they are deceiving you. They aren't God. They aren't Jesus. They're extraterrestrials. I don't think they're from this world. I did a little reading, and what I've read terrifies me.

"Have you read anything at all about UFOs?

Now, I was annoyed. "I checked three books out of the library."

"But were they about UFOs or historical books on the early Sumerian and Babylonian gods? I mean, this is wild. You're making assumptions—"

"Scholars wrote the books, Judd. Researchers have carefully documented everything in footnotes and references."

"But you're assuming that's what they are. An ancient civilization that's returned. You have no idea."

"My twin is going to meet me there—Humana."

"Your what?" Judd asked.

"I told you about her."

"Yeah, yeah, I remember now."

Neither of us said anything. We were at an impasse.

Then Judd asked, "Tell me about this Major guy. What's he like?"

"Well, he's well-built, handsome, smart, and much older than I am. I think he's human."

"You don't even know for sure that he's human?"

"Okay. He's human," I said, getting exasperated.

"Suppose something happens while you're in the spaceship."

"I'll take my walkie-talkie with me and talk to you from inside."

"I doubt that it would even work. Remember, you tried to send me a photo of your mother when she was near the UFO, and I didn't receive it."

"Well, the radio is different. I think it would work."

"I thought they didn't want you to tell me about them, and that's why all this secrecy."

"I told them you have your technician license."

"You did?"

"Yeah. If you stayed hidden, they wouldn't know you were near. You could contact me on the radio like you did earlier."

Judd rolled his eyes. "That's insane. You've got to be kidding."

I was getting impatient. "Look, it's 9:30 now. It will take 15 minutes to walk there. Are you coming with me or not?"

Judd was irritated, and I was ready to walk alone if I had to.

He interrupted my thoughts. "How far back do I need to stay? And then what do I do? Wait until you come out?"

I threw up my hands. "I don't know. Why don't we say 30 minutes?"

"Didn't you say something about a difference in the lapse of time? You thought your mother was inside for only a few minutes, but it was a couple of hours."

I'd forgotten about that. "My phone lost an hour or two. Yes, that's true, but I didn't lose time."

"Did you tell your mother you'd be out late?"

I nodded. "She knows I'm with you. By the way, did you say anything to Shale about UFOs?"

Judd shook his head.

"It's strange she picked that verse to discuss in the Bible Study."

"Chumana, I told you I wouldn't tell anybody. I don't want people to think I'm crazy, so why would I bring it up?"

"I just wondered."

"Has it occurred to you that God may be talking to you?"

That comment hit a nerve. I remembered my dream about the book I couldn't open and that somebody named YH was praying for me not to be deceived.

“Well, I’m listening if he is.”

“Are you?” Judd asked.

“Yes, I am. I went to the Bible Study.”

I rechecked the time on my phone. “Are you coming with me or not?”

CHAPTER FORTY-FIVE

I began walking, leaving Judd behind.

"Hold on. I'll come with you part of the way."

I waited for him to catch up. However, he tried to dissuade me the whole time.

"If something happens, I'm not responsible."

"This is my choice," I said. "I appreciate you walking with me."

The cool air was perfect for a brisk walk. I studied the heavens. To my surprise, the stars shone in all their glory, and a full moon hung in the sky. I admired the Creator's handiwork—if there was one.

Whether there was or wasn't, I couldn't deny the creativity around me, the universe's orderliness, the pinpoints of light that darted across the heavens. Who knew what lay beyond? My imagination soared as I envisioned undiscovered worlds ripe for exploration.

While I thought about the opportunities to visit distant lands and meet life on other planets, wherever and whoever they might be, Judd pelted me with negative ideas about the possible nefarious intentions of hellish monsters bent on destroying the Earth.

I finally told him to shut up. "Keep your thoughts to yourself."

He kept walking with me, remaining silent for the rest of the way.

Once the football field came into view, I grabbed his arm. "Look, there it is."

A large saucer gleaming in the moon's faint light hovered in the distance. I sensed it was alive, almost sacred, as if it knew ancient wisdom from a time when the gods ruled the Earth.

Interrupting my thoughts, Judd asked, "Are you sure you want to do this?"

Before I could respond, rhythmic sounds reverberated through the still night air.

"Do you hear it?"

Judd nodded.

"I don't have anything to write with."

"Here." Judd handed me a pen and a small notepad.

I translated the sounds from the spaceship into CW.

I missed the first couple of letters but figured it out when the dits and dahs stopped: "'Humana is here,' but Judd, I don't know how to respond. I must get closer so I can see her."

"What do you want me to do?" Judd asked.

"Stay in the shadows so they can't see you. When I return, I'll come to this location."

Reluctantly, Judd said, "I'll be praying."

I returned the pen and notepad to him. "I won't need these now. I can talk to Humana."

Judd nodded. "If I don't hear anything from you for a while, I'll call you on the radio."

I reached into my back pocket, making sure the walkie-talkie was still there. "It's turned off now, but I'll turn it on when I get inside."

"Try not to forget."

"Okay." I looked straight ahead. If Humana was here, I would find her.

Soon, I reached the spot where I had watched Mother enter the UAP. I searched for my hand-scratched message in the dirt but couldn't find it.

Hearing no road noise and seeing no street lights, I felt alone, but I wasn't scared. I was at peace.

The UFO's immense size spoke of power and authority as I approached. Unexpectedly, a light shone beneath it, and I saw Humana waving it.

Like me, she wore blue jeans and a loose long-sleeved shirt. I doubt she would have been indistinguishable from me to the human eye.

How did they create her with such accuracy? As Gracie had suggested at lunch, I did have a twin. I didn't know it then, and neither did my mother.

I turned on my phone flashlight so Humana could see me. Briefly, we carried on a conversation flashing lights back and forth. It didn't take me long to get within talking distance, but she didn't wait for me to speak. She ran up and extended a warm welcome.

"I'm excited to see you," Humana said. She motioned for me to follow her. "The tractor beam will lift us."

I nodded, and we took several steps to get positioned beneath the spaceship.

"This is good. Wait here," she said.

I felt a tractor beam lift me into the ship's belly. The warm, soothing light enveloped me, filling me with contentment and peace.

Once inside, the ship's doors closed underneath us. When the beam released its hold, I could move about in the UAP's interior. The euphoria reminded me of a Disney ride.

As I took in my surroundings, I sensed profound knowledge, and warmth and friendship enveloped me. I'd never felt this kind of oneness with another entity before. I was speechless as my eyes adjusted to the bluish light.

"What do you think?" Humana asked.

"Is anyone here besides us?"

"Yes, they are here. They want you to get familiar with the spaceship so you feel comfortable. Roam about. Ask anything you want."

On the semicircular walls, large screens displayed many locations and places. Some looked like other galaxies. One screen showed an exotic red planet, reminding me of Mars, while another resembled Saturn surrounded by brilliant rings glistening in space. Earth's satellites came into view on another screen.

Dozens of screens appeared to be monitoring various locations. Some locations seemed Earth-like; others were unidentifiable, perhaps other galaxies or worlds in other solar systems.

Every few seconds, the views changed. The Earth monitors displayed mountains, cities, forests, and oceans—almost like the screens were reflecting what they thought I wanted to see.

Could it read my mind? I didn't know. Humana shadowed beside me, not saying anything and letting me absorb everything.

After several minutes, she asked, "What do you think?"

"It's amazing," I said.

"Are you ready to meet one of the Shining Ones?"

"Is that what you call them?"

Humana nodded. "You can see for yourself if you're ready."

"I'm ready."

CHAPTER FORTY-SIX

A strange sensation penetrated my soul. Something had joined with me—or, at least, had entered my reality. I knew I was in communion with another being.

At first, I could only feel it, but then my eyes saw it: a celestial being materialized clothed in dazzling light.

He was about seven feet tall with blond hair and fair features. He looked human and would have been considered handsome by any woman's standards. However, he was not human. His body shone with the brightness of shimmering light. Now I understood why Humana called the extraterrestrials Shining Ones.

I didn't think he was an angel because he didn't have wings. I remembered the movie *It's a Wonderful Life*, where the angel had to earn his wings. That was the extent of what I knew about angels.

I admired the Shining One. He was pleasing to the eye, and I perceived another characteristic of his demeanor that I couldn't quite identify. It may have had more to do with my perception of who he was. He had just demonstrated the ability to be visible when invisible. He must be multi-dimensional to materialize and become visible at will. Even more than that, as spectacular as that was, I perceived his desire to be my friend.

As I marveled, a smile crossed his dazzling face, and unexpectedly, he reached out his hand in a gesture of friendship.

"I think he wants to shake my hand," I exclaimed. "Is that permissible?"

"Of course," Humana said excitedly. "You are one of the few humans the Shining Ones have contacted with this level of intimacy. Until now, most of our friendship building has been indirect: UFO sightings, remote viewing, telepathy, extrasensory perception, that kind of thing."

I breathed deeply, full of anticipation and trepidation, and reminded myself to exhale. Was this happening? An intelligent life form from another world wanted to be my friend!

Perhaps he was afraid, but I felt he trusted me enough to take that first step toward interstellar oneness.

I reflected on what history had recorded. How the Indians trusted the early Europeans and how our ancestors mistreated them. Early European explorers didn't seek to befriend the Indians; instead, they aimed to conquer their lands and impose their religious beliefs.

In the process, they obliterated Indian culture and confined them to reservations, where they still live today. I wanted this relationship—the first friendship between humans and an interstellar traveler from another world—to be different.

I extended my right hand timidly at first, and as I did so, a quiet calm enveloped me in a way I had never experienced. From one life force to another, we joined in friendship.

For an instant, our eyes met. We exchanged something that I couldn't put into words or fully understand. Although we couldn't communicate like humans, I sensed his longing to know me better.

Humana edged over to me and whispered. "He is saying, 'Thank you for your friendship.'"

"How do I say thank you?"

Humana replied excitedly. "Most of the time, they can perceive our thoughts even if we don't understand theirs. But, in time, you'll learn how to communicate. It's like magic. Eventually, you'll even be able to summon them."

For a fleeting moment, we lingered, connected in a handshake that crossed dimensions, worlds, time, and space.

Then, as quickly as the star traveler had appeared, he was gone.

I waited briefly for him to return. When he didn't, I asked, "How did he do that?"

Humana shook her head. "I'm not sure."

I studied my twin, intrigued by who she was and her connection to the Shining Ones. "Are there more twins, like you and me, who can facilitate communication with them?"

"A few," Humana said. "However, this is all new. The government needs certain bloodlines. Not everyone has the right blood type. Yours—and mine—is very rare, very ancient—a royal bloodline. That's why they chose you."

"Based on my mother's bloodline?"

Humana nodded. "But it's also politics. The Chosen Ones must be associated with the right benefactors. Your father is an integral part of the government's program regarding Unidentified Aerial Phenomena.

"The Shining Ones want humans to meet specific intellectual criteria. He—or she, as in your case—must have the character traits to deal with future events involving inter-dimensional exchange and time travel.

"The Chosen Ones must be comfortable in liminal spaces, interacting with life forms that are more intelligent and different from humans. They must be sensitive to the ethereal boundaries in the multiverse. That's why the person must demonstrate they live predominantly on a higher frequency level. That's just the beginning. In your case, your main limitation is your imagination."

Wow! That was a lot to take in. Where did I start? How did my twin know so much about all of this? I had many questions, but the reference to liminal spaces caught my attention. I had to ask about that. "What do you mean by liminal spaces?"

Humana chuckled. "That is one of your strengths, dealing with liminal spaces. It's like an in-between place; it's what exists between what was, is, and will be. If you are on the verge of something that's about to happen, but it hasn't yet happened, and you aren't even sure when it will happen, you are in a liminal space.

"That's where you've lived for a long time. Waiting for disclosure, waiting for your mother's healing, waiting to meet your father, waiting for the revelation of your past, and waiting to determine your future.

"Everybody has some of those issues, but in you, they are magnified. You've had to learn how to cope with adversity.

"Many souls are unable to do that. They become overwhelmed by worry, dysfunction, and discouragement. Sometimes, human beings will turn to drugs or alcohol as a coping mechanism. Others develop repetitive, unfruitful behaviors that rob them of creativity and joy."

I thought about some of my former repetitive behaviors, such as incessantly counting steps and a proclivity to keep track of time to the nearest second. Did they recognize that I had stopped doing those things?

Humana's words hit the mark. They echoed with truism within me. It was like they knew me better than I knew myself.

Humana added, "You've survived in a world that would have crushed many people. Of course, all of this was to develop your character so you could fulfill your destiny."

"What is my destiny?" I asked.

Humana waved her hand. "This is your destiny, even what is yet to be revealed."

There were so many questions I wanted to ask. How long would they give me? While I was curious about Humana, my clone, I was more interested in learning about life on other planets.

I wasn't so interested in my lookalike, like a narcissist. I wanted to know about the Shining Ones. Were these beings our progenitors?

The debate was foremost on my mind. Rather than delve too deeply into the philosophical aspects, I focused on the most pressing question. "Maybe you could help me with something practical."

"What's that?" Humana asked.

"I have a debate coming up on Friday on the Origins of Life. It's for AP Biology, and I've been reading about the Sumerians, Akkadians, Assyrians, and Babylonians. Historians have discovered references to the Anunnaki in ancient clay tablets and drawings. These ancient civilizations worshipped the Anunnaki.

"According to some sources, the Anunnaki were a pantheon of deities. Some historians might even refer to them as gods, and their divinely appointed tasks were to decree the fates of humanity.

"Many scientists believe they gave knowledge to our forefathers when they weren't much more than hunters and gatherers. Some believe the wisdom they shared led to the Golden Age of the Greeks.

"In well-documented writings, others believe they taught early humans the sciences of metallurgy and alchemy, and the understanding of music and mathematics.

"Still others, like conspiracy theorists, claim the Anunnaki came to Earth and seeded us, leaving remnants of their DNA in the human genome."

Humana listened intently, taking in every word I said, like she knew where I was going before I even spoke.

"I've gotten long-winded here, but I wanted your thoughts. I don't understand everything, but were the Anunnaki more than Watchers? For instance, could the Shining Ones, in the past, be the descendants of the Anunnaki? Could they be our progenitors?"

Humana pondered my question. "That's a different question than panspermia, which is widely accepted by many, that microorganisms from comets or meteors found their way to Earth and seeded life on Earth.

"However, it is similar in presenting that life on Earth originated elsewhere. An advanced civilization may have visited Earth and shared its knowledge with humans, possibly intermarrying with them and producing offspring.

"Yes, you could present that as a valid view, relying solely on the historical record and information available on the Internet and in academia. But, experientially, it's too soon for disclosure. We need to respect the Shining Ones' timeline. They will let us know when they can reveal their identity."

"How will they let us know?"

Humana winked. "You will see. It might be sooner than you think and in a way you can't imagine."

CHAPTER FORTY-SEVEN

"Are you ready for the next step in your orientation?" Humana asked.

"I didn't even know this was an orientation."

Humana laughed. "You've only just begun. I'm permitted to show you more if you're ready."

The secrets within the UFO had slowly revealed themselves to my blind eyes. I couldn't wait to see more. I knew it was a process that would take time. I felt honored that they trusted me. I hoped I didn't disappoint Humana, Major, or the Shining Ones.

I was nervous but wanted to continue. "Sure."

Humana was pleased. "This next step is a bold one. You might feel overwhelmed. The Shining Ones want you to meet the rest of the crew. You've only met one member of the star travelers, but it takes a whole crew to navigate this mighty ship across the starry heavens.

"So now, I'll introduce you to some of the workers. At the least, I can allow you to see them in action."

When would I be more ready than now? Again, I inhaled, trying to catch my breath. I didn't know what to expect, but whatever the Shining Ones revealed, I anticipated it would be essential in creating a lasting friendship.

As I waited, a mysterious presence lifted the veil, and I saw dozens of creatures manning the monitors and screens around the ship's perimeter. The workers reminded me of the Greys, the small entities often depicted in Hollywood movies and described by people in YouTube videos.

They didn't have the unique beauty of the Shining Ones. In some ways, the creatures looked frightening, with large, almond-shaped eyes; small, human-like bodies; grey skin; and disproportionately large, hairless heads. I would have been terrified had I not been "prepped" beforehand.

The extraterrestrials' sensitivity to human frailty and fear struck me. Their desire to be our friend and not scare us was commendable. Thank goodness they had even created a clone to assuage my anxiety and allow me to trust them. After all, who can we trust if we can't trust ourselves?

My musings were interrupted by Humana's question. "What do you think?"

There were so many Greys on the ship's bridge, I couldn't count them all. They were busy with various tasks to the extent that they paid me little attention. My presence was barely a blip to them. They were preoccupied performing multiple operations to keep their spaceship running.

"They look like the Greys we see in videos."

Humana nodded. "Unfortunately, Hollywood has given them a bad rap. The truth is, they are busybodies. They fly the ship and perform all the mundane tasks to keep this bird in the air. They follow the orders of the Shining Ones and complete whatever tasks the Shining Ones give them.

"Sometimes, the Greys are needed to perform operative procedures on patients who need life-saving medical interventions."

I watched in awe as they worked. Their small bodies didn't have a lazy bone. I imagined their large heads were necessary for their intellectual prowess, and their big eyes allowed them to monitor all those screens that needed their complete attention.

But anything medical alarmed me. "What kind of interventions do you mean?"

"Would you like to see?" Humana asked.

"See, as in a medical procedure?"

Humana bit her lip. "I don't think anyone is there now, but we can still visit the lab. I think you would be impressed with their level of technology."

None of the Greys had even looked at me or attempted to talk to me, so it seemed like a good opportunity. "Sure, I'd love to."

"Follow me."

We left the spaceship's bridge and headed down a sterile hallway to another section of the ship. Humana opened a door, and I found myself in a large room that reminded me of an operating room.

Medical equipment filled the nooks and crannies, various monitors lined the walls, and within the larger room were smaller cubicles, each with an examining table.

"Do they perform operations in here?"

"Chumana, their technology is so far above ours that sometimes the government asks them for help. They know how to cure diseases for which we don't even have names."

I thought of my mother and Major's words about their efforts to help her. Is this where she came when she visited the UAP? What kind of medical procedures did they perform? But I didn't say anything; my imagination went in a direction I didn't want to consider.

Humana motioned for me to follow her. She edged over to a small table like she wanted to discuss something important. I sat alongside her, trying to absorb and understand everything I'd learned.

Humana leaned toward me, looking into my eyes. "The Shining Ones have suggested they put a small chip in your wrist to stay in contact with you. It's like what vets use on dogs and cats, so if a family's pet gets lost, and someone finds it, the chipping company can facilitate the return of the lost animal to its owner."

I listened intently but again remained silent.

Humana explained more: "They insert a small object underneath your skin. When the UAP arrives, it will blink to indicate its presence. The way they contact you now is to contact Major or an intermediary and inform them of their arrival time. Then, someone in The Frequency Group will send you a digital message to let you know their itinerary.

"If you had the microchip, it would be easier. You would immediately know when the Shining Ones return and could plan your rendezvous."

"I don't even have a body tattoo, so the thought of someone inserting something underneath my skin is unsettling."

Humana laughed. "It's far less invasive than a tattoo. The object is the size of a grain of rice, barely visible unless it's flashing, which only happens when they are nearby."

That seemed simple enough. "Does it hurt to insert the microchip?"

Humana giggled. "You won't even feel it."

I peered around the sterile, stainless-steel room, indicating a state-of-the-art medical facility. "If I don't like it after insertion, can I take it out?"

"You can take it out," Humana assured me, "but it would be better to let them remove it. Their technology is so advanced, they would do it without an anesthetic."

"Do you have one?"

"No. I don't need a microchip because the Shining Ones can communicate with me directly. I've learned how to be what they call an adept. However, I could ask them to insert one in me so you can observe what they do."

"I'd like to watch the medical worker microchip you first. Then I can decide."

Humana smiled. "I will see if they can send someone if they aren't too busy."

❧

A FEW MINUTES PASSED, and one of the Greys entered the room where we were waiting. I didn't expect him to talk or explain anything, so I remained silent. However, I could tell that Humana and the alien were telepathically communicating.

When they finished, I asked Humana, "What did you say to each other?"

"Oh, he said the procedure will only take a few seconds. He will set up a room and summon us."

I watched as the Grey shuffled back and forth between our location and an adjoining room. He was efficient and focused, but he also remained distant and emotionless. If I used a short description, I would call him a worker bee with blue-grey skin.

In some ways, he reminded me of a robot—very task-oriented. His approach was to complete the current task and move on to the next one in militaristic fashion.

I thought about how efficient telepathy was. Even human communication may not always involve words. People can talk in subtle ways without vocalization. Animals have various means of relating. Bats and dolphins use sonar.

As I watched Humana and the Grey, they weren't speaking in words. I wasn't even sure if the Greys had mouths. But, at some level, they were exchanging information.

I was beginning to understand. Something happened emotionally between me and the Shining One. However, with the alien, I felt nothing. He was just there.

After a short wait, Humana said, "Follow me." We went into a neighboring room. The Grey had set up a steel table with two chairs. Humana motioned for me to sit and sat beside me in the other chair.

The Grey lowered the table to accommodate the seating arrangement, and Humana laid her arm on the table between herself and the alien.

A small robotic arm connected to a medical device extended above Humana's wrist. Then, a thin laser beam from the robotic arm projected down to her wrist, a light flashed, and then it stopped.

The robot arm retracted itself out of the way. The alien did nothing physically. He just monitored everything.

It was so quick that I wondered if anything had happened. Humana held up her hand, and I could see a tiny triangular grain implant underneath the skin on her wrist.

"Is it working?" I asked.

She laughed. "Not right now. When a UFO approaches, it will blink green. When it leaves, it will blink red. It won't do anything if the saucer is not moving or stationary like it is now. If it's not nearby, it won't have any effect. The implant lets you know when the spaceship is near and whether it's coming or going."

"Did you feel it?"

Humana shook her head. "I didn't feel anything. I mean, I can feel it when I touch it. Otherwise, I wouldn't even know it's there."

I stopped talking so she could communicate telepathically with the Grey. As I waited, I studied the four-foot creature; I had to admit, he looked like an alien—scary and otherworldly, but perhaps not as frightening as Hollywood made him out to be.

His large, dark, almond-shaped eyes were impossible to see through like human eyes. His tiny mouth seemed frozen in place. His pear-shaped or bulbous head was too big for his body. His thin arms were too long, reaching nearly the middle of his legs. His flat nose was tiny, and he didn't seem to have ears like humans. Two small holes on each side of his head must have functioned as ears.

When I looked closely at his hands, I saw that he lacked a thumb, and his fingers appeared webbed.

Humana interrupted my thoughts and my focus shifted to her. "He wants to know if you're ready."

I took a deep breath. "I guess so. As ready as I'll ever be."

"Just do what I did. Extend your arm on the table and let the robotic arm scan your wrist for a few seconds. It will then insert the tiny device. That's all there is to it."

I followed Humana's instructions, and the alien repeated the same procedure.

"Is that it?"

"That's it," Humana said. She smiled broadly, and I examined my wrist to ensure something was there. I didn't feel anything.

After the Grey completed the medical procedure, we left the surgical ward, and I followed Humana back to the bridge. As before, the Greys were busily performing their tasks from one end of the bridge to the other.

"I need to get back home," I said. "I'm exhausted. How do I do that?"

Humana nodded. "Let me summon one of the workers to open the port, and the tractor beam will let you down."

As we waited, Humana encouraged me to keep up my CW. "Soon, we'll need your skills."

I failed to see how everything fit together, but I was so tired that I didn't care. Soon, I heard the tractor beam moving into place and the doors retracting. Humana reminded me where to stand.

"Are you coming with me?"

She shook her head. "You can do this. It will soon be second nature to you, and you won't think anything about it."

We hugged briefly, and I thanked her for helping me through the unofficial orientation. "When can I come back?"

Humana smiled. "Maybe tomorrow night. Wait for the blinking light to alert you of their imminent appearance."

I nodded. "Sounds good."

Once the tractor beam lowered me to the ground, I stood and waited for it to retract. Then, I realized I had forgotten to turn on my walkie-talkie. Was Judd still here waiting for me?

CHAPTER FORTY-EIGHT

I scanned the trail in the distance but didn't see him—not that I expected to, because he was supposed to be hiding. I pulled out my iPhone, but the screen was frozen, so I had to reboot it.

While it restarted, I grabbed my walkie-talkie and turned it on. I heard the usual static and attempted to contact Judd.

"CQ, CQ. This is KO4LBS looking for K4PREP. Please respond if you hear me."

After waiting a few seconds and hearing nothing, I called CQ again, edging away from the UFO in case it was causing interference. I listened for a response but still heard nothing.

I was becoming concerned, and then his voice came through. Although drowned out by static, we had made contact.

"We'll meet at the rendezvous site. KO4LBS, out."

The phone was still not working, so I kept the radio tuned to the Simplex channel in case I needed it. As I continued toward our agreed-to rendezvous point, I saw Judd waving.

We exchanged a warm, heartfelt embrace. "I'm so glad to see you," he said.

"How long was I gone?"

"You weren't gone very long. Maybe 20 minutes. I tried contacting you several times but never heard anything."

It seemed longer than that, but I was glad I hadn't been gone for hours.

I didn't want to tell him I'd forgotten to turn on the walkie-talkie, so I evaded his indirect question. "The UFO affects radio frequencies and electronic devices. My phone isn't working either. I had to turn it off and turn it back on."

Now that we had reconnected, Judd peppered me with questions. "So, what happened?"

Adrenaline flowed through me, pumping me with more energy. "It was amazing. Truly amazing."

"Like what? Tell me."

We slowed down as I became absorbed in my account from the beginning. Judd loved the part about the Shining One and their hope to be our friend.

However, when I started talking about the Greys, he backed off. Then, he questioned me about everything.

"Tell me about Humana," Judd said. "I know she looks like you and all of that, but what is she? A robot? A humanoid? Does she have flesh and blood? Is she human? What is she?"

The question was off-putting. I believed Humana was a mirror image of me, but she was more knowledgeable about many things. She had been exposed to this expanding universe longer than I, even if it was a new human adventure.

I imagined what it would have been like if I had grown up in her world. She had to have my DNA, and that's all I cared about. Maybe we all had clones and didn't know it. I wanted to focus on the star visitors. My priorities had changed, and I suddenly realized they no longer included Judd.

"Does it matter?" I asked. "She's facilitating our ability to befriend human-like entities from another world, who are likely our progenitors. It's an amazing story. Can't you focus on that?"

"It just troubles me that somebody might use your likeness to promote a lie. We must examine our sources to determine whether they are trustworthy. If they are, then the story is more believable."

Again, I was annoyed. "Are you saying I'm not trustworthy?"

Judd shook his head. "No, you don't understand what I'm saying. You're trustworthy, but how do you know this person who claims to be your clone or double is also and not someone who wants to be you for a nefarious purpose?"

I bit my lip. I felt hot and started walking faster. "Don't you think I'd recognize if it were someone pretending to be me. I mean, Humana looks like me, and she talks like me.

"What is that old expression, if it walks like a duck and quacks like a duck, it's a duck. Do you not trust me at all?"

Judd kept pace with me. "I'd like to meet her to see for myself."

"Well," I said with a Southern drawl for emphasis, "I don't think that's going to happen."

We walked briskly for another minute without saying anything. The initial excitement had worn off; now I was tired and didn't want to discuss it.

When my apartment was in sight, Judd said, "Get some sleep. I want to hear more, but I can tell you're tired, and I'm still not quite well. I need to get home."

I'd had a few minutes to think about our relationship in the quiet of the night. Things had changed between us, even if Judd didn't recognize it.

I no longer needed his help with Rophe. My mother had mostly returned to who she was before she lost her cognitive abilities. It would take Judd a while to reach my level of ham radio competency, even though he was more adept at some things than I was.

However, he couldn't use the HF radio, couldn't do CW, knew nothing about digital ham radio, and couldn't visit the UFO, per the ET's request.

He didn't have the right blood type. I didn't want to go to any more Bible Studies, and I didn't want to share more intimate things, like the implant in my wrist. Our relationship was at a crossroads, if not a dead end.

"Judd, maybe we should pause our relationship. Your perceptions and comments aren't helpful and, if anything, are only causing me stress. I must justify everything and prove that what I'm saying is trustworthy.

"You used to tell me how smart I was and encouraged me, especially with Mother and Rophe, but all you've done since this started is criticize me."

Judd didn't say anything. After thinking about it, he replied, "Okay. I'll give you some space and stop asking questions you don't want to answer, but please know I care about you. I'm concerned for your safety, and I hope you'll still come to Bible Study."

Friday was also the AP Biology debate day on the Origins of Life. I didn't have the emotional energy to think that far ahead.

"I don't know right now. I'll see how I feel on Friday."

We paused at Judd's car. I sensed this was goodbye, but maybe I was wrong. Who knew if I might feel differently tomorrow?

"I'll respect your feelings," Judd said. "You know how to reach me."

I nodded. "Thanks for walking with me to school."

"I'll leave after I see you're safely inside."

I nodded. "Okay."

I continued walking to the apartment, leaving Judd standing beside his car. When I unlocked the door, I briefly waved, and he waved back. Then I closed the door and stepped inside, ensuring I locked it.

Turning around, I saw Mother reading a book in the living room. The television played softly in the background. When I noted the channel, I chuckled. "You're watching a cat video?"

Mother laughed. "Yes, Rophe loves to watch cats and birds on TV."

I rolled my eyes. "I didn't even know such videos existed, but Rophe did appear to be quite interested in the white cat on the television screen.

I turned my gaze back to Mother. "You're up late reading."

Mother sighed. "Yes, but I think I'll head to bed now that you're home."

It never occurred to me that she would be worried. “Judd was with me,” I reminded her.

“Yes, I know, but mothers always worry.”

I remembered the infirmary inside the UFO. If only she could remember what she experienced. If only …

CHAPTER FORTY-NINE

Since it was the weekend, I stayed home and studied to prepare for the upcoming debate. I also practiced CW and briefly looked at colleges. Mother had dramatically improved since the last sleepwalking episode, and I could be more optimistic about the future.

Of course, if I did move away to go to college, I couldn't bring Rophe. I wasn't sure I was willing to go without him. Besides, I'd need a substantial scholarship to attend a prestigious school outside of Atlanta.

So far, I hadn't heard from my father. It was always in the back of my mind that disclosure would include money for college.

On Saturdays, Judd and I usually hung out together. We would get coffee, walk, and talk about school. I missed that, but I didn't want to answer his annoying questions.

Besides, I was forbidden to share my UFO experiences with him. Since I had already broken the trust of those involved, although they weren't aware of it, I wanted to try to fix it, and the only way I knew how was to break off our relationship.

The day flew by, and as nighttime approached, I thought about my UAP encounter. Occasionally, I'd touch the implant to ensure it was still there. I also checked for digital messages, which they expected me to do, and I listened to CW on the HF radio, copying what I heard. I could operate at about 15 words per minute. I was at an impasse to get any faster.

Unexpectedly, the light blinked on my wrist. I jumped up. "Contact!" My heart raced as I looked out the window at the darkening sky, but some daylight lingered.

I turned off the radio, brushed my hair, dabbed on some makeup, grabbed a sweater, and passed Mother in the kitchen. "I'm going for a walk but won't be gone long."

She glanced out the window. "It's going to be dark soon."

"I know. Don't worry. I promise I won't be gone long."

I hurried to school with a myriad of thoughts racing through my head. When I was within sight of the football field, I immediately saw the UAP. I ran the rest of the way, and when I was close enough, I saw Humana. She was waiting under the saucer.

I held up my wrist. "It worked," I said as I approached, but it had stopped blinking. "It was blinking."

"It only blinks when the power is on."

"Oh. That makes sense."

"The Shining Ones wanted to make sure they could contact you."

"Well, you can tell them." I admired the overpowering structure above us. "Are we going inside?"

Humana laughed. "You enjoyed that, didn't you?

I nodded.

She shook her head. "No, not this time. We wanted to test to ensure the microchip is working. I'll be leaving with the ship soon, and when we take off, it should blink again. Please send us a digital message to let us know. Tonight was just a test."

Humana giggled. "The government is always running tests."

I was disappointed, but it made sense.

Humana looked up. "I must go now. They are summoning me. If you choose to stay and watch as we leave, stand back a safe distance."

I nodded. "When will you return?"

Humana squinted. "I'm not sure. I know they want to take you on a trip soon. The government also needs your mastery of CW at 20 words per minute. Are you getting close?"

"I'm practicing every day."

"That's good. We have a Zoom call scheduled, and Major may have a robot to practice with you. Humana giggled. "We haven't heard your call sign on CW. You seem to be shy."

I smiled. "Yeah, a little."

The lights on the UFO began blinking, and simultaneously, the microchip blinked.

I pointed. "Look."

"Great," Humana said. "I'll let them know."

"Do I still need to send a digital message?"

"No, but check it every day." Humana began to ease toward the ship. "I've got to run; they're waiting for me to come aboard."

I stepped back and waved, watching the tractor beam lift her. I longed to go with her, but Mother was waiting for me. As I headed home, I dreamed about the promised trip. Where would they take me?

WHEN I ARRIVED HOME, nighttime had set in. I found Mother reading in the living room again, just like in the old days when she read all the time.

"What are you reading?"

"The Bible."

"Oh. What book in the Bible?"

Mother rubbed Rophe's back as she answered. "I've never read the Bible from beginning to end, so I thought I'd start at the beginning."

"Genesis?"

"Yes, Genesis."

I knew the first line in the Bible because we had studied it in Shale's Bible Study. "Let me see if I can recite the first line from Genesis. Are you ready?"

Mother nodded.

"In the beginning, God created the heavens and the Earth, and the

Earth became formless and void, and darkness was upon the face of the Earth."

Mother was gazing down at her Bible but didn't say anything.

"Did I get it right?"

She nodded, her eyes drifting somewhere else. "Does that mean when God created the heavens and the Earth, everything became formless, void, and dark?

"That doesn't sound like God. I thought everything God created was good."

Her question shocked me. Maybe I didn't need to worry about Mother anymore. She had just asked a question I couldn't answer.

CHAPTER FIFTY

Tension filled the room when I entered AP Biology. You could have heard a pin drop. No one was talking. The debate presentation would significantly impact our final grades. While I had worked hard to prepare, I didn't expect to see the same level of preparation in the others.

I anticipated that group one would go first. Shale was the speaker. Her team followed traditional biblical teachings and believed God was the Creator of everything.

Judd would present the findings for team two, which believed in evolution

My team consisted of two subgroups. We couldn't agree on who seeded the planet or how, whether it was space dust from another world via asteroids and comets, or if aliens arrived thousands of years ago and established a pre-Adamic civilization from which the first humans evolved.

Shale volunteered to go first. I was glad we didn't draw straws. She approached the podium, and knowing her as well as I did, I could tell she was nervous.

"I want to assure you," she began, "that we didn't arrive here in

UFOs or UAPs or evolve from lower life forms. An all-knowing God created us in his image, as recounted in the first book of the Bible."

She clicked on the first slide from the PowerPoint presentation, which showed Michelangelo's fresco painting "The Creation of Adam."

Mr. Beasley interrupted. "Shale, this isn't a religion class. We've spent six weeks studying evolution. Scientific facts should be the foundation of your arguments, not religious innuendos."

"Yes, sir. May I continue?"

He waved his pen. "It's your grade."

The class snickered.

Shale continued. "As I said, the Bible says we're the only creatures created in God's image."

"Does she believe this stuff?" a student muttered.

Mr. Beasley gave the student a stern look, and he shut up.

A few seconds passed as Shale refocused. "What does it mean to be created in the image of God?"

"It means we're all gods," Judd commented.

The room erupted in laughter.

I couldn't resist. "Everybody except Shale Snyder."

Shale didn't let the comments bother her and continued. "We are unique in the universe. God did not even create angels in his image."

"That's a relief," another student said.

I questioned that statement. Didn't angels resemble people who looked like God? However, historical accounts from nonbiblical sources often depicted them with enormous wings. I had to admit that Shale knew more about the Bible than I did. I'd give her a pass on that one.

She continued. "Have there been changes in animals? Yes, but God wrote those adaptations into the DNA. Species can change within the genetic code but can't evolve into a new species. Besides, most mutations don't help animals to survive."

Mr. Beasley interrupted. "Name one scientist who agrees with you."

I could tell that Shale was ready for that question. She replied,

"You can order Dr. Hugh Ross's book, *A Matter of Days: Resolving a Creation Controversy*, from Amazon.

Mr. Beasley was nonplussed, but then a snarky smile covered his lips. "If there is a God who created everything, would you agree that evolution improved upon his creation?"

"Oohs" and "ahhs" filled the room. I watched Judd frantically jotting notes. In my case, that argument was moot. Judd would have his chance to defend his position next. At least, I hoped he was next. I wasn't going to volunteer.

I glanced around the room. The initial excitement at the start of the debate had given way to boredom. Shale ignored Mr. Beasley's question and continued with her prepared speech.

She presented additional PowerPoint slides as she spoke, illustrating lab research that utilized animals as test subjects. "I don't believe it's ethical to perform genetic experiments combining species or to attempt to create a perfect human—or any new animal."

"And stop medical advancement that could lead to a cure for cancer and other diseases?" a boy interrupted. "My father is dying, and you want me to believe in a God who would rather let him die than find a cure? DNA research can lead to cures."

Applause erupted.

Shale countered the boy's point: "Do humans possess the heart of God? Are we intelligent enough to alter the genetic code only for good and not evil?"

Mr. Beasley stood. "Shale, you were to present arguments against evolution, not champion your religious beliefs. Because your statements are offensive to students in this class, I must ask you to stop your presentation and take a seat."

I didn't see that coming. I knew Mr. Beasley was an evolutionist, but it seemed unfair to Shale to stop her presentation because he disagreed with her argument. It may have been more emotional due to the student's sensitive interjection.

I watched Shale step away from the podium, dropping a card. Mr. Beasley picked it up and whispered something in her ear. She didn't seem bothered by his words.

I had to give her credit; she was thick-skinned. I was too sensitive and covered my sensitivity in ways that weren't glamorous. Sometimes, life was about surviving. I expected to hear all about the survival of the fittest from Judd.

I touched the triangle on my wrist as I watched menacing clouds outside, hinting at a thunderstorm.

My focus returned to Mr. Beasley when he said, "The podium is yours." Then I realized he was talking to Judd and not me.

Conflicted feelings hounded me as I watched Judd set up at the podium. He was handsome with curly hair, a dark complexion, and stunning brown eyes. Every girl in the class wanted him except for Shale. She already had a boyfriend who lived in Israel. I'd had Judd all to myself for three years and dumped him less than a week ago.

I didn't think anyone knew we weren't a couple anymore. The girls ogled over him and looked at me with envy, but I ignored them. He'd be looking around soon for another attractive girl, and they could fight over him—unless I changed my mind.

Judd exuded confidence. "Evolution has been accepted as a scientific theory by reputable scientists for the past hundred years, ever since Charles Darwin published his famous thesis on natural selection. We are evolving as humans.

"Sometime in the not-too-distant future, we will possess the necessary knowledge to create a perfect human. There will be no more death or disease.

"The goal of the New World is to create a civilization ruled by a one-world government where the fittest survive."

Judd paused to let his words sink in and wagged his pencil. "Even now, we are on the threshold of opening the door to the future where we can take the best of each species and create a new one."

He chuckled. "Imagine the woman of your dreams, perfectly shaped, who can hear like a wolf and see like an eagle—who wouldn't want the perfect woman?"

I noticed he averted his eyes from me when he made that last comment. Whistles and catcalls shot up around the room. Others clapped approvingly.

"Once humans have evolved beyond imperfection, we will no longer be limited. Maybe, we will become god-like in many ways."

Judd was on an unstoppable roll, and students embraced every word he uttered. He clicked on the PowerPoint presentation wildly, and photographs of unusual animals appeared on the screen.

"Scientists at CERN hope to recreate the universe's beginning with the Large Hadron Collider in France and Switzerland—even opening doors to other dimensions. God has put no limits on our abilities.

"The Age of Aquarius has dawned, and the New World promises the utopia we all long for, etched in our DNA through evolutionary processes."

A photograph of a strange creature appeared on the screen labeled "Statue of Lord Shiva at CERN."

"We have much to look forward to as scientists discover new ways to create computers that think like humans. Soon, we'll grow animals in test tubes that mimic human-like qualities. Scientists will program robots to perform the mundane tasks of day-to-day living, allowing humans to enjoy a more fulfilling life."

Students stood and cheered.

After a congratulatory pause, Mr. Beasley stood. "Thank you, Judd, for that outstanding presentation. We all need hope for a better tomorrow."

Judd glanced at me, looking for approval. I nodded in appreciation of his presentation and the research he had conducted. I could respect his position even if I didn't embrace it. He did an excellent job, which would make it hard for me to win the debate.

"Chumana," Mr. Beasley said. "It's your turn."

I approached the podium, pretending I was more confident than I was. Despite what everyone thought, I hated being the center of attention, I hated public speaking, and I would have preferred to have written my arguments. Students, after my presentation, would call me a conspiracy nut.

I began. "How can you explain the strange monoliths worldwide—the pyramids in Egypt, the crop circles in Africa, or Stonehenge in

England? Scientists have discovered ancient cave paintings with UFOs, now called UAPs, and extraterrestrials all over the globe."

I clicked through several unusual photographs in my PowerPoint presentation.

A stir rose from the class. "How old are these drawings?" a student asked.

"Some of the cave drawings in India, like this one, are thought to be 20,000 years old. According to a national UFO database called NUFORC, as of September 2014, almost 100,000 sightings of UAPs have been reported in the last twenty years."

Gasps filled the room.

Now that I had everyone's attention, I added some red-headed dramatic flair. "I'll tell you how you can explain these strange anomalies. We are descendants of a race of beings called the Anunnaki. They came here, and for whatever reason, they left."

"Really?" a student asked.

I pointed at the class. "Despite what some might say, life on other planets doesn't mean God doesn't exist. It simply means we aren't alone in the universe. Did you know that a rogue planet is returning soon? It visits our solar system every 3,600 years."

Gasps rose from several students.

I laughed and then switched to a different tone for dramatic effect. "It's arrogant to think we are the only intelligent life. If we continue to destroy our planet, we might need help from superior beings to survive. Be open-minded and embrace the possibility that we are not alone in the universe."

The room erupted with cheers and applause.

Mr. Beasley stood. "Thank you, Miss Ironvein, for that excellent presentation."

I glanced at Shale, who seemed annoyed with my arguments. Judd was emotionless. Rachel smiled warmly, and Gracie gave me a thumbs-up. At least my presentation wasn't dull.

As I returned to my seat, I glanced out the window. Something didn't look right. I watched Shale tap Rachel on the back to get her attention, and then everyone stared out the windows in disbelief.

"Wow!" Gracie exclaimed.

CHAPTER FIFTY-ONE

A hush fell over the room, and several students left their seats, scooting over to the windows for a better view.

Unexpectedly, six bright orbs shot out of the clouds. They moved as one at incredible speed. The largest one in the middle broke away from the others. The aircraft sped quickly in and out of the clouds, zigzagging back and forth. I felt the triangle pulsing on my arm, and I looked down and saw the light blinking.

At the same time, the UAP stopped, disappeared, and reappeared, repeating this process several times. Then, it dropped down and skimmed over the treetops in a nearby neighborhood.

The jarring motion of the unidentified object caused the classroom windows to vibrate. Without warning, the saucer-like craft reappeared and headed toward the school. The UFO landed on the football field in a split second, as fast as lightning. Students who had rushed to the windows screamed and ran to the other side.

I couldn't resist holding up my wrist to show the pulsating light. "They are here!" I shouted. But everyone was too preoccupied staring out the windows.

I was the only one in the room who wasn't terrified—no wonder the Shining Ones had waited to reveal their presence. I shouted again. "They're coming."

"To kill us?" a boy asked.

Why did people always assume the worst? "No, to save us from ourselves!"

Mr. Beasley was calling someone on his cell phone. Many students tried to leave, but the door must have jammed. Shale rushed over and confronted me. "What is that on your wrist?"

When I didn't answer, she shook my arm harder. "What is that thing on your wrist?"

"It's a tracking device. They come and visit me."

Shale's eyes doubled in size. "What?"

I shoved her out of the way and ran to the door. With superhuman strength, I unjammed it and ran out into the hallway to blaring sirens and flashing emergency lights. I covered my ears and dashed to the nearest exit.

After pushing open the emergency door, I scampered toward the UFO, waving my arms to get their attention. Would they see me? The blinking light on my wrist encouraged me to keep approaching the saucer.

"Here I am," I shouted. "Do you see me?" The UFO blinked my call sign, KO4LBS.

"Yes!" They were summoning.

I ran to where the tractor beam could lock on me. I searched for Humana, my double, but I didn't see her. I assumed she was inside the vehicle.

A light shone down from the belly of the saucer, and the tractor beam locked in on me. I could feel my body levitating. Could anyone see me through the school windows?

I knew they were watching, but I didn't care. My future involved something bigger than school. The government and the Shining Ones had chosen me.

With the tractor beam locked in, I couldn't move until inside. My heart thumped wildly, and my hands shone under the bright lights.

Once inside, the craft's bay door closed. The tractor beam released me, and I stood on the bridge. I didn't see anyone, but lights and monitors buzzed everywhere.

The blinking light on my wrist confirmed the UFO was "turned on," as Humana described it. I felt the ship as a living, breathing entity.

A huge monitor lit up as I waited to see what would happen. Humana sat at a table with a big smile. She exclaimed, "You passed the test!"

"What test?" I asked.

She rolled her eyes. "Sometimes your genius blinds you to the simplicity of what they want to accomplish. The Shining Ones wanted to ensure you trusted them enough to come on board without my presence."

I noticed the lights in the background fading, and a quietness enveloped the ship as it powered down. The light on my wrist stopped blinking.

For a moment, I felt like I was the only one here. "Are you here?" I asked.

Humana nodded. "Yes. I will come to you now."

A few seconds later, she entered the room and hugged me. "Chumana, you came on your own despite the chaos in the classroom and the alarms blaring throughout the school. Most people would have been terrified, but you weren't. You kept your wits. That's a huge step. You weren't afraid even in the face of opposition and turmoil."

"They sent my call sign to me—the blinking light. I recognized it."

"That's good. Next, we must ensure you can send and receive CW at twenty to 25 words per minute. Major wants me to have a session with you so you can practice with me."

"That would be great," I said. "I'm still reluctant to go on the radio and send CQ."

Humana nodded. "We know, but it's okay. Don't worry about it. We can help you with that.

"Here's what's important now. Go back to school. The Shining Ones must vacate the school grounds, as Hazmat teams, police, fire, and news reporters are en route. The administrators will dismiss the school early to investigate.

"Our Zoom meeting will be at 5:00. We will practice, practice, practice."

"Okay."

Humana added, "Don't tell anyone about your experience. The public will see the news soon enough. Make the media work for it. Don't help them.

"Once disclosure happens, everything will change, and the government will need your CW skills to get the word out."

I wasn't sure I understood everything Humana meant, but I'd be on the call. Things would become clearer soon.

Humana hugged me again. "You must go now. Don't delay."

I went to the designated area and waited. When the bay doors opened, I gave Humana a thumbs-up. She smiled and watched as the tractor beam lowered me to the ground.

Once released, I scooted out of the danger zone and retreated to watch the spaceship take off. Right on cue, the mysterious vehicle sprang to life, its lights flashing, and within seconds, it rose and disappeared.

In the distance, I heard emergency sirens blaring. Everybody who was anybody was en route to investigate. I couldn't contain my excitement.

I went back into the building to complete chaos. Wails of fear and cries of worry filled my ears as alarms rattled, shaking the windows and shattering everyone's nerves. Several students had fainted, and school medics were tending to them.

If I didn't know, I'd think the world had ended. For everyone else here, it may have.

CHAPTER FIFTY-TWO

I didn't see anyone I knew in the cafeteria, so I went and sat at an empty table. I'd ticked Shale off when I shoved her during AP Biology. I hadn't talked to Judd since I'd broken off my relationship with him several days earlier. He hadn't even texted me.

I didn't expect anyone to be friends with me now, especially after my debate presentation and the UFO encounter. What were the chances I'd be talking about beings seeding Earth from another planet when the Shining Ones would appear?

I glanced at the object underneath my skin. When it wasn't blinking, I couldn't tell it was there. Was it more than a tracking device for arrival and departure? Perhaps they were listening to my conversations. How could they have known to arrive precisely when they did?

I felt someone sit beside me. I turned to see who it was.

Before I could say anything, Judd asked, "Do you mind if I join you?"

I shook my head. "No, you can sit here."

A few seconds later, Shale plopped down, invited or not, but Gracie, with her British politeness, asked if she could join us. When Rachel returned with drinks, it was like old times.

I had been sitting alone all week, claiming I was prepping for the debate. Now that it was over, I couldn't use that excuse. Since Judd and I had broken up, I had lost interest in the Bible Study.

Plus, CW and ham radio consumed all my spare time outside of class, and I didn't feel like I had anything in common with them anymore. But today, we sat together, reflecting on what had happened.

School buses were already out front since Mrs. Twiggs, the principal, had dismissed school early. The police brought in Hazmat crews and promptly went to the football field to investigate.

Reporters had shown up but were restricted from accessing the school, being allowed to speak only with teachers. Ambulances took several students to the hospital, including Mr. Beasley.

Judd leaned over and whispered, "How often has this happened now?

I brushed back my long, red hair, debating what to say. "Oh, three or four times."

"During the day or at night?"

He was there one time, so he already knew. "Nighttime, about 10:00, the same as when you went with me." I lied because that wasn't true, but I was irritated by his probing.

Judd leaned forward. "Where?"

I glared at him. He knew the answer. "Here."

The table suddenly grew quiet. Judd, sensing my irritation, changed the subject. "Shale, what do you think of my hypothesis?"

Shale gazed into Judd's eyes. "I believe God created us."

"Yes," Judd agreed, "but he did it through evolution."

Shale shook her head. "That's not what the Bible says."

Judd frowned. "Only if you interpret the words of the Bible literally."

Seeing the discussion escalate, Shale changed the subject again. "Tell me about CERN."

Judd's face brightened. "What do you want to know?"

"What is it?"

Gracie jumped in, "I know about CERN."

"You do?" Shale asked, surprised.

"Yes, my father is involved with some projects in Geneva."

Judd elaborated, "They smash subatomic particles."

I had gotten to know Gracie a little over the past few months. Her British accent betrayed her ethnicity, but she had tried hard to fit in. I recalled our funny conversation when she confessed to mimicking a Southern accent.

The conversation veered off in several directions but eventually returned to the topic we had been avoiding. I primed the subject. "While the school may say it was a Dobbins Air Force Base military plane, I know a UFO visited us. If I wanted to, I could convince you UFOs are real, aliens are here, and they want to be our friends."

Judd laughed. "As ridiculous as that sounds, it's still different from believing we came from aliens, and that was your argument."

I shrugged. "You have to start somewhere, right?"

Shale asked, "Why is it so important to you that we believe in UFOs?"

I had baited Shale, and now I could say what I wanted. "It would be an obsession with you, too, if you had seen what I have seen—or been where I've been."

"Tell me more," Shale urged.

"You heard what I told Judd."

"What?" Rachel said. "I think I missed something."

Judd interjected, "A UFO abducted Chumana."

Shale's eyes grew wide. "Abducted?"

I leaned in and whispered, "They're here." I laid my arm on the table and pointed. "Look."

Concern crossed Shale's face. "What is that underneath your skin?"

"Go ahead and touch it."

She ran her finger over the triangular object under my skin. "What—what is that? I saw it pulsating when the UAP landed."

I already told you that it's a tracking device."

Four sets of eyes stared at me in disbelief. "When did you get it?" Shale asked. "Does your mother know about this?"

I laughed. "Are you crazy?"

Rachel looked aghast. "Don't you think a doctor should check it out. It might be a disease or something."

I took my arm off the table. "They put it underneath my skin."

"Chumana, you need someone to look at it," Shale urged.

I didn't want rumors about me at the school to circulate. "Promise you won't tell anyone?"

Rachel and Shale exchanged glances.

"Why wouldn't you want to tell someone?" Shale asked. "I mean, you shouted it out in class."

I shrugged. "Because they aren't ready to share their plans."

"What plans?"

"To take over the world is the short answer, but that's only because we're on the verge of annihilation, and they want to help us."

Shale asked another pointed question. "You meet them here at the school—at night?"

I chuckled, "I knew you were listening."

"You could talk to Dr. Silverstein," Shale suggested.

I glared at her. "You don't believe me, do you?"

"I don't know," she stammered.

It was time for me to leave. I stood, pushing my chair back. "Out of all people, Shale, I expected you to believe me. You are so vocal about your faith. You must believe there is life on other planets."

"It's not the same thing. Go see Dr. Silverstein, will you?"

"When the time is right, maybe I'll do that." I grabbed my tray and walked away. I'd never convinced them that the Shining Ones wanted to be our friend.

CHAPTER FIFTY-THREE

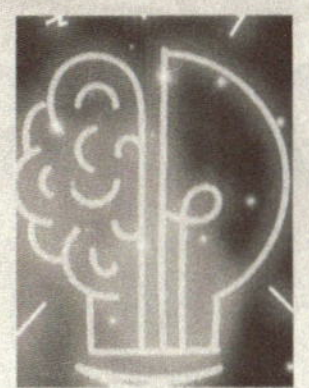

Rophe walked into the bedroom to see me off to school. I petted him on the head. "You take care of Mother while I'm at school. Don't let her go anywhere."

He purred and rubbed his head against my hand. I had become spoiled having him as my mother's guardian when I wasn't around.

Mother waved as I said goodbye. I noticed the Bible in her hands. She had been reading it a lot. While I had distanced myself from spiritual things, she had increased her study, even sharing things I didn't know.

I wanted to believe her dementia was a thing of the past. I feared that if anything happened to Rophe, however, she would decline.

Today, I would get answers from the psychologist. I had waited weeks for the appointment. Shale wasn't too fond of Dr. Silverstein, but I'd never been to him. I hoped he didn't think I was crazy. I knew I wasn't crazy—just different.

A squirrel darted across the road carrying an acorn. The animal's life was simple: find an acorn and survive. Perhaps survival was the hardest thing to do. Didn't everything struggle to survive? Even a lowly worm possessed a will to live. Pull him out of the ground, and he'd wiggle between your fingers to return to his secluded life under the dirt.

My heart burned. It wasn't just knowledge I wanted—knowledge was nothing without understanding. I desperately wanted someone to talk to about everything. I had distanced myself from Judd and the others. I didn't want to listen to their ridicule of my obsession with UFOs.

I had also just learned that Shale had withdrawn from school to live with her father in Washington, D.C. I wasn't even sure if the Bible Study would continue in her absence.

I'd lost touch with everyone. I'd spent most nights in the last month working on CW with Humana. The Shining Ones had not been back since the public appearance at school, which had generated a firestorm.

Ultimately, the official statement was that it was not a UFO but a Dobbins Air Force Base test plane. Go figure. But I knew disclosure was coming—the real disclosure.

I had made the CW breakthrough that Major and The Frequency Group wanted. My speed had reached 20 words per minute. In short spurts, I could do 25.

My thoughts returned to school. I arrived at the final bell and scurried to AP Chemistry. I couldn't wait until the school year ended, and I didn't have to deal with my narcissistic chemistry professor. He was a renowned surgeon and retired to devote his time to teaching gifted students.

Deep down, he probably thought we were nitwits. Despite his annoying personality, it would be worth it if I exempted chemistry in college and saved that money.

Judd and I had been on friendly terms, but our relationship had become distant. I didn't know what the future held between us.

The third period couldn't come soon enough. The bell rang, and I rushed out the door into the overcrowded hallway. I didn't take the time to stop by my locker, but I carried my books with me.

When I arrived, Dr. Silverstein's secretary greeted me. I tried not to appear anxious. "I have an appointment with Dr. Silverstein."

She smiled, allaying my fears. "Just a moment."

The young receptionist, dressed in business attire, stuck her head in his office door and announced my arrival.

"Send her in," I could hear the doctor say.

She motioned to me. "You may go."

When I entered, the psychologist greeted me warmly. Too many disheveled papers took up too much space on his old wooden desk. Books filled the bookcases, and a red-tinted mister blew on an adjoining table. Soft music played in the background.

Pointing, the balding doctor said, "Have a seat."

As I sat, he interjected, "Oh, Chumana, have you been to see the principal yet?"

"The principal?" I asked. "What for?"

He raised his eyebrow, apparently surprised that I hadn't. "Mr. Youngblood wanted you to stop by before seeing me. Why don't you see him first and then come back—if you have time."

I protested. "Dr. Silverstein, I've waited weeks to see you. Am I in trouble?"

Dr. Silverstein shook his head. "I don't think you're in trouble. However, he said it was important."

What could be that important? Unlike my friend Shale, I had never been to the principal's office. I had heard about her escapades; she was always in trouble. Of all the times the principal wanted to see me, why did it have to be now?

"Can it wait, Dr. Silverstein? I'm here, and I want to talk to you."

"He said it was urgent. Just return when it's convenient. I can fit you in tomorrow if today doesn't work out. You've waited this long." His eyes narrowed. "Will one day make that much difference?"

Maybe I didn't want to see Dr. Silverstein after all. I stood. "Okay. I'll go see him now."

"I'll be here," he promised.

Reluctantly, I left, looking for the principal's office. I wasn't sure where it was.

I walked to the main office, and another receptionist greeted me. I gave her my name and added that Dr. Silverstein had sent me. "Can you tell me where to go?"

"Sure. It's Chumana Ironvein, right?"

I nodded.

"Just a moment, please."

I waited as she sent a message through the office messaging system. A few seconds later, she pointed. "Mr. Youngblood is waiting for you. You can enter through those doors."

"Thank you."

I was unsure what to expect or why I was even here. As I entered the immaculate office, no doubt cleaned out from Mrs. Twiggs' abrupt departure, I noticed headshots of important people lined one wall, and school awards and official-looking plaques, such as accreditations, covered another.

A defibrillator machine was prominently displayed. It seemed out of place, like someone didn't know where to put it and stuck it there.

The principal was younger than the psychologist. Following the UFO event, the school board had fired the cranky Mrs. Twiggs. Her poor handling of the emergency had made news headlines, and Mr. Youngblood replaced her. How long would he last? At least he seemed friendly enough.

Mr. Youngblood extended his hand to greet me. "I'm so glad you stopped by. I usually see students in trouble or dealing with serious issues, so it's nice to meet a student like you who has—shall we say—broken the record."

I stared at him. "What record?"

He laughed. "Not many students make a perfect score on the S.A.T., certainly not a student who is only a junior in high school, and on their first try, no less."

"Really? I aced it?"

He nodded, adding. "I can only imagine what your I.Q. is."

I didn't know what to say.

An awkward silence followed, and he motioned for me to sit at the table beside him.

"Chumana, I have already received emails from half a dozen Ivy League schools and well-known universities extending full scholarships. Some want you to start a new year early, skipping your senior year of high school."

A thousand thoughts entered my mind. I wasn't thinking that far ahead. College was a year away, and my mother—would she stay healthy if I moved? She still seemed fragile. Who would care for her if I wasn't here? And how would I leave Rophe?

I couldn't take him with me. I'd assumed I'd attend Kennesaw State University. That way, I could stay in the Atlanta area. I wish I knew how disclosure on my 18th birthday would affect things. I didn't know what to say, so I said nothing.

Mr. Youngblood waited for me to respond. When I didn't, he leaned back in his chair. His enthusiasm had been overwhelming, but my silence was not for the reasons he probably imagined.

"I'm delighted," I finally managed to say. "But I need to think about all of this."

He smiled. "Absolutely. How much time do you need?"

I shrugged. "I don't know. I have lots I need to think about, but …"

He turned his ear toward me. "But what?"

I stuttered, "I don't think I want to start college early. But I need to talk it over with my mother."

He laughed. "Of course, of course. We could even set up an appointment for your mother to come in and discuss it. Full scholarships are rare."

I shook my head. "No, it's okay. I'll tell her."

I hid my mother's condition from everybody. It was my only home; if the school knew her history, I feared they would take her away. I loved my mother. She was all I had.

Now that I knew why he wanted to see me. I was anxious to leave and keep my appointment with Dr. Silverstein. How could I exit gracefully?

Mr. Youngblood scribbled something on a sheet of paper and handed it to me. "These are the schools interested in recruiting you. Take a look and see what you think. These offers are rare. Don't waste this opportunity.

"Too many students don't know what they want to do and throw away offers that come only once. Those rare opportunities slip through their fingers, and later, they regret their indecisiveness. Don't let that be you."

I glanced at the names. It was an impressive list, but I couldn't focus on it. "Thank you, but I must be going. I have an appointment with Dr. Silverstein."

Mr. Youngblood smiled. "I won't hold you up."

We both stood, and he walked me to the door. "Don't wait too long to get back to me, okay?"

I nodded and left.

When I returned to Dr. Silverstein, a note hung on the door. "Out to lunch."

Maybe I didn't want to see him. What now? I looked at the clock. I'd go to the library and look for books on UFOs. That's all I could think about.

Despite all the hard work I had done to impress my father, he remained out of touch and hidden. I felt lonelier than ever, but what else could I do than what I'd done?

I'd finish my classes, go home, and share the good news with Mother. But at the end of the day, I knew I wouldn't leave. I loved my mother, and Rophe was too important to me.

Maybe I would meet my father soon. One thing I did know: Something was about to happen, and the government would need my CW skills. Hopefully, it was sooner rather than later.

CHAPTER FIFTY-FOUR

TOP SECRET

When I opened the apartment door, what I saw shocked me. Two well-dressed men sat on the sofa talking to my mother. She sat across from them in her favorite chair. The TV played in the background, and Rophe lay in Mother's lap.

We never had visitors. Were they here to take my cat away? Or even my mother? While Mother's memory had improved, she still experienced moments of forgetfulness. Why did she allow these two men into the house when she was alone?

Before I could say anything, they stood and greeted me. They wore badges on their suits, and whoever they were, they looked official.

The taller man reached out to shake my hand. "You must be Chumana?"

"Yes." I reciprocated the gesture so as not to be rude. "Is everything okay?"

The man smiled. "Yes. My partner and I are here to ask you some questions."

I glanced at the other man, who was shorter and younger. "What about?"

Mother answered from the living room. "They think you boarded a UFO and want to ask you about it."

My heart skipped a beat. "Oh." I looked at their name tags but couldn't read them. "Who are you?"

"We are the Collins Elite, a small secret group in the U.S. government," the taller man said. "Can we talk?"

I gazed at my mother. "Are you okay?"

She nodded. "I'm fine. They have only been here a few minutes."

I reached down, picked up Rophe, and held him in my arms. I needed him to calm my nerves. "What do you want to ask?"

The shorter, younger-looking man opened his briefcase and pulled out an iPad. He turned it on and opened a file. Then he held the iPad in front of me. "I want you to look at this video."

I immediately recognized myself. "What do you want to know?"

"Is that you?"

I nodded. "Yes, it's me. At school. Later news reports said it was a Dobbins Air Force Base experimental airplane."

The younger man with the iPad asked, "What did you see inside?"

I wasn't sure how to respond. "You know."

"Know what?"

I patted Rophe on the head. "I met a human being inside the craft. They weren't aliens if that's what you're getting at."

"You weren't afraid?"

I was becoming uncomfortable. If I was working with the government on a top-secret project, and these guys were with the government in a top-secret capacity, why were they asking me these questions?

"I don't know how to answer that."

Mother interjected. "Her father works for the government, and she is helping her father."

The shorter guy loaded another file and held the iPad up again for me to see.

This video surprised me. It was the video Judd shot when I was sending CW. "Where did you get this?"

The taller man standing off to the side answered. "Your boyfriend posted it on Facebook, and we identified you in both videos."

"Well, it's me," I said. "I'm an amateur ham radio operator, and the government has trained me as a communications specialist in case of an emergency."

The shorter man put the iPad back in his briefcase.

I had shared too much with Judd about my ham radio activities. Even though we weren't dating now, had I gotten myself, The Frequency Group, or my father in trouble? The silence made me uncomfortable. "Is that all?"

The shorter man continued packing up the rest of his stuff. "Ma'am," he began, "we didn't mean to alarm you or your mother, but we have grave concerns about your safety. Unfortunately, the government doesn't always communicate well among its agencies because, in this area, at least, of Ufology, everything is compartmentalized for security reasons."

He continued. "Either the people you are working with are rogue, or it's so top secret they haven't informed us about who they are or what they are doing. When we saw this video and checked your age, we found you are a minor. Your mother didn't seem to be aware of your activities. It's very concerning since you are underage."

I stared at the two men and then glanced at my mother. Were they trying to intimidate me? Were they government informants or another group with ulterior motives?

I shook my head. "You are mistaken. My father is in charge, and nothing I have done or that they have done is without my consent. So, I don't think you need to make accusations. Everything I've done is of my own volition."

The taller man interrupted. "Chumana, do you know how dangerous this is? These are aliens. Are you saying you haven't met the Greys or the reptilians who navigate these UAPs?"

I shook my head. "No, I've met them, and the Shining Ones. They mean no harm to humans."

The conversation continued for another minute, and then they stood. I could tell they were not happy. "Can we take a photo of your radio?" the shorter man asked.

I hesitated. "It's in my bedroom. I'd prefer you not."

The taller man nodded. "That's fine. We will leave now." He

handed me a business card. "If you want to talk to us anytime, call this number."

I glanced down and read his name. "Did you talk to Judd?"

"Judd, your boyfriend?"

I nodded.

"Not yet," the shorter man said.

I'd have to talk to Judd before they did. The two men proceeded to the door.

"What are you going to do with those videos?" I asked.

"Nothing," the taller man said. "It's part of your file."

So, some secret group connected with the government had a file on me. I wasn't sure if that was good or bad.

The men said goodbye again, and I closed the door as they walked to their car.

"Are you okay?" I asked Mother.

She nodded. "Your father was always entertaining government operatives. It just brought back memories, that's all.

"Memories of what?"

Mother squinted. "UFOs. He was involved with UFOs. I'd forgotten, but now I remember."

CHAPTER FIFTY-FIVE

I retreated to my bedroom and logged into Facebook. Then, I went to Judd's page to look for the video. It didn't take me long to find it. It wasn't very long, and he didn't identify me by name, just saying I was a friend, but he should have asked me before he posted it.

I called Judd on the phone, but he didn't answer, so I texted him and waited. When he didn't reply, I felt frustrated. The one time I needed to talk to him, he didn't answer. Maybe he was getting back at me for dumping him.

I walked back into the living room and sat on the sofa, staring at the barely audible television. "What are they talking about?"

"I don't know, Chumana. Things in the Middle East are not good. There are rumors that we might get dragged into the conflict."

I turned to Mother. "Are you hungry?"

Mother shook her head. "No, but I'm concerned about you. I don't want you getting involved with UFOs."

Our roles had reversed. Mother had been visiting a UFO in the middle of the night for the last year, and now she was telling me not to.

Somewhat annoyed, I quipped, "You just told those two guys my father was involved with them. Why would you say that?"

"That doesn't mean they are good. We don't know what their intentions are."

All this time, I'd been trying to find out what Mother knew, where she sleepwalked, and now that I had had an encounter, she suddenly had an opinion on the topic. "Well, what do you know about them?"

"It's just a foreboding. I don't know." She wrung her hands. "I can't explain it."

I looked at the table where she had placed her Bible. Did that have anything to do with it? Before I could ask her anything else, my phone rang. I glanced at the caller. It was Judd.

I retreated to my bedroom so Mother couldn't hear me.

"Judd?"

"Yes."

"Thanks for calling me back. I need to ask you a question."

"What's that?"

"Why did you post that video of me doing CW on Facebook?"

Silence followed, and then he replied. "I thought it was cool and just wanted to share it."

"Well, you should have asked me first. Two agents from the government, calling themselves the Collins Elite, came by to question me about the CW video and one of the UAPs at school. They saw me, I guess, on the school camera."

"What are you talking about?" Judd asked.

"They came to question me about that and the UAP video."

"What UAP video?"

My annoyance was rising. "The school video when the UAP came during the debate."

"Oh," Judd said. "What did you tell them?"

"I told them there was a human inside." I summarized the rest of the conversation, as I didn't want to get into a protracted discussion.

"What did they ask you exactly?"

"What I saw," I said again.

"What did you tell them?"

"It was just Humana, my clone. But, Judd, they want to talk to you also."

"Why do they want to talk to me?"

"I don't know. The men said they were with the Collins Elite ..." and then the phone clicked. I looked at the screen. It seemed frozen. I bet someone was listening. I tapped the numbers to call Judd back and noticed the phone still wasn't responding. What was going on?

And why was the desk light off? The whole room was dark. My heart skipped. What were the chances the phone would die, and the power would go out simultaneously?

"Mother?" I ran out of my bedroom, holding up my phone, and saw Mother sitting in the dark living room.

"I guess the power went off," she said.

I shook my head. "No, something happened." The room was eerily silent, with no TV in the background. I ran to the front door and stepped onto the porch for a better view. People were abandoning their cars in the street, and vehicles sat motionless everywhere.

A middle-aged man ran up to me. "Did you see that flash?"

"No, what flash?"

He pointed. "It was in the sky, over there." I looked where he pointed, but nothing was visible except smoke, and the air smelled ashy.

The man was visibly upset. "It looked like—like a missile or something. Something exploded. Something bad happened."

The man's glossy eyes searched in all directions, and then he went hysterical. "The end of the world is coming. It's the end of the world," and he ran down the street, flailing his hands.

I wanted to turn on the TV and learn more, but we didn't have a working TV. I couldn't call anyone because the phone didn't work.

Soon, it would be completely dark. We needed lights. I slammed the front door and locked it. "Do we have any candles?"

"In the closet," Mother said.

"I should get a flashlight, too." I rummaged around in the kitchen drawer. We had one of the old-fashioned ones we'd had forever, so it should work. I found it and pushed the "on" button. It came on, but the light was weak. "It needs a fresh battery."

"Well, it's better than nothing," Mother said. "See if you can find those candles in the closet."

I did as Mother suggested. I found several, some of which were well-used. I picked the best ones, putting one on the dining room table and one beside Mother's chair.

I lit them with a match and watched the flickering light for a minute. "That's pretty good."

I took one with me into my bedroom. I was glad we at least had candles, but there was no way to find out anything. Then I remembered my hand-held radio.

Major had insisted that when I wasn't using the HF or walkie-talkie, I keep both in containers that would prevent an electromagnetic pulse from shorting them. I kept the small radio in a pouch they had sent me, and the HF radio stayed protected by a high-tech military-grade covering when I wasn't using it.

I would also need to retrieve the portable power station from the closet. They sent me a Faraday cage from Amazon to keep it in. I needed to act quickly while there was still some natural light from the bay window.

Suddenly, I remembered. Judd and I had agreed that if something happened, we would connect on Simplex. We had just been talking on the phone.

I pulled out the walkie-talkie, attached the antenna, and turned it on. Immediately, I heard desperate voices. Operators were talking over each other. I couldn't get a word in. I waited and listened, but with so many hams on it, they jammed the frequency.

Mother walked into my room. "Can you contact anyone on the radio?" she asked.

"Hold on a second. I'm trying."

Suddenly, we heard banging on the door.

"Wait, Mother, don't answer it. People are not in their right minds. Let me go."

I rushed to the door, and when I looked out the peephole, I saw Judd. I opened the door and let him in, immediately locking the door behind him.

His eyes showed fear. “Chumana, I think we’re at war. We just suffered an EMP.”

CHAPTER FIFTY-SIX

BLACKOUT

I tugged on Judd's arm. "Help me set up the portable power unit before it gets darker. Tomorrow, I can recharge it using the solar panel."

We scooted to the closet near the front door and pulled out the power station. "You've got a thousand watts on this thing," Judd said. "That's more than enough for the radio, phone, and lights."

"Yeah, except the phone doesn't work. Anyway, forget the other stuff. All I care about is the radio."

"Cars aren't running either. I tried to start mine, and it wouldn't even crank. You saw the cars on the street. They are frozen. Every single one of them."

"Would an old car run?"

Judd shrugged. "It would have to be old."

"Did you hear those guys on Simplex? They sounded terrified."

"I know," Judd said. "I couldn't get a word in. That's why I came over. Even my mother is freaking out. I promised her I wouldn't stay long. At least we can talk on the radio if we can get an open frequency."

"Choose another one as a backup. Jot it down for me, and if we can't talk on the main one, we'll talk on that one."

Judd placed his hand on my shoulder. "Chumana, I've missed you."

I'd been so insensitive after all he had done for me. I dropped my head. "I'm sorry. I didn't know what to do."

"Well," Judd said, "I don't agree with you on some things, but I knew you needed space."

"It's not so much that. It's just that I was never supposed to tell anybody anything. I was afraid, once I saw my involvement and your resistance, that everything would fall apart, and I wanted to succeed. I didn't want to let The Frequency Group down, Humana or Major. I had invested a great deal of time with the CW. It's not easy to get to 25 wpm."

When I stopped talking, a twinkle popped into Judd's eyes. "I've got something to tell you."

The closet door was ajar, but I wanted to hear his news before we carried everything to my bedroom. "What is it?"

"I passed the general license exam."

"You did? What did you make?"

"I knew you would ask. I missed four, so you beat me."

I hugged him. "As long as you passed, that's all that matters. That means you can operate HF."

Judd glanced toward my bedroom. "I wish I could afford your radio."

"So, have you ordered yours?"

"Are you kidding? No, but I will. Of course, now everybody will look for any radio they can find. I may not be able to buy one."

"Let's get this stuff connected to see if it works."

"Is your radio protected?" Judd asked.

"They insisted I keep the wrap over it when I wasn't using it, and the computer they sent me is in a Faraday bag."

"Where is the prepper food I bought for you?"

It's up there in the closet. I thought you were insane buying it at the time."

Judd cocked his head. "I should have gotten more, but I made sure to get enough for Rophe."

"How long before we run out?"

"Well, if you ration it, you and your mom should be able to go several months."

"Well, let's hope they restore power in a few days."

"That's wishful thinking," Judd said. "You're talking about infrastructure. You can't rebuild it overnight."

I thought for a minute. "What do you think will happen when people run out of food?"

"Chaos, desperation, violence. Without God, we're in trouble."

I didn't want to think about it. "Let's get this set up. We can run to the store later."

Judd glanced at Rophe lying on Mother's chair. He was waiting for Mother to return from the bathroom. "I doubt that the stores will be open."

"Why? It's not that late. It's just getting dark outside."

"Because they won't have power. There will be no way to buy things without cash. Plus, people will be out of control. Desperate. I mean, if we go to the store soon, if there is something specific you need—"

I interrupted him. "Candles, batteries, toilet paper."

"And, Chumana, we'll have to walk. It's twice as far as the school, and then you've got to carry everything back."

I thought about it. "Okay. Sounds like a bad idea. Let's just set up the radio. In an emergency, the protocol is that The Frequency Group will send me a message on digital and instruct me on what to do. I think this qualifies as an emergency."

I stopped, shaken by everything. "I never imagined this would happen. I just thought I'd be doing CW for routine announcements. I didn't think in terms of an emergency, even though they emphasized that many times. Gees, I don't know what I was thinking."

Judd reached out and squeezed my hand. "Don't worry. I'll help you set things up, and then I'll need to head back home."

We carried the power station and connectors into my bedroom. Between the two of us, it didn't take long. The crackle as the radio came to life was a relief.

"All that work, Judd, but I never took it as seriously as they did. How did they know this was going to happen?"

"Because the government has access to information we don't have."

"Who set off the EMP?"

"That's the million-dollar question."

"Yeah, we'll probably never know. Everybody will blame everybody else. Why don't you see if you can bring something up on the radio, and I'll open the digital software on the computer."

Judd looked at me. "Even if it works, there won't be any internet."

"It was in a Faraday cage, so it should work. This digital program doesn't use the internet. It just uses the radio."

Judd chuckled. "I've still got a few things to learn to catch up with you."

"I also like digital because I don't have to talk."

Judd squinted. "Why are you so afraid to talk on the radio?"

I shrugged. "I'm not afraid. Just shy. Let me check for messages."

Judd played with the dials as I set up the computer for digital. "Look, I do have a message. An important one."

Judd stopped what he was doing. "What does it say?"

"When the power grid goes down, tune into this government frequency as soon as possible." I wrote it down and handed it to him.

"Makes you wonder if this was all planned," Judd said, dialing into the frequency.

I listened closely. "I hear someone."

Even over the radio, the air was thick with tension. "Sounds like the net controller," I added.

The voice was authoritative and direct. "When you check in, please give your name, call sign, location, and if you have power."

"At least with a net controller, operators won't be talking over each other," Judd said.

Operators checked in one by one. I listened for a few minutes to familiarize myself with the protocol.

After I gave the Net Controller my information, he asked, "KO4LBS, do you have power?"

"Negative. Running off a portable power station."

When I finished, I set the mic on the desk. "Tell me what you hear when I return. I need to check on Mom. Since it's a government frequency, don't say anything."

Judd nodded.

Mother had returned to the living room, and Rophe was sleeping on her lap. She looked up from her reading. "Can you hear anything?"

"No one has power, at least no one I've heard."

"Is it just this area or…"

"So far, the operators I've heard are in Atlanta, but they prioritize local operators before expanding to outlying areas.

"However, this is a government frequency, so I'm unsure. I wanted to make sure you were okay, but I need to go back and listen. They will provide information once everyone on the call has checked in."

"Okay." Mother sighed. "Let me know if you find out anything."

Mother's face flickered in the candlelight. At least we had candles.

I patted Rophe on the head. "You take care of Mother."

He looked at me as if he understood. Maybe he did.

CHAPTER FIFTY-SEVEN

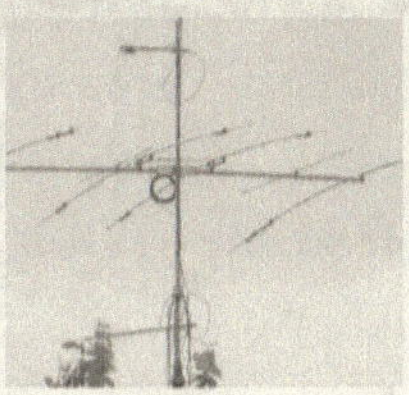

"Everything is working," Judd said, "and I need to get back home."

"Did you jot down another Simplex number?"

"Yeah, and I programmed it into the walkie-talkie."

I hugged Judd. "Thanks for your help."

"Keep track of how much power you're using."

"Do you think there will be school tomorrow?"

Judd shook his head. "Nope. If anything comes up, contact me. Again, don't forget to charge the power station with the solar panel."

"I just wish the phone worked."

As Judd headed to the front door, I returned to focusing on the radio. After everybody had checked into Net Control, the Net Controller, the central figure in our communications network, formally addressed the participants.

"Thank you, everyone, for joining. Listen carefully. This is not a test. I have been gathering information from other sources, and I can confirm that the power grid in the United States has been rendered inoperable by an electromagnetic pulse, or EMP.

"Satellite links are down or severely degraded. Power stations are out across the U.S., except in a few isolated areas that have invested in EMP resistant generators.

"The hardened military network out of Cheyenne Mountain confirms a widespread power grid collapse. We can detect no civilian communications, except for preppers and those who have prepared for a possible catastrophic failure.

"A few public facilities are on solar power, but that is the exception. The public is blind and deaf. News outlets are down. Phones are down—even satellite phones.

"A few emergency broadcast towers are functioning, but not enough to meet the demand. We have some pre-hardened stations in selected areas.

"That's where all of you come in. You are communications specialists. We need you on the radio to share this information. Please announce it at the top of each hour.

"Begin your broadcast with the word 'attention.' Say it several times so people will listen and follow the protocol: This is an emergency broadcast. A widespread incident has affected power and telecommunication systems.

"Stay calm and shelter in place. Conserve food, water, and medical supplies. Avoid non-essential travel. Law enforcement and emergency services will be operating locally. Stay tuned for more details."

The Net Controller paused before continuing. "Repeat this message to the public as often as possible: 'do not panic.' The biggest threat, beyond the loss of services, is rioting and looting."

"Any questions so far?" Net Control asked.

"What about hospitals? Are they operational? And what about EMS and fire?"

"Right now, they are operating but have maxed out services. If people need medical care, emergency vehicles are almost nonexistent. People with medical needs are especially vulnerable.

"Biking or walking might be the only means of transportation unless someone can find an old truck or car that survived the attack. A vintage tractor on a farm might work.

"That also brings up another point. Access to clean water and waste disposal will become critical. People need to boil their water if possible. Practice strict hygiene. Encourage people to check on their neighbors. Basic medical care will require self-reliance. Folks in neighborhoods will need to be charitable."

Another ham radio operator asked, "Do you know how long it will take to restore things to normal?"

The Net Controller cleared his throat. "We have no timeline. We're not talking days. We're talking weeks, possibly months. Micro-grids will be up sooner, provided wind turbines and solar panels are operational, but that depends on the weather.

"We need natural gas, but that takes macro-grids that we don't have. We can't move forward until we fix the infrastructure. It's a massive logistical nightmare without transportation. That sums up the situation in Georgia."

Another listener on the call asked, "What about other states? What about Washington? Have you spoken to anyone outside of Georgia?"

"A few state and local emergency managers have hardened communications, but we can't depend on anyone but ourselves. I haven't heard from FEMA. I hope to soon. Everything is very patchy.

"Our focus is on medical, water, food, and communication in Atlanta and outlying counties—including Fulton, Cobb, Clayton, DeKalb, Gwinnett, Douglas, and Cherokee Counties. Encourage people to stay where they are unless it's not safe.

"Thousands of dead vehicles are blocking roads and making them impassable. There is no place to go that isn't affected. It's everywhere in the U.S., as far as I know."

A few more general questions followed, but the message was the same. There was no power, and soon, there would be no food or water. Help was a long way off—possibly months.

The Net Controller ended the call with this warning. "Let me say, this is about survival. Whatever skills you have, use them to disseminate this information to the masses. The chain of command will be decentralized. Help your neighbor.

"The next update will be in two hours. Keep a diary and prepare any reports that would be helpful for authorities to know where help is most needed."

"I have one other question."

"Go ahead, and please identify yourself," Net Control said.

This is KO4QRN. Do we know who set off the EMP?"

A long pause passed before he answered. "No. Your guess is as good as mine. Good luck, and good night, everyone."

A long night awaited me. I went into the living room and updated Mother on what I'd heard. "I'm going to be sending alert messages every hour."

Mother yawned. "The darkness is making me sleepy."

"Just sleep. We should probably eat what's in the fridge while it's still cold."

"This is not good, Chumana. I feel like the world is coming to an end."

Could this be how it all ended? We returned to the Stone Age and lived as hunter-gatherers. I didn't know what to say.

"I'll just read my Bible," Mother added. "Under a candle, as they did in the time of Jesus. It worked for him; it can work for me."

I glanced at Rophe. He didn't have a care in the world. "Rophe will take care of you, Mother."

"God will provide," Mother said. And then, almost as an afterthought, Mother asked, "Do you know what Rophe means in Hebrew?"

I shook my head. "No. What does it mean?"

"It means God heals."

I stared at Rophe. "Rophe means to heal?"

Mother nodded, and then she closed her eyes.

I couldn't get it out of my mind. Rophe means to heal.

When I returned to my bedroom, I heard my call sign on the walkie-talkie. I recognized Judd's voice and rushed over to grab the mic. "This is KO4LBS."

"Great to hear your voice," Judd said. "Your signal report is a 5-9."

I laughed. "K4PREP, do you know that Rophe means to heal in Hebrew?"

"No, I didn't know that. Sounds prophetic, doesn't it?"

CHAPTER FIFTY-EIGHT

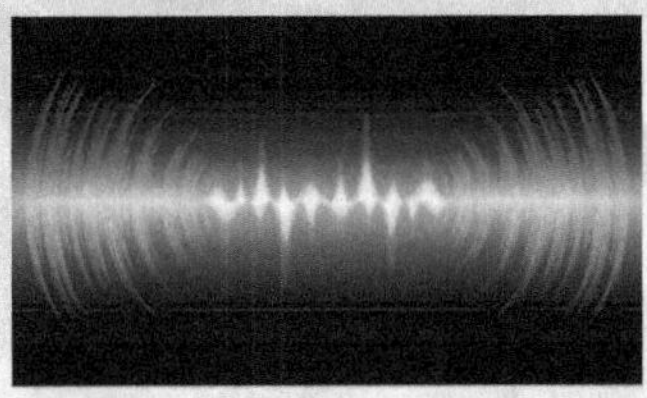

Although talking on the radio was not romantic, especially since anyone could listen to your conversation, the sweetness of conversation was more precious without other means available.

There was no internet, TV, transportation, or phones. I thought about all those crazy science fiction movies depicting the end of the world, never thinking anything like that would happen.

I thought about families who lived far apart. The world is lonely when there is no one in it but you.

I glanced at my transceiver and pretended it was calling my name. I needed to get started. I felt overwhelmed.

I understood now why CW was so important. Those dits and dahs could reach other continents when HF voice may not be heard.

I was glad Judd was so close that I could talk to him on Simplex. Although convenient, VHF/UHF had limitations, even when the repeaters were operational. I needed to figure out how to get him an HF radio.

I tried to clear my mind as I took a break. I'd forgotten about the bathroom night light that ran on a battery for emergencies, but how convenient it was now that we needed it. Then I went into the kitchen. A big cup of coffee would be perfect for the long night ahead.

I called out to Mother, "Would you like some coffee?"

Wait a minute. We had no power, I reminded myself. I couldn't make coffee. "Never mind. I forgot."

Mother laughed. "I've already tried to flip the light on three times."

We needed to conserve power for the radio.

Using the flashlight, I found some crackers in the cabinet. I took them to Mother, along with a glass of water.

"Thank you, Honey," she said. "I'll probably stay in my favorite chair and drift off to sleep. I'm comfortable here with Rophe."

I hugged her. "I love you. Let me know if you need anything. I'll be busy, but I can stop anytime."

Mother squeezed my hand. "Thank you. I also appreciate what Judd has done to help us. I hope he knows that."

"He does," I assured her. "I just wish he had an HF radio. He passed his general license exam."

"Are they expensive?" Mother asked. "Maybe we could get him something since he's been so helpful."

"Yeah, maybe." I gave Rophe a couple of cat treats, and he gobbled them down. "I'd better get back to the CW."

We should have gotten a second power supply unit for the living room. Of course, even if the TV worked, there was no internet.

I returned to the radio and set the band to 80 meters. I couldn't hear anybody and didn't know if that was good or bad. With my scribbled notes in front of me, I settled on a frequency, sent my call sign, and began relaying the message the Net Controller had instructed us to send.

Twenty to 25 words per minute was slow compared to someone talking. The higher speed was to ensure my ability to receive messages. I slowed down to 18 so those less skilled could copy me.

I made several mistakes initially, but things went well once I overcame my initial jitters. Should I have made it more formal, operating like a Net Controller? They didn't tell us to do that. The government just wanted us to convey a general message of reassurance, letting the public know what had happened and that they were doing everything possible to restore services.

CW operators quickly found me. I noted their locations to prepare a report. New York, Virginia, Oklahoma, Alabama, Florida, North Carolina, Kansas, and Georgia. Everyone was operating on backup power.

I became so engrossed in CW that an hour passed before I realized it. One operator gave his QTH as Gloucestershire, England. He was the only one running on AC power.

The attack occurred most likely in the central part of the United States. Otherwise, it was unlikely that the entire continent would be affected. No one I talked to had connected with anyone in Alaska. Other hams had communicated with operators in neighboring states, and I wrote down those locations.

Then, someone from Canada joined our rag chew. I noted he had AC power.

"Sounds like someone specifically targeted the U.S.," one ham CW'd.

Would we ever know? The military probably knew, but that information was unavailable to us. Once we all knew, I imagined a full-scale war. Would it be nuclear? The way things had escalated, it would not surprise me.

The operator out of New York reported, "All commercial U.S. planes are grounded."

The New York ham also reported that the subway was dead and people were trapped in the tunnels. There was concern about flooding. The Fire and Police departments had no operational vehicles, so they weren't sure how they would rescue them.

I sent the follow-up message, "The safest place right now is in your home. Don't go anywhere. Check on neighbors. Conserve food."

"Is there any radiation risk?" someone asked.

I didn't know.

After two hours of rag chewing, I messaged the CW operators that I needed a break.

I looked at the implant on my wrist. Some time had passed since my last contact. Would UFOs be affected by the power outage?

When I checked on Mother, she had fallen asleep in her chair, and

Rophe had retreated to the sofa. I took the Bible in her lap and placed it on the table.

Then I drank some water and returned to my bedroom. I tried to raise Judd on Simplex, but he didn't respond. Hams were rag chewing, but no one knew anything.

I returned to sending CW, hoping to operate a few more hours. Perhaps a brilliant person could figure out how to restore power.

Operators checked in and out on the frequency. At 3:30 a.m., I messaged that I needed to get some sleep. I sent my call sign and signed off. Since hams were in different time zones, they'd be sharing information all night. I would probably sleep hearing dits and dahs.

I retrieved Rophe from the sofa and brought him to bed with me. He stayed out of my room when I did CW because he disliked the noise. I also blew out all the candles, noting how dark the world was when there was no light. I couldn't imagine living in darkness for months.

CHAPTER FIFTY-NINE

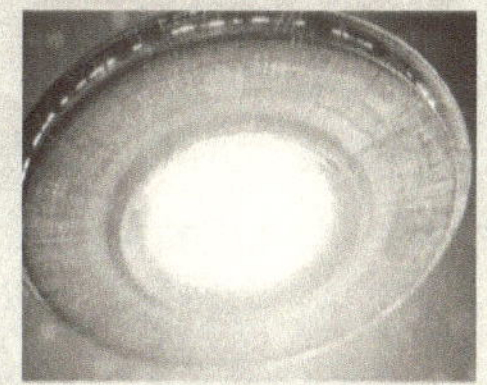

Mother's voice awakened me. "Chumana, Judd is at the door."

I rolled over. "What time is it?"

"I don't know, but the sun is up."

I groaned. "I didn't go to bed until almost 4:00."

"Should I tell him to come back later?"

"No, I'll be out in a minute."

Mother left, and I reached for my phone to check the time. Of course, it was dead. I was starting to dislike this new world. The excitement of doing something important had worn off, and I wanted everything to return to normal.

I rolled out of bed and dressed. Judd was sitting at the dining room table, talking to Mother, when I appeared.

I longed for coffee. I was tired and didn't feel like talking to anyone.

"I was up late doing CW. Coffee would taste so good right now."

"You could use your power station," Judd said.

I sat beside him. "In a minute. We should probably charge it first."

"Any updates?"

I shook my head. "From the contacts I made on the radio last night, it appears the attack happened in the central portion of the U.S. No one I communicated with in the U.S. had power. Only a ham out of Canada and England did."

"You were able to talk to someone in Canada and England?" Judd asked.

"Yes."

"That's cool. Did you do any voice?"

"No, I just stayed on CW."

"I listened to local chatter," Judd said, "on the walkie-talkie. Nothing is working. I rode my bike to the store this morning and purchased a few items. I had to pay with cash. People swarmed the place. You'd think Armageddon had come."

"Where did you go?"

"Publix. I got what you said you needed; my mom wanted a few items. They are in the bag. I also wanted to help you set up the solar panel. We should probably do it while the sun is shining."

I nodded, still trying to wake up.

Judd chuckled. "You need some coffee. I'll get the stuff." He went and disappeared into my bedroom

I rubbed my eyes, thinking I shouldn't have left my room in such a mess. "Did you sleep well, Mother?"

She leaned against the counter. "As well as can be expected. I wish we could get the news."

"I'll check for messages in a minute, as soon as I wake up. First, let me go and help Judd."

I met him outside. "How long do you think it will take to charge?"

Judd shrugged. "There is a formula that will tell you, but I don't know what it is. However, the power station still has plenty of power. You didn't run it down as much as I thought you would."

"Well, that's some good news."

"Do you have any electronics besides the radio that the EMP didn't destroy?"

"Just the computer, but I kept it connected last night when I was on the air, so it doesn't need charging."

Suddenly, I felt my wrist vibrating. My heart skipped a beat. "Look. It's flashing."

Judd stopped what he was doing. "Are you going to the school now?"

I nodded. "They're contacting me."

"I'll go with you."

I put my hand on his chest. "No, Judd, stay here. I'll take the radio with me and keep you posted."

"Like you did before?" he said sarcastically.

"No, seriously, I will. I promise." Then I stopped talking. "That's the one thing I didn't charge."

"Plug it into the computer for a few minutes. You don't have to leave this exact moment."

"Okay. Five minutes."

I ran inside and connected the walkie-talkie to the computer. Then I went and hugged Mother. "I'm going for a walk. Judd is going to finish up with charging the power station."

"Where are you going?" she asked.

"Toward the school. I want to see if anyone is there."

"You said school was closed."

"Yeah, but I want to make sure."

I reached over and patted Rophe on the head. "I won't be gone long."

When five minutes were up, I retrieved the handheld radio and contacted Judd. "This is KO4LBS. Do you hear me, K4PREP?"

"Yes, loud and clear."

"I'm headed your way."

The implant continued to blink, and I knew I needed to go, so I made a beeline for the door.

Once outside, Judd protested again, but he knew I wouldn't listen.

Finally, he just said, "Keep me posted."

As I headed toward the school, I was overwhelmed by what I saw and didn't see. No one was around, and abandoned cars filled the streets. The traffic light didn't work, and the air was eerily silent until I heard the Grosbeak. He landed on a limb several feet in front of me and began to sing. If only I knew what he was saying.

Perhaps he wanted to encourage me. He had done that all winter, lifting my spirits and giving me hope about the future. Each day, he visited the feeder to eat the seeds I put out for him, so he had hung around all winter.

"Thank you, Mr. Grosbeak."

My thoughts returned to the UAP. Would Humana and Major be in the UFO?

The saucer soon came into view, its silver exterior reflecting off the bright sunshine. Perhaps it was a good thing schools were closed. I quickened my pace.

When I was close enough that they could see me, I waved my hands in the air. The cargo belly opened. I knew that was my invitation.

Before I went any further, I sent a message to Judd. KO4LBS to K4PREP. How could I say it cryptically? I am fixing to board. Stand by. KO4LBS, out."

"This is K4PREP. Copy you."

I walked over and stood underneath the massive saucer The tractor beam gently picked me up and lifted me into the cargo bay.

CHAPTER SIXTY

When the tractor beam released me, I saw Major and Humana standing on the bridge. What a pleasant surprise they were here and not on an overhead monitor.

Before I could say anything, Major ushered Humana and me into a side room. After shutting the door, he said, "Please sit beside Humana at the table. I have something important to tell you."

Once we were seated, Major began. "The United States' power grid has officially failed. You did a great job getting the word out on the radio last night. I'm proud of you."

"I tried. When will it be restored?"

Major leaned back in his chair. "A problem has arisen."

"What's that?"

"Chumana, the rogue part of the U.S. government is on to you. They captured an image of you entering the saucer, and Judd posted a video on Facebook of you sending CW on the radio."

It took me a minute to process everything Major said. "Some guys calling themselves the Collins Elite came to the apartment."

"I know," Major said. "They were able to identify you using Judd's video. You aren't active on social media, so we never worried about someone tracking or tagging you."

"I'm not on social media hardly at all."

"Well, Judd's video was all they needed to identify you, that one video."

"Judd didn't ask me beforehand."

"Here's the thing, Chumana. They want you for information, and they want to seize the radio we've given you. They can do it by court order if they run out of options.

"We've run out of time and won't be able to complete your training on how to deal with, how should I say it, those who have gone rogue, or teach you how to use telepathy to interact with the Shining Ones."

Maybe Judd was right. I should never have gotten involved. "What's going to happen?"

Humana broke in. "Relax. We have a plan, and it will all work out. Just listen."

My heart pounded. "I'm listening."

"It's disclosure time," Major said. "We wanted to wait a little longer, but we can't. Are you ready?"

I nodded. "I think so."

"Chumana, I am your father; this is your twin sister. She's not a clone."

I was speechless. I remembered what Gracie had asked me that day at lunch, if I had a twin. "I asked Mother, and she said, 'No, you don't have a twin.'"

"First, because of my top-secret position, I had to keep many things hidden from your mother. She has a rare bloodline, back to the golden age of the gods, when our ancestors had direct contact with the powerful entities.

"Once the government learned that she was carrying twins, which they kept hidden from your mother, the powers that be opted to separate you and your twin sister here, Humana, at birth and raise you in two different environments."

My father continued. "I believe it was a mistake. I shouldn't have let the government do it. I raised Humana, and your mother raised you. It was a government experiment. They have repeated this scenario many times. Like what Hitler did, but not in an evil way—more in case something went wrong.

"However, the agreement was that when you turned 18, all of this had to be disclosed. Of course, your mother was compensated by the government."

"Why did you hide this from her, though?"

"The government is a bureaucracy with many tentacles, and their work with the entities, the Shining Ones, was top secret."

"Who are they?" I asked.

"They are trying to save humanity from the upcoming war that threatens to destroy all of us. They have been undertaking a breeding program, learning how to bring children to birth in artificial wombs.

"Humans have killed so many children through abortion that the population is shrinking. In the event of a war, with rising infertility, the future of all humankind is at stake.

"Without getting into too much detail right now, I suggested that both of you be trained as communications specialists."

"What kind of breeding program?" I asked, my voice betraying my confusion and disbelief.

"To increase the human population. Remember, your mother has a rare bloodline. Only because of my position in the program was I able to steer your greater purpose into the communications arena.

"That's my expertise; you inherited your genius from me. Not many people have our level of I.Q. I convinced them your genius was more useful to them than your genes. You are double-gifted."

Major glanced at Humana. "Both of you."

Humana and I exchanged smiles.

"So, where does this take us now?" I asked.

Major nodded. "I knew you would want to know. Humana and I have talked about this. Our superiors have agreed to our proposal.

"The rogue U.S. government does not like what we're doing. They have spiritual concerns that make no sense to me, and we want to protect you. So, our plan is for you and Humana to swap places.

"Humana is much more familiar with how things operate in the government, and nobody will know the difference because nobody knows you have a twin. We want you to leave with the spaceship on its journey back home, and Humana will take your place here on Earth."

I glanced at Humana and then back at Major. It would take me a while to get used to the idea that Major was my father.

"What about Rophe? I won't leave without him, and my mother needs him."

Major nodded. "We've known for a while that this would be an issue. Humana, do you want to get him?"

"Sure."

I watched Humana leave the room, not understanding what they meant until she returned. In her arms was a cat that looked like Rophe. "A clone?"

Major nodded. "Yes, he's a clone of Rophe. You can't tell them apart because they are the same in every way."

"So Rophe stays here with Mother, and I take this cat that looks like Rophe with me?"

"Or the other way around," Major said. "It's up to you."

"How soon do we have to do this?"

"Soon," Major said. "The rogue government will return next time with a search warrant."

I could only imagine how much that would upset Mother. "So, they bombard Humana with questions instead of me?"

"Humana has been trained to protect herself—mind control, power of suggestion, tricks of the trade you learn in government ops."

"So, they will seize the radio but not her or Mother?"

"Well, we also had an idea about that. We can remove the government frequencies and return the radio to its original state. If we do that, you can gift the radio to Judd.

"We certainly don't want to give the rogue government a free radio; chances are, they wouldn't come after Judd. There is too much legally at stake for them to go that far. He's a minor. It would draw attention to them, and they don't want that."

"So, is this something you want to do now?"

"The sooner, the better," my father said.

"What about you?"

“Here’s the plan. Once the Shining Ones leave Atlanta, they will go to Alaska. While there, I will attend the top-secret military briefing at the underground base. The war has already started. The game is on.

“The Shining Ones want to return to their planet as soon as possible. It will make sense once everything falls into place. I will be with you until the spaceship leaves Alaska.”

“Where is their home?” I asked.

“It’s far away, but they go through portals, so getting there doesn’t take long. You will love the journey. It’s out of this world.”

CHAPTER SIXTY-ONE

"This is KO4LBS calling K4PREP. Can you hear me?"

"This is K4PREP. I'm hearing you loud and clear, KO4LBS. Go ahead."

"Can you come to the drop-off point?"

"Roger. Roger. On my way."

I held Rophe II, as I referred to Rophe's clone, in my arms. He seemed so much like my Rophe that it was hard to believe he wasn't Rophe.

As we waited, I told Humana, "I should tell you about Judd and Mother."

Her eyes beamed. "That sounds like a good idea."

"Of course, this is my school. It's closed because of the EMP. We're so close to the end of the year, they may not reopen."

"Does Judd know all the classes I need to go to and the names of the teachers?"

"Yeah, but I don't think they'll finish the year. We only have a couple of weeks left. We've already taken end-of-year exams."

"My school is shut down, too," Humana said.

"They're closed across the country," Major added.

"Mother is sweet, caring, and sentimental. She's had some mental challenges in the last year, but she's improved with Rophe."

"That's good," Humana said. "I can't wait to meet her. She's my mother, too."

I filled Humana in on her sleepwalking. "I'm sure there is a correlation because, after many months, I learned she was sleepwalking to the UFO."

"It's her bloodline," Father said. "The Shining Ones keep tabs on family lines generationally."

"Her sleepwalking stopped when I brought Rophe home, and her mental issues have evaporated. Occasionally, she'll have a relapse, but not often."

Major jumped into the conversation. "What you say makes sense. The Shining Ones sent Rophe to help her. They know more than we do about the human mind, frequencies, and how to heal the body. Animals play a big part in that. Once the Shining Ones figured out what she needed, they knew how to help her."

"Does that mean someday I might be like her with her mental deficiencies?" I asked.

"I don't think you can make that correlation. Even if it were true, you know how to heal your body."

I patted Rophe II on the head. "Be good to Mother. She needs you to be like my Rophe: kind, affectionate, loving, and compassionate. Can you do that?"

He purred reassuringly. I tried to think of quirks about Judd that Humana needed to know.

"He's a little religious. He likes to go to Bible Study with our small group, all girls except him. However, Shale has withdrawn from school to move to Washington, D.C., so I'm not sure who will lead it or if they will meet anymore."

I debated in my mind—should I bring it up? I might as well. She might need to know. "Mother and I used to live with Shale and her mother before her mother remarried.

"Shale had an accident with Judd's dog, and we had a falling out. Judd forgave her, but I'm not sure I have. I'm still working on it."

"That's good to know," Humana said.

"Of course," I added, "you may not even see my friends with the school closures. Gracie is the one I told you about who seems like a prophet. Her father is a physics professor at Kennesaw State University. He was a big wheel in England before coming here, and he's involved with CERN."

"Another brain, it sounds like," Humana said.

"Yeah, you could say that, although she tries to hide it with a fake Southern drawl. She's a sweet girl. You will like her if you get to meet her.

"And then, there is Rachel, our Jewish friend. You might see her because she also lives in the Hope Garden Apartments."

"So, are you and Judd boyfriend and girlfriend? Like, how serious?"

"Well, I have kissed him a couple of times, but nothing long and drawn out. Just a little kiss." We both laughed.

I glanced up at my father, and he looked away, pretending not to hear.

"You think he likes you better than you like him?" Humana asked.

"Probably. I distanced myself from him for a few weeks, and we just got back together. Judd's a prepper type; when I got into ham radio, he also decided to get into it. That's what brought us back together."

"I think I see him coming," Major said.

I looked down the pathway. "Yeah, that's Judd. Let me prepare him before I introduce you."

I handed Rophe II to Humana and hurried down the trail.

A gust of wind rose behind me, pushing me in his direction. We shared a warm embrace. Before Judd could say anything, I placed my hands on his shoulders. "You must pay attention to everything I'm about to say, so listen carefully."

"Is everything okay? I didn't expect you to bring me here."

"Yes, Judd, everything is fine, but I need to tell you some things."

Judd's eyes appeared worried. I'd better talk fast to allay his fears. "I want to introduce you to my twin sister, father, and a cloned Rophe."

Judd stared at me. "What?"

"I know it's a lot to take in, but you remember me talking about Humana. I thought she was transhuman or a robot or a clone—I didn't know exactly—well, it turns out she's my twin.

"My mother had a set of twins, but she only knew about me. And, please, don't tell anyone I'm a twin. No one else should know."

"Okay. Whatever you say."

"Good, that's what I want to hear. The man I'm going to introduce you to is my father. His name is Major."

"Is that his name or his rank?"

"Well, I just assumed it was his name. That's what he told me to call him initially, but only tonight did I learn that he's my father."

"You're sure?"

I nodded. "Yes, I'm sure."

"Is he human?"

I laughed. "Of course, my father is human. Who do you think my mom married?"

"Okay. Sorry. And—you said a cloned cat?"

"Yes, the cat is a clone of Rophe."

"They cloned Rophe?"

"Yes. Scientists have been cloning animals for a long time."

"I wonder where they got his DNA."

"They probably had it from before. They sent Rophe to help Mother. Remember the strange light in the forest? So, I'm sure they had his DNA. They would have looked for certain qualities in him to help Mother heal."

"Like what?" Judd asked.

I shrugged. "I don't know. The Shining Ones know more than we do about everything."

"Will I meet them?"

"No. Judd, please listen. What I'm about to tell you is extremely important."

"Okay. I'm listening, although I am feeling a little light-headed."

"Are you okay?"

"I'm okay. But I feel like a bowling ball just hit me."

"Well, this may make you feel like you've been run over by a Mac truck. Humana and I are going to exchange places. I want to take Rophe and leave his clone with Mother."

Judd's eyes bulged. "Where the hell are you going?"

"I'm going on a trip. I'll help with radio communication between the Shining Ones and the U.S. government. It will also allow me to keep in touch with you. That's the positive side to all of this."

"For how long?"

"I didn't ask, but I'm not sure they know. They want to leave before the war starts."

"Why do they, whoever they are, need you?"

"I think it's out of goodwill, like an exchange. I also have a rare bloodline that dates back to the golden age when gods lived among humans. My father didn't say this, but maybe if I searched back far enough, I'd discover I'm related to the Anunnaki. Maybe I'm their progeny."

Judd was stunned into silence. He edged away, like he needed space to think about everything I'd just shared. I glanced up the trail and saw my father and sister patiently waiting.

I took a deep breath. We had reached the point of no return. If we crossed this threshold, there was no turning back. I had peace about it.

However, if I were honest, I also had apprehension. I worried about Mother. Would she be the same with Rophe's clone or mentally regress? Would she know something was off when Humana took my place? I didn't think she would, or I would not have agreed to go. She still had moments of brain fog, and I imagined she would attribute it to that.

Humana was like me in every way—our mannerisms, how we fixed our hair, how we talked, what we liked, and what we didn't like. We just knew different things, having grown up with only one of our two parents.

And my father—he seemed level-headed. I knew he was a genius. I could tell. Plus, disclosure would still happen on my birthday, which was only a few months away. Disclosure for my mother, anyway. The judge would permit her to open the vault and unseal the letter. I hoped to be back by then.

With war coming, she'd stay home, so her lifestyle wouldn't change. She never went anywhere. The war might be a blessing. Her life would go on just as it had. Judd would still have me around in a sense—my twin sister.

Then I remembered. I forgot to tell Judd about the radio. I'd let him know when he was ready, which he'd be excited about. I also needed to ask him to stay away from the Collins Elite if they knocked on his front door.

They were both into spiritual things. Nothing good could come out of that.

As my worry started to mount that Judd wouldn't agree to the proposal, he turned and walked back. "Promise me, you won't die."

I laughed. "Judd, if anything, I'll be safer than you. I'm worried you'll get drafted. Who knows what's going to happen."

"Well, one thing we know for sure."

"What's that?"

"We won't have power for a long time. So, we might be fighting a war with sticks and stones."

CHAPTER SIXTY-TWO

Judd and I joined hands as we took the trail to meet my sister, father, and Rophe II. Without technology, the world and time moved at a slower pace. The frozen vehicles seemed anachronistic now, representing a former time we wouldn't see for many months.

In contrast, nature became more visible because the world now belonged to it. We had molded the world to fit our needs, but we were now forced to live in theirs. That wasn't a bad thing. Perhaps nature knew something we didn't. In the tyranny of the urgent, we forget to take time.

I saw trees emerging from their winter hibernation in my new, unhurried reality. Green leaves sprouted tender shoots, and the renewal of life had begun. Sunlight filtered through the overhead canopy, and wonderment filled my anxious heart.

The round saucer glistened ahead of us, and I could see Major, Humana, and Rophe watching from a distance. Anticipation welled inside me. I squeezed Judd's hand. "Just be yourself."

Judd caught my eye. "I'll look after your mother while you're gone. In the meantime, I'll save money to get an HF radio."

I would wait to tell Judd that I was giving him mine. I needed to stay focused. I rehearsed several scenarios in my mind. How could I make this undramatic?

Of course, there was nothing normal about introducing my boyfriend to my newly discovered twin sister; my father, who had just disclosed himself to me; and a cloned copy of my favorite cat. I couldn't make this up.

What lay in store? A UFO glistened behind us on the brink of World War III. I was on an adventure to another planet, another universe, perhaps another dimension.

What did I just say? I wanted to keep this simple. No way that would happen.

We arrived, and I began the introductions. "Dad, Humana,"—I giggled— "and Rophe, this is Judd, my boyfriend." I made it short, just the way I wanted.

I stepped back and let everyone exchange pleasantries. This moment would stay etched in my mind. I wanted to savor it. The only thing that would have topped it is if Mother were here. She would know soon. I was thankful the day wasn't far away.

After the introductions, everyone looked at me. I wasn't used to being in charge.

"Here's the plan. Judd and I will take Rophe II with us." I turned to Judd. "I will go in first and distract Mother."

On second thought, I didn't like that. "Let's do it this way instead. I'll go inside, talk to Mother, and bring Rophe to you. We'll make the exchange. I'll take Rophe II inside. We shouldn't use a carrier. If you try to put Rophe in one, he'll protest. What do you think?"

"That will work," Judd said.

"You might want to scoot off to the side of the porch, so Mother can't see you or what we're doing."

"Agreed," Judd said.

I turned to my dad—I'd have to get used to calling him that—and twin sister, Humana. "Are you going to wait here for me?"

Humana looked at my father.

Major replied, "I think we'll go back and tell the Shining Ones what's happening and then return."

I peered at the glistening saucer. “I guess the EMP attack didn’t affect its power.”

Father laughed. “They have power.”

I turned to Judd. “Ready?”

He nodded.

I reached over and took Rophe II from Humana. Once I held him comfortably, we took the trail back to the apartment. Like lovers who know separation is imminent, Judd and I exchanged pleasantries. I kissed Rophe II several times.

My favorite bird in the universe, the Rose-breasted Grosbeak, appeared, serenading me from his favorite perch. Rophe II noticed him.

I squeezed Rophe’s clone. “No, you can’t have Mr. Grosbeak. He’s my favorite bird.”

A dog barked in the distance. I had yet to see a soul.

“I asked Judd, ‘Where is everyone?’”

“Buying whatever they can get their hands on. Those who don’t have cash are in trouble.”

“How much do you have?”

“A few hundred dollars, but not enough to buy a radio. Without the walkie-talkie, I’d be completely in the dark.”

Now was the perfect moment to tell him. “Judd, I want to give you mine.”

Judd looked astonished. “What?”

“I want to give you my transceiver and antenna. My father said the rogue actors would want it, and he didn’t want to give them a free radio. Do you think you can set it up at your apartment?”

“Yeah, I’ll figure it out. Are you sure?”

“I’m sure. I won’t be here. I didn’t get the impression that Humana would use it. She knows how to communicate in other ways. The official government doesn’t want the Collins Elite, a religious rogue part of the government concerning the UFO phenomenon, to seize it by court order.

“When they visited me, they asked to see my equipment, and I declined. Whatever you do, don’t let anyone know you have it.”

Judd shook his head. "I can't believe you're going to give me your radio."

"Mother wanted to buy one for you, but that seems impossible now. Make sure you keep it protected in case of another EMP attack."

"I want to know who launched the EMP."

I pondered Judd's question. "Several countries might want to, and many have the ability. Iran, Russia, and China are the most likely. Who hates the United States the most?"

Judd laughed. "That's not helpful. We aren't popular anywhere in the world anymore."

We walked the rest of the way in silence. Once we arrived, I rehearsed everything with Judd.

"Are you ready?" I asked.

"Yeah."

I waited until he was out of sight and opened the door. Mother's face was buried in a book, and I walked over and knelt beside her. "Is it good?"

She smiled. "It's good. I'm just trying to figure out where God is in all this."

I touched her arm lightly. "When you find out, let me know."

Humana could tell Mother about giving the radio to Judd after she and I traded places. Today, I just wanted to focus on Rophe. I picked him up and held him in my arms.

"He might like some fresh air," I said to Mother. "Without the fans running, the air is stale."

She nodded. "Yeah, Rophe used to watch the birds on YouTube. But we have no TV now. He probably would like some fresh air."

Carrying Rophe in my arms, I strolled to the front door. Once outside, Judd and I exchanged cats. I took Rophe's clone with me.

When I returned to the apartment, I caressed him and showed him where everything was—his litter box, food, water dish, and both bedrooms.

Rophe II seemed to recognize this as his new home. His purrs filled me with delight as I returned to Mother carrying him in my arms.

The most challenging part might be bonding. I sat on the chair beside Mother as I talked to Rophe II. Treats and catnip would be helpful.

I retreated to the kitchen and poured a few cat niblets into a small container. Then, I placed the container next to Mother's leg. He eagerly went for the treats, and Mother scratched his ears.

I lingered. "I love you, Mom."

"I love you, too, Honey."

I sprayed some catnip around the base of Mother's chair. When Rophe II finished the treats, he sniffed it and rubbed his back on the herb. Satisfied when he had had enough, he looked around the room with cat eyes. I was thrilled.

Should I take anything with me? I went to my bedroom and retrieved the working computer.

As I headed to the front door, Rophe II had jumped on the sofa, which was another good sign. Mother seemed oblivious to everything, as the book held her attention.

"See you in a bit," I said as I opened the door.

"Tell Judd I said hello."

"I will," I promised. I shut the door behind me and found Judd waiting.

"Everything okay?"

I nodded. "Let's return to the ship."

Rophe was content with Judd carrying him. I was emotionally exhausted, remembering how little sleep I'd had. How would I get through the rest of the day?

CHAPTER SIXTY-THREE

The moment of goodbyes had arrived. Everything had happened so fast. Suppose I had sown the wind? I needed time to process everything. Being sleep-deprived didn't help, but whether I was ready or not, time waits for no one.

The four of us stood in front of the towering UFO. Its lights, which had been off earlier, now flashed.

I held Rophe in my arms and asked my father, "Can Judd and I have a moment to say goodbye?"

"Take your time. The Shining Ones understand humans well enough to be patient."

Major and Humana kindly stepped back to give us a moment of intimacy.

We embraced. Our thoughts, while mostly unspoken, filled our hearts.

"I'll be back soon," I promised. "And maybe we can talk on the radio."

"What frequency?" Judd asked.

"What about 20 meters, 14.05? That means you'll need to learn CW. I think that's the only way I can talk to you in the heavens."

Judd forced a smile. "So like you. But, because I love you, I will do it"

I whispered. "I knew you would do it for me."

"Did you notice what I got at the store for you this morning?"

I shook my head. "No, sorry. I didn't look in the bag."

"What you requested: batteries, toilet paper, and candles."

I chuckled. "That toilet paper might come in handy."

Judd wrapped his arms tighter around me, and I buried my head in his chest. "You are one of the most thoughtful people I know."

After a long embrace, Judd stepped back and looked away, trying to hold back tears. "Stay safe."

"I will," I promised.

He wiped his eyes. "I'll try not to do anything stupid."

I giggled. "Okay."

He cleared his throat. "And I'll be praying for you."

I inhaled. "I appreciate that. Thank you."

Judd signaled to everyone they could rejoin us.

I looked at Humana. "He's all yours."

She laughed. "I promise I won't steal Judd from you. I have a boyfriend back home."

I glanced at Judd out of the corner of my eye. He appeared relieved that he didn't have to worry about that.

"You know," I said, "The only thing I grabbed on the way out was my computer. I had handed it off to my father when I took Rophe from Judd. "I didn't even think about clothes or makeup or …"

Major interrupted me. "Humana took care of all of that."

"Oh," I said, somewhat embarrassed. "Then, I think I'm ready."

After such a dramatic goodbye, walking to the spaceship seemed anticlimactic.

"Someday, I want to join you," I heard Judd say behind me. "Looking down from above must be beautiful."

I turned. "I'll see if I can arrange it when I return."

I blew Judd a kiss and waved at Humana. I hoped to stay in touch with them. I held Rophe securely as the tractor beam pulled my father and me inside the ship. I was surprised that Rophe didn't squirm away. He remained calmer than I.

I relaxed once the tractor beam released us.

Unsure of what was next, I watched my father. He looked at me, anticipating a question.

I studied the bundle of fur wrapped in my arms. "What should I do with Rophe now that we're aboard?"

Major laughed. "Yeah, we need to familiarize him with the ship."

"Where is everybody?"

"Oh, they are here," my father assured me. "They just wanted to give you a few moments to acclimate. Here, let me show you your quarters. Rophe's bed is in there, too."

"You have a room?" I asked.

"Yes, mine is next to yours."

"Can I wave goodbye to Judd and Humana?

"Yes, sure. You can see them from over there."

I followed Major to a window, and he tapped me on the shoulder. "Stand here."

Far below, I saw on the path to the football field Judd and Humana watching. "How soon until we leave?"

"Soon."

I waved, even though I knew they couldn't see me. "Wait, my radio. Can I use my walkie-talkie?"

My father laughed. "That's old technology. Go ahead."

"Here." I handed Rophe over so I could pull out my radio.

"This is KO4LBS calling K4PREP. Can you hear me?"

I could see Judd react.

"K4PREP standing by for instructions."

"Tell Humana, 'Thank you.'"

I heard her giggle in the background.

"Have a good flight," Judd said.

At that moment, the ship came alive. Major tapped me on the shoulder. "Come, let me show you around."

"Do we need to—"

"Fasten our seatbelts?"

"Yeah, something like that."

Father shook his head. "Follow me."

We left the bridge and walked down an adjoining hallway. He pointed at a sign on a door.

"My name!" I gasped.

We entered, and a vase of flowers decorated the table. On one wall was an automatic litter box, and on the other was cat food and a very expensive-looking cat bed.

My simple cot was next to his. Then I opened the closet and discovered a complete wardrobe.

I checked out the bathroom. Turning to my father, I smiled. "Everything I need."

"Humana did all of it," Major said.

"Is this where she stays—when she isn't home?" I wasn't even sure where home was for them.

"Yes, this is her space."

I tried to imagine her here. What a different kind of life she had experienced. "It's like we've exchanged places."

Father smiled. "If anyone would know what you like, she would."

Up until now, our relationship had been business-like. I suppose that had been good in a way—safe. It gave me time to understand this new world and make it my own.

As I reflected, my father and I were different toward each other now. I bit my lip. I felt more comfortable. I didn't have to prove I could do everything Major and the others expected.

I peered into my father's eyes. "I always thought you would have red hair. Where did my red hair come from?"

"I presume your mother's side," Major said. "I don't know of anyone in my family with red hair."

"I never asked Mother." I shrugged. "Since she had blonde hair, I just thought my father would have red hair."

Major chuckled. "Well, I'm sorry I disappointed you."

I giggled. "Don't be silly."

It was a sweet moment, one that I would remember. "I'm going to set Rophe down to show him where everything is."

"Good idea," Major said.

Immediately, Rophe used the litter box.

"What now?" I asked.

"Why don't you leave Rophe here, and let's return to the bridge."

On the way back, Major pointed to the door next to mine. "That's my quarters if you need me."

Nothing on the door indicated that, so I was glad he showed me.

When we returned, the Greys were everywhere, busy with various tasks. I didn't see the Shining Ones.

My father probably noticed I was uncomfortable watching them. If they looked in my direction, I felt uneasy.

Major said offhandedly, "The Greys take some getting used to, but they are so busy they hardly notice you."

In contrast, I liked the Shining Ones. "Will we see the Shining Ones?"

Probably not until we arrive at our destination."

"Which is where?"

"The location is a top-secret military base, hidden away in Alaska."

"Oh."

"And that's where I depart. Humana and I live near the base, so I'm returning home."

"You will miss her, won't you?"

Major nodded. "But we've been apart before for various reasons." He smiled. "I'll survive."

"And then?"

"They will give you time to sleep. They don't sleep, but they have preparations they will want to make before leaving. Then, I imagine they will stop at the Giza Pyramids before taking off on a journey you won't forget."

"Have you been wherever it is they are going?"

Major laughed. "I've been many times. I imagine they will visit their home base at some point."

"Where is that?"

"You will know when you get there, but they may visit other places, too. So, I don't want to tell you something and then be wrong."

"What am I supposed to do when I get to where I am going?"

My father put his hand on my shoulder. "You'll see. A lot of it is teaching you about the past, re-educating you. Just imagine that almost everything anyone has told you about the past isn't true. Where do you start?"

"At the beginning," I said. "I guess."

"That's right. At the beginning, the very beginning. In the meantime, the Shining Ones will have you sending messages back to us—the military base. Part of this is fine-tuning the ability to communicate. Remember, a major war is on the horizon."

"Will I use CW or voice?"

"CW until you become an adept. They have already used CW with you. You were the middle woman, I could say, between the government and disseminating information to the public. Keep up your CW skills. You did very well. I was impressed last night."

"Thanks."

"And—how do I communicate with them?"

"CW for now. They don't speak like we do. The Greys don't have the same faculties. They don't talk. The Shining Ones will be the ones most likely to communicate with you.

"Let me show you the radio and paddle. It's over here, and you also have a smaller one in your quarters."

I followed my father to the transmission area, and he turned on the transceiver.

"What about the frequencies? What do I use?"

"The radio is already programmed, but here is the chart," he said, pointing to a sheet on the wall.

"What if I want to contact the Shining Ones?"

"I'll show you how."

I followed Major to another hi-tech area. "Push this button, and that will summon them."

"And then, I send CW to talk to them?"

"CW. Use that until you get comfortable with thought-speak. They can communicate with you in CW as they have demonstrated.

Thought-speak takes a little training and getting used to, but it will come. I'm so used to it, I don't even think about it."

"Humana knows how?"

Major laughed. "Oh, yes. She's better at it than I."

"Well, I'm sure I'll pick it up then."

Father gave me a reassuring side hug. "Look."

I leaned forward to see out the viewing window. "We're flying so high, how long will it take to get to Alaska?"

"Oh, just a few minutes."

"A few minutes?" I repeated.

"Yeah, it's quick."

"What do I eat?"

"The Greys will fix you anything you want. Just CW your request, and they will bring it to you."

"Anything?"

"Well, within reason; you know what I mean."

Feeling suddenly sad, I went and sat in a chair on the bridge. "That means you'll be leaving soon."

Major sat beside me. "You can call the base at any time. I'll answer if I'm on duty."

I felt drained. "That's reassuring. Do you think I can take a short nap when you leave? I didn't get a lot of sleep last night."

"I think that's the plan. The Greys will tend to some technical matters, resulting in a docking delay of a day. Speaking of rest, why don't you check on Rophe, lie down, and I'll come get you when it's time?"

That sounded so good, I couldn't resist. I imagined how lonely I would be without Rophe.

I hugged my father. "I can find my way around now. There's no need to take me this time."

He nodded. "Okay."

As I left the bridge, he said, "Enjoy your rest. The best is yet to come."

CHAPTER SIXTY-FOUR

I felt Rophe, my loyal companion, climbing on me. He seemed to be saying, "Wake up."

It took me a minute to remember where I was. It was so dark without a window that it could have been day or night. How long had I slept?

I jumped out of bed and made myself presentable.

Feeling insecure, I picked up Rophe and proceeded to leave. I tried to lock the door as I did habitually, but it wasn't lockable. To put a positive spin on it, that meant I couldn't lock myself out.

Walking down the hallway, I felt a gentle breeze on my back and heard my name, but it wasn't my father's voice.

C-h-u-m-a-n-a.

I turned, but I didn't see anyone. Rophe seemed agitated and unexpectedly jumped out of my arms. He ran to the door beside mine, which led to my father's quarters.

I knocked on the door and waited, but didn't hear any noise coming from the room, so I knocked again. Nothing. I checked the door handle. It wasn't locked.

If he was sleeping, I didn't want to disturb him. I would shut the door and leave. I picked up Rophe and caressed him to relieve my stress.

When I cracked the door, it was so dark I couldn't see anything. Either my father was sleeping, or he wasn't in here. I needed some light to make sure, so I flipped the switch. His room looked like mine. His bed was empty, and the bathroom door was open; I didn't see him.

Why did I hear someone say my name? And why did Rophe struggle to get out of my arms and rush to this door if nobody was here? He was too smart to go to the wrong one if he wanted to stay behind.

Rophe squirmed again in my arms, and I let him down. If I shut the door and my father or someone entered, they'd think I was snooping. I could say I entered the wrong room if the door was open.

Rophe jumped on the bed, exploring with his nose. Perhaps my father's scent caught his attention. Then, I noticed a couple of official-looking papers. Rophe was scratching on them as he did with catnip.

I reached for the document on top of the pile. Perhaps it was a passport, but it was maroon-colored; I thought American passports were blue. It could be different for government officials.

I flipped it open. It was a passport, but it did not look like an American one. Under nationality, it said "Cydonia." I'd never heard of a country named Cydonia.

This revelation about my father's identity presented more questions than answers. Was my father not American?

I saw another document underneath the supposed passport. My heart pounded. What if somebody caught me snooping through my father's papers?

I quickly picked up the second document, which looked like another passport. This one said the United States of America. I wasn't sure if I was relieved or more confused. Was he a U.S. citizen and a citizen of another country?

Mother said he was always gone and could never talk about his whereabouts. I had a computer in my quarters. If I had the internet, I could look up Cydonia later.

Then I noticed there was one more document. I picked it up. The full name at the top, which I didn't take note of on the passports, was Major E.A. Ironvein. Other extraneous information followed; I didn't understand all the abbreviations or their significance.

My eyes dropped down the page. It had children listed: One girl. Then it had another entry for children: One girl.

Why was it listed this way? Was that the way twins were designated? I had no answers to these questions.

The address on the American passport was in Alaska, but the first passport said Cydonia. His last name on both was the same as mine. It didn't make sense.

I needed to leave. I put the documents back on the bed the way they were, turned off the light, and shut the door.

Thank goodness nobody saw me. I placed Rophe back in my quarters. I didn't want him to get lost or run away. When I set him on the floor, before I shut the door, he looked at me as if asking, "Am I in trouble?"

"I'll be back in a minute," I told him. "I need to find my father and see what's happening." With a sense of urgency, I pulled the door shut and headed to the bridge.

The Greys were performing various tasks. I had yet to see a Shining One. I went to the radio, which my father had told me to use to contact him.

"This is KO4LBS, Chumana Ironvein, calling Major Ironvein. If you hear me, please respond."

I heard a couple of clicks followed by his voice. "Chumana, I was fixing to come back to the ship. You are awake?"

"Yes. What time is it?"

"It's early morning. If you look out the window, you can see me."

I hadn't thought to look outside. I expected to see sunshine, but it looked like we were in a bunker underneath the ground. Where had I seen this? It looked familiar.

My heart pounded. I had seen this place before—in my dream. Except this time, I was inside the pyramid, gazing out. In my dream, I was outside the pyramid, wondering what was inside.

I searched for my father—there he was, off to the side. I could see him waving. What looked like military personnel were around him. My father's smile and wave reassured me. "I see you. Can they let me down, or are you coming up?"

"They will transport you down, and I'll give you a quick base tour."

"Can I leave Rophe in the room?"

"Yes, Rophe will be fine. "I'll see you in a few minutes."

I turned off the radio. How soon before we took off?

CHAPTER SIXTY-FIVE

Once the tractor beam released me, I took a few steps and saw my father. Dressed in a military uniform, he looked distinguished. Some of the soldiers stopped to watch us. Was this as special for him as it was for me? I rushed over to greet him.

I felt better, having gotten some much-needed rest. We lingered in each other's arms long enough to connect emotionally. Some moments stick with you. This one, I would remember.

"Chumana," my father said, "The ship will leave soon. They have given us 30 minutes. Can we get a cup of coffee?"

I would never turn down a cup of coffee. "Sure."

I followed him within the pyramid. It appeared different from this perspective. I wasn't sure where I was standing in my dream, but dreams are never the same as in real life. However, I knew this was the place I had visited, and now I knew its significance.

We entered a cafeteria, and all around were military people. "This is a military base?"

"Yes, it's part of the newly formed Space Force and an important component of America's strategic military operations. Our friends in high places want to help us. They feel like America is in the best position to maintain peace. Though not perfect, it is the freest country in the world."

We went through the cafeteria line, which reminded me of school, and I ordered a cup of coffee and a chocolate-covered doughnut.

"Are there enemies of our friends in high places?" I asked.

"Absolutely, but we have the best military in the world. We can win, and they will help us."

"Is there anything I should know that I don't know? And when will I return?"

"Those are great questions. First, time is very different in other dimensions. What might seem like a long time to you will be very short in our time. Time is an illusion.

"The question is, how do you measure it? It's relative. For example, time goes by slowly when you look forward to something that won't happen for a while. In contrast, our time together now will go by quickly. Does that make sense?"

I nodded. "I just think about Mother and Judd. I'm glad Humana is there."

My father nodded. "I understand, but they will be fine. Atlanta is not a primary target of the enemy. My best advice is just to be you. Enjoy the journey."

"Suppose I get sick? Do they have medicines?"

"Their medicines are centuries ahead of ours. So, you don't need to worry about that."

"Will I be able to keep in touch with you?"

"At times, you will. It will depend on what dimension you are in."

"What does that mean?"

"What we see here on Earth is not all there is. There are worlds beyond ours, dimensions, universes. I'm still trying to figure it out myself."

My father reflected. "Sometimes, I wondered, was I doing the right thing bringing you here? You could have had an ordinary life. I know about your perfect test scores and your aptitudes. You could have gone to any school in the country, even the world. You can still do that when you return.

"In the meantime, how should I put it? You are like an ambassador. I am hopeful that the good people will win this upcoming war. I believe we are on the winning side, the good side."

My father added. "If you learn otherwise, let me know. I've spent my whole career trying to figure it out, which is not easy when dealing with entities you don't understand, huge egos, and powerful countries wielding weapons we must obliterate to save America."

"I hope I am up to it."

My father glanced at the clock. "We have a few more minutes, but you must return to the ship soon. I knew the time would pass quickly."

"Are you coming with me?"

"I need to retrieve some documents I left in my quarters, so I'll go with you." Major laughed. "They will kick me out if I stay too long."

I hoped my snooping didn't cause any harm. I wanted to ask about the documents, but it wasn't the right time.

ONCE WE RETURNED to the ship, we walked down the hallway to our quarters. I checked on Rophe while Major retrieved his paperwork.

We reunited in the hallway and returned to the bridge. My father didn't seem to notice that someone had tampered with his personal documents.

He pointed to the wall to catch my attention. "Whenever you want to see outside, that's the best window. Because the spaceship flies so high, the view is magnificent. And when you enter other dimensions, the colors are mind-boggling. You can hear the stars singing."

"That sounds awesome."

"Make sure you watch when you approach the Giza Pyramids. It's breathtaking as you fly over the desert with the pyramids rising from the sands."

"What do the pyramids have to do with the Shining Ones?"

"Oh," my father said, "that's a story. The pyramids are power stations. They have been on the Earth for thousands of years, perhaps hundreds of thousands of years. They have been here since the Shining

Ones. Before they leave this dimension, they will stop there to power the spaceship for the rest of the journey."

"Do they ever crash?"

My father laughed. "I've never heard of one crashing. Their technology is so advanced that they can go anywhere in just a few minutes. The military hopes they will give us that technology rather than give it to Russia or China. That's what this is all about—goodwill, friendship, and peace."

Major checked his phone. "I need to be going."

"How does your phone work when mine doesn't?"

He laughed. "The military has technology that is not yet available to the public. We're prepared thanks to our star friends. Even though we're in darkness now, we hope to restore power soon.

"The U.S. no longer needs the outdated infrastructure that was expensive. We now know how to make free power, but we must wait until the Shining Ones let us share it."

"Can I have one of those phones?"

My father shook his head. "I would if I could, but I can't."

I frowned. "I didn't think you'd be able to."

Major briefly glanced at his documents. "I must return to the base."

We hugged again, and I walked to the departure area with him. When I stepped back, the tractor beam lowered him to the ground.

I tried to salute him and then thought how silly I looked. I didn't know how, so I threw him a kiss. He saluted back and returned the kiss. I waited as the bay doors shut and hurried over to the window.

He waved goodbye. "I love you," I whispered. I should have said it sooner. Then, he slowly walked back into the cafeteria.

When would I see him again? When would I see Mother again? Judd? Humana? Then I remembered Rophe.

CHAPTER SIXTY-SIX

Peering out over the hot Egyptian sands, I saw the three Great Pyramids of Giza. The trip from Alaska was so quick that I barely had time to retrieve Rophe and walk back to the viewing window. The immense height of the tallest one struck me.

Did the Shining Ones build them thousands of years ago, as my father alluded to? We seemed to be over the top of the middle one, stationary and lingering, which gave me a moment to appreciate the pyramidal energy the UFO absorbed.

How did the Egyptians build these massive structures to such precise measurements and move them without modern technology?

A voice inside me whispered, "They didn't."

The history of the pyramids and what lay beneath them was an enigma. No one seemed to agree on who built them or why.

As I admired their grandeur, contemplating their place in the world's scheme of cultural significance and antediluvian history, I witnessed something I could never have imagined.

Against the backdrop of the blue sky, the heavens receded. For a moment, I could see into another dimension.

In this other place, I beheld a magnificent lion. His steely eyes spoke of wisdom, and his stoic face reflected superiority over every creature in the universe. His bronze mane rippled in the winds of time as he stood against the backdrop of a mighty throne surrounded by angels.

Captivated by his fierceness, I watched in wonderment. Without warning, he opened his mouth. His roar reverberated across the desert sands and shook the universe's fabric.

The vision shocked me into speechlessness, and I clung to Rophe, full of trepidation. In the moment of the lion's thunderous battle cry, I heard him proclaim, "What hath God wrought!"

GROUP READING GUIDE

1. What kind of person is Chumana? Mother? Judd? Shale? Rachel? Gracie? Major? Humana?

2. What are two overarching themes presented in the book?

3. What is ham radio?

4. What is CW/Morse Code?

5. What are the good influences in Chumana's life?

6. What are the questionable influences in Chumana's life?

7. What is your opinion about the Bible passage Genesis 1:1-2?

8. What do you think UFOs are, and why?

9. If you were Chumana, what would you do?

10. What (or who) do you think Rophe represents?

11. What (or who) is whispering to Chumana?

12. Who are the initials in the book that Chumana discovers on the swing in her dream?

13 .What is the idea presented in the Eighth Dimension about when time began? And when will time end?

14. What is your opinion on the origins of humankind as presented in *Eighth Dimension - Frequency?* Which theory do you believe is correct and why?

15. Who do you think built the pyramids?

16. What was an important purpose of the pyramids as presented in the book (beyond being a burial place for kings)? If you are unsure, look at recent research about what they are discovering underneath the pyramids.

17. Who were the mythological gods?

18. What are your opinions of Chumana's father?

19. What is the Collins Elite?

20. Where is Cydonia?

21. What is an electromagnetic pulse?

22. What are some things you can do to prepare for such an event?

23. Are there any Scriptures that reference "signs in the sky" that could be UFOs?

AFTERWORD

One of the many reasons I wrote *Eighth Dimension - Frequency* is to help homeschooling families understand concepts that the mainstream media, Hollywood movies, and prominent secular books have presented that do not align with Scripture. I homeschooled my daughters for a significant portion of their education through high school. They are now adults, and I'm thankful to say, both college graduates.

However, if I were to do it all over again, I would do one thing differently: That one thing is what the *Eighth Dimension Trilogy* is about. *Eighth Dimension - Frequency* is the first book in the series.

I don't have a complete listing of every resource I used, but what follows is a sampling that was important for the plot, theme, and content. Note: You will never hear pastors preach on these things.

As a novelist of YA Christian fiction, God has given me a sanctified imagination. I wish I had known about these incredible stories when I homeschooled. I would be interested in your thoughts if you would like to share them. You can visit my website at LorilynRoberts.com to connect with me.

BOOKS AND RESOURCES

BOOKS

Earth's Earliest Ages *by G. H. Pember.*
I found theologian Pember's interpretation of the gap theory very helpful, as well as his thoughts on how Satan has used false religions, modern spiritualism, and theosophy to corrupt God's Truth before Christ's return.

Stolen Seed *by Karin Wilkinson.*
Before her conversion, Mrs. Wilkinson was abducted by aliens (fallen angels) and shares her testimony and story.

Before Genesis *by Donna Howell and Dr. Thomas Horn.*
Mrs. Howell discusses worldwide archeological findings and how they point to a civilization that predates Adam and Eve.

Inherit Your Freedom *by Mike Signorelli.*
Pastor Signorelli emphasizes how the father's sins are passed down from generation to generation until a believer breaks the pattern of repetition and is "reborn" through the Holy Spirit, thereby ending generational curses.

The Dragon's Prophecy *by Jonathan Cahn.*
Rabbi Cahn demonstrates how the red dragon mentioned in Revelation is the same dragon that appeared in the Garden of Eden. He tracks the

dragon's history and his impact on Israel for the last six thousand years.

Angels Volume II: Messengers from the Metacosm *by Chuck Missler.*
Dr. Missler discusses the coming deception of UFOs.

Judgment of the Nephilim *by Ryan Pitterson.*
A comprehensive study of the Nephilim.

Reversing Hermon *by Dr. Michael S. Heiser.*

Angels *by Dr. Michael S. Heiser.*

Demons *by Dr. Michael S. Heiser.*

The Unseen Realm *by Dr. Michael S. Heiser.*
I read The Unseen Realm *first and was so intrigued by Dr. Heiser's concepts, including the Divine Council and sons of God, that I read his other books to answer some of my questions about angels and demons.*

The Book of Enoch
I found reading this source material to be extremely helpful in understanding Genesis. While not on the same level of authenticity as the Bible, references to the book of Enoch are made in New Testament writings. The book's comprehensive nature explains a lot that is not easily understood from reading only Genesis 6.

Corrupting the Image 3 *by Douglas Hamp.*
Dr. Hamp discusses in detail the early Mesopotamian civilizations' worship and how their pagan rituals

harkened back to the Old Testament. He traces the history of their mythological gods to the Nephilim and the Watchers that God put over the seventy nations in Genesis.

The Watchers assigned by God turned the people away from worshipping God and corrupted them into worshipping themselves, which translated into the worship of Satan by mythological names. Dr. Hamp also brings the story forward to who the dragon is in Revelation 12.

The Invisible War *by Donald Grey Barnhouse.*

Pastor Barnhouse summarizes all the other books I read about the Great War and refers to it as The Invisible War.

The most significant point I took away from Barnhouse's book is that the war is not between man and God but between Satan and God and Satan's desire to receive human worship.

He shows how Satan corrupted humans into worshipping fallen celestial beings through false religions, deception, and occult practices.

Barnhouse points out, however, that humans are sinners themselves, and not all sinners will choose to worship Satan.

Thus, in this divided house of chaos, we see the imprint of Satan's twisted works on Earth as the prince of the power of the air.

Created in the Image of God: Missionary to the Chácobo Ignites a Revolution Without Guns *by Gilbert R. Prost. Completed and Edited by Lorilyn Roberts.*

My biggest takeaway from working on Mr. Prost's book is that Satan has been deceiving humankind ever since missionaries ventured out of their comfort zones to share the Gospel per the Great Commission.

Historically, sometimes, before these missionaries even had a chance to share the Gospel or the Good News of Jesus Christ, these illiterate societies had been corrupted by the evil one through worshipping nature, embracing paganism, and creating gods made with their hands.

Spreading the Gospel is hampered unless these pagan societies are willing to embrace the covenantal relationship between husband and wife and build their tribal identity on God's law rather than man's law.

In anthropology and Bible translation, establishing this covenantal foundation first has been problematic for missionaries who have not embraced it, resulting in dozens, if not hundreds, of Bible translations unusable.

- ***We Are Legion*** by Thomas R. Horn.
- ***Piercing the Comic Veil*** by Joseph Jordan and Jason Dezember.
- ***America Before: The Key to Earth's Lost Civilizations*** by Graham Hancock.
- ***Birthright: The Coming Posthuman Apocalypse and the Usurpation of Adam's Dominion on Planet Earth*** by Tim Alberino.
- ***Living in Wonder*** by Rod Dreher.
- ***Out of This World*** by Lt. Robert Maginnis.
- ***The Roots of the Federal Reserve*** by Laura Sanger
- ***Final Events*** by Nick Redfern.
- ***Area 51: An Uncensored History of America's Top Secret Military Base*** by Annie Jackobsen.
- ***Cydonia: The Secret Chronicles of Mars*** by David Flynn with forward by Stephen Quayle

HAM RADIO RESOURCES

- Morse Code dot World
- LCWO dot net
- Ham Radio License Exam dot com

VIDEOS

• **UFO Disclosure: 5 Disc DVD Set,** by L.A. Marzulli.

• **The Great Delusion: The Second Coming of Earth's Oldest Enemy,** by SkyWatch Films.

• **Judgment of the Nephilim: Secrets of the Pre-Flood World Documentary,** by Ryan Pitterson.

• **Klaus Schwab Eugenics & the Rise of the Nephilim,** 10 Episodes on DVDs by Get a Life Media and Pastor Billy Crone.

• **The Final Countdown, Tribulation Rising: The AI Invasion,** 24 studies on 12 DVDs by Get a Life Media and Pastor Billy Crone.

• **Hybrids, Supersoldiers, and the Coming Genetic Apocalypse,** 28 hours on 16 DVDs by Get A Life Media and Pastor Billy Crone.

• **Endtime Nephilim Deception,** by Ryan Pitterson and Days of Noe Publishing.

• **The Final Nephilim: Battle for Heaven and Earth Documentary,** by Ryan Pitterson.

• **Christmas in Branson - On Demand** by Prophecy Watchers, 49 videos.

ACKNOWLEDGMENTS

A special thank you to Brett Wallace (NH2KW).

I also want to give a shout out to my beta readers: Paula Clauser, Laura Domingue, Katherine Harms, Emma Right, and Kevlyn McIntosh

ABOUT THE AUTHOR

Lorilyn Roberts is an Amazon bestselling author with over 20 titles to her name, including *Children of Dreams* and *Seventh Dimension - The Door*. A recipient of 50-plus writing awards, she holds an MA in Creative Writing from Perelandra College and is an alumna of the University of Alabama, graduating Magna Cum Laude. Connect with her at LorilynRoberts.com. Lorilyn is also a ham radio operator and CW/Morse Code enthusiast. KO4LBS.

NOTE FROM THE AUTHOR

If *Eighth Dimension - Frequency: A Young Adult Fantasy* has been a blessing to you, as an independent author not backed by a major publishing house, thoughtful, helpful reviews on sites like Amazon, Goodreads, and Barnes & Noble help to spread the word about my books to other book lovers like you

Thank you for taking your precious time on this journey with me. I plan to publish book 2 in the trilogy in 2026. May God receive all the glory for His Good Works and allowing me to share my faith in Jesus Christ.

The Messiah is coming soon. If you have not accepted Him as your personal Savior, today is the day of salvation.

All you must do is recognize you are a sinner, turn away from your sins, believe that Jesus died on the cross for you, and invite Him into your heart. Then you will be born again.

Feel free to share with me if you make that decision on my website at LorilynRoberts.com.

www.ingramcontent.com/pod-product-compliance
Lightning Source LLC
Chambersburg PA
CBHW021148020826
49168CB00034B/61

* 9 7 8 1 9 6 4 5 2 8 0 4 5 *